DELIVERING DANTE

A MADE MARIAN NOVEL

LUCY LENNOX

Cover Designer: Angstyg - www.AngstyG.com

Editor: Hollie Westring - www.HollieTheEditor.com

Professional Beta Reading: Leslie Copeland (lcopelandwrites@gmail.com)

Sign up for Lucy's newsletter for exclusive content and to learn more about her latest books at www.LucyLennox.com!

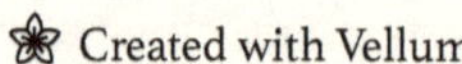 Created with Vellum

KEEP IN TOUCH WITH LUCY!

Join Lucy's Lair
Get Lucy's New Release Alerts
Like Lucy on Facebook
Follow Lucy on BookBub
Follow Lucy on Amazon
Follow Lucy on Instagram
Follow Lucy on Pinterest

Other books by Lucy:
Made Marian Series
Forever Wilde Series
Aster Valley Series
Twist of Fate Series with Sloane Kennedy
After Oscar Series with Molly Maddox
Licking Thicket Series with May Archer
Virgin Flyer
Say You'll Be Nine

Visit Lucy's website at www.LucyLennox.com for a comprehensive list of titles, audio samples, freebies, suggested reading order, and more!

TRIGGER WARNING

Delivering Dante includes references to conversion therapy as well as domestic violence.

THE MARIAN FAMILY

Thomas and **Rebecca** Marian

Their children (oldest to youngest):

Pete, married to **Ginger** - they have twin girls and a baby boy

Jamie (meets **Teddy** in *Taming Teddy*)

Blue (meets **Tristan** in *Borrowing Blue*)

Thad (dating Tristan's cousin **Sarah**)

Jude (meets **Derek** in *Jumping Jude*)

Simone (hmm....)

Maverick (meets **Beau** in Moving Maverick)

Griff (meets **Sam** in *Grounding Griffin*)

Dante (turn the page to find out)

Aunt Tilly - Thomas Marian's aunt

Granny - Tristan's grandmother

Irene - Granny's wife

PROLOGUE
DANTE - 8 YEARS AGO

I don't remember much about it, honestly. One minute I was curled up in a painful, broken ball, crying on the nasty bathroom floor of the church basement, and the next, a guy's soothing voice was in my ear telling me I'd be okay.

It was the middle of the night, but god only knew *what* night it actually was at that point. I'd been kept awake and off-kilter for days by then, in hopes of getting my attention so I would realize how serious the situation was. As if getting jumped by the entire high school football team several days before hadn't gotten my attention enough as it was.

I suspected some of my fingers were broken and probably a rib or two. Other than that, all I knew was hunger, pain, confusion, exhaustion, and the sense of finally, after two full years of trying to keep my head down and get through it, deciding I couldn't do it anymore.

I couldn't stay in that town, in that church basement with my abusive father and his circle of religious henchmen preparing to put me through our small town's own homegrown version of conversion therapy. Again. Had I been able to walk without puking, I would have tried to escape.

The Reverend Richard Lawton hadn't been happy when his one

and only child refused to obey, and the man was hell bent on teaching me my place. By the time my guardian angel found me that night in the basement bathroom, I was close to caving. I'd pretty much decided if I couldn't just go ahead and die, which would have been the preferred choice, I might as well agree to the church's plan for me. At the very least, it would buy me time to get the hell out of town.

I was half naked and covered in filth. The clothes I'd worn when the football team caught me kissing one of their own had been quickly covered in dirt during the scuffle. Once Officer Johns had found me, instead of taking me home, he'd met my father at the church and taken me straight to the basement, repeating the made-up story he heard from his son: I'd attacked one of the football players and forced myself on him.

After I puked the first time, I took off my filthy shirt and just lay on the bathroom floor. What was even the point in trying to get out of the bathroom anyway? I'd only end up back at the sink to wash my face or try to choke down some water.

So that's how the stranger found me. A guy I only ever knew as "Angel." He must have been heaven sent, because I'd never seen him before and I knew all the other kids in my small town. He couldn't be real. And part of me wished he wasn't. That maybe he was an actual angel, come to deliver me to heaven. Or hell. And that would be all right, I supposed.

"Shhh, it's okay," his comforting voice murmured in my ear as he gathered me up in his arms. "You're safe now. I've got you."

The young man made shushing sounds and I could smell the clean scent of him—such a drastic contrast to however nasty I must have smelled at the time. He smelled like faded cologne mixed with an earthy smell I couldn't quite place. It wrapped around me like a warm blanket, making me feel as if the possibility of safety might exist in this world.

"You smell so good," I told him, not realizing my thoughts were going to come out of my mouth. "I'm sorry."

A deep rumble came through his chest as he lifted me. "You're sorry I smell good?" he asked quietly.

I wanted to tell him I wasn't. But I couldn't bring myself to move my mouth anymore. My ribs screamed in pain as he carried me, and it was all I could do to keep breathing shallow gulps of air.

As he snuck me out of the church, I knew I should have been afraid. What if my father or one of his friends saw us? What if they caught us and dragged me back? But somehow, cradled in the stranger's arms, I knew I would be okay.

I remember a car, a drive, a couch. I remember him carefully tucking a blanket around me, murmuring reassuring words into my ear about a doctor coming for my injuries. I begged him not to leave me, but he said he had to. I begged him not to take me back to my father, and he promised he wouldn't.

He urged me to put my past behind me and start fresh. Forget everything, including him.

I told him I could never forget him; he'd saved me. After all the years I'd prayed for someone to save me from my father, my prayers had finally been answered in the form of that man—my angel. I wish I recalled what he looked like. Vague memories suggest he had a shaved head and tanned skin, but my eyes were swollen and I'd been so dizzy. I don't really recall more than that.

The last thing I remembered was his kiss on my forehead, a last inhale of his scent, and the distant calling of a gentle female voice.

"Angel," the voice said. "Is that you?"

He really was an Angel.

1

AJ - 8 YEARS LATER IN JUNE

I was seventeen years old when I committed my first felony—the kidnapping of Daniel Lawton. Luckily, the operation was a success, and I was never caught. Eight years later, I did it again. Same mission, same target. Only this time he was known as Dante Marian. And he was significantly more difficult to steal.

I was in a car on my way from the San Francisco airport to Aunt Londa's house. Whenever I left my home in Chicago to visit my aunt, I felt a familiar nervous excitement in my gut. Would this be the time Dante saw me and figured out who I was? Would he recognize me after all these years? What would he say if he did? What would *I* say if he didn't?

In the past, my trips to San Francisco had been short and sporadic, making it easy to avoid Dante. This time, though, I wasn't just visiting. I'd accepted a consulting gig with On Your Six Security and was moving to the city to work with Joel Healy. Living and working in San Francisco meant it was time to stop avoiding Dante. I was bound to run into him at some point, and chances were high it would be sooner rather than later.

Even though I'd avoided him like the plague for fear he'd recognize me, I'd kept tabs on him from a distance for eight long years. Most of what I knew about his life in San Francisco was from Aunt Londa. He'd been taken in by the large Marian family shortly after arriving at the youth shelter my aunt helped run. The Marians were committed volunteers at the shelter and had already adopted two other teens from the program into their family.

Knowing Dante had ended up in a loving, supportive family had finally allowed me to let go and stop stressing about him. I'd worried for months about whether my father and I had done the right thing by essentially stealing him and sending him out west with my aunt instead of calling the police to report the abuse. Had we followed the rules, the law in that small town wouldn't have done a single thing to help him, and they would have closed ranks to protect each other if anyone so much as came sniffing around. The abuser was not only the town preacher, but he was also the mayor. No, my father and I knew better than to notify the authorities when we went in for an extraction like that. It never ended well for the victim. Dante would have been hurt worse, possibly permanently.

Instead, he was able to spend the rest of his childhood healing and experiencing family, love, and the fresh start I'd so desperately wished for him. At eighteen, he was officially adopted by the Marians after three years of being a Marian in everything but name. He'd gone to college and taken over the shelter expansion duties after his brother Thad had gone overseas.

Over the past several months, raving about Dante Marian had become one of Aunt Londa's favorite pastimes. They worked together full-time at Marian House—she watched over the kids and he managed the shelter itself. It was obvious from the pride in her voice that she considered him one of her success stories from her tenure as director of the shelter.

After I arrived at her house and stowed my suitcase in the guest room, Londa began bragging about him again.

"Dante's going to be in charge of all of the administrative nonsense and the programming so I can focus on the kids going forward," she said as she heaped food onto my plate at the small dinner table in her kitchen. "You know he got his master's degree in nonprofit management, right?"

"You never said it was a master's," I said in surprise. "I assumed it was a bachelor's."

"He graduated high school early and then got his degree in sociology. Worked his tail off and went straight into the master's program for a year. Finished a year ago. When Thad and Sarah left last October for their Doctors Without Borders thing, Dante took over the expansion project. He's done an incredible job. Well, you'll see while you're here." Aunt Londa looked at me with a big smile." Thanks for coming this week, AJ."

"I wouldn't have missed it. You know that."

"The grand opening gala is going to be super fancy. You brought a tux, right?" she asked with a worried look on her face.

I leaned over and rested a hand on her arm. "Yes, ma'am. I brought the monkey suit. Don't worry. You and I both know I'd never let the queen bee go to the ball without a properly outfitted escort," I teased.

"I wish your parents could have come," she said with a sigh.

"They do too, but they booked their anniversary cruise over a year ago. We'll take lots of pictures to show them. How about that?"

She grinned. "Your mama will be green with envy when she sees my dress."

"Sisters," I muttered, shaking my head. "You two are just as bad as my own. They're in their thirties and still one-up each other."

THE FOLLOWING night when we entered the hotel for the gala, I was impressed. The enormous ballroom was decorated with sparkling china and crystal, and each table was dominated by heaps of elegant fresh flowers and flickering votive candles. A stage sat at one end of the ballroom and a live band played instrumental music while servers offered wine and finger foods.

It was obvious from the people mingling this was an extremely wealthy crowd. Beaded dresses glittered in the warm light of the chandeliers and candles. Whoever had planned the guest list for the grand opening gala for Marian House had done an amazing job at targeting San Francisco's elite donors. The evening was sure to bring in heaps of money for the shelter and its programs.

Aunt Londa preened like a proud peacock as she worked the crowd, shaking hands with familiar faces and introducing herself to new ones. After several rounds of introductions, I made my way over to the bar to get something other than the white wine being passed on trays.

As I stood in line, I felt the hairs on the back of my neck prickle and turned to see what set off my sixth sense. I scanned the area, seeing nothing out of the ordinary until my eyes landed on a man in one of the open doorways to the ballroom.

He was stunning, and my entire being homed in on him while the rest of the crowd seemed to fall away. My heart began banging stupidly in my chest at the same time I felt my throat tighten. The man was familiar but different. I knew right away it was Dante, but it wasn't the Dante I remembered.

That Dante had still been a bit of a kid—a gangly teen, hurt and scared. This Dante was all man. Lean muscled and fit, he seemed to carry his frame like a panther. He wasn't tall, maybe five eight, but he stood straight, elegant poise hiding taut energy below the surface. The tuxedo he wore fit him like a second skin, and he looked like he would be right at home on a red carpet somewhere. His dark brown hair was shiny and seemed to fight his attempts to smooth it to one side.

The man was perfection, and everything about him called out to me.

His eyes scanned the room as if he was looking for someone in particular. When they got to me, they stopped. Did he recognize me? Without realizing it, I took a step forward as if I was going to walk over to him. What the hell was I thinking? Dante Marian was off-limits. Thankfully someone nudged me out of my trance before I could make a fool out of myself.

"Huh?" I stuttered. "M'sorry, what?" The woman in line at the bar behind me smiled politely and gestured with her head it was my turn. My eyes flashed back over to where Dante had stood, but he was gone.

2

———————

DANTE

I was nervous as hell. It wasn't as if I didn't love my job—I did. I absolutely did. But if I could cut out the part where I was supposed to give a major speech at the Marian House fundraiser gala, I would love my job that much more.

Before entering the ballroom, I took one last deep breath and held it. I hated being in the spotlight, but even more than that, I hated crowds. No, that wasn't quite accurate. I *despised* crowds. Crowds made me crazy and messed with my sanity. Even being with my large family sometimes freaked me out, and I had to struggle to regulate my breathing lest I tumble into a full-on panic attack.

But I could do this. I *would* do this. Hell. I was downright *required* to do this.

I felt like a lamb leading my own damned self to the slaughter. Whose idea was this stupid fundraiser shindig, anyway?

Oh, right. *Mine.*

Here went nothing. I let out a breath and stepped across the threshold, expecting it to be anticlimactic. I knew I was being melo-dramatic, after all. I scanned the room to look for a familiar face to anchor me. Griff, Maverick, Simone, Mom—anyone, really.

As my eyes ran across the group of people in line at one of the bars, my pulse jumped. A man stood there staring at me. Well, not me probably. He must have been staring at something behind me, but I couldn't take my eyes off him long enough to look to see what it was.

Instead, I stared at him like an idiot.

He was tall compared to the people in line near him, and he had thick brown hair styled up with gel or something in a trendy look— long on top and short on the sides and in the back. His eyes were intense, and staring into them was a bit like being hypnotized. As long as I looked into those eyes, I couldn't look away. Didn't *want* to look away.

Was I salivating too? *Jeez, moron, get a grip.*

The beautiful man in line at the bar turned to speak to the woman standing next to him, breaking the spell. Of course he was there with someone. It was probably his wife.

I shook my head and stepped forward. Maybe my subconscious clamored for any excuse not to focus on what I was really supposed to be focusing on—my speech. Oh, and schmoozing wealthy patrons.

Not long after venturing farther into the room, I found my brother Pete and his wife, Ginger, talking to some friends of Ginger's parents I'd met before.

My sister-in-law smiled warmly when she saw me. "There he is, the man of the hour. Dante, you remember Leonard and Patrice Mallon, don't you?"

I tried to be discreet about wiping the imagined sweat off my palm before offering my hand. "I sure do. It's nice to see you again. We really appreciate your support tonight. Thank you so much for joining us."

Apparently, my competent-adult act was convincing, because they smiled and tittered about what a great cause Marian House was. By the time I wrapped up that conversation, I was on to another and another until I heard Maverick's voice over the sound system in the giant room.

Oh dear god. It was time for my speech. My eyes tilted up to take in the endless groups of people seated at the dining tables, and I realized what a monumental mistake that was. It was packed. There were quite possibly a thousand people in attendance, including the press.

I hated having my picture taken. It was a leftover fear of my biological family finding me after all this time. Even eight years later I held a tremor of unease about being discovered by anyone from Gordon, Indiana. I hoped the press in attendance was all local. Surely no one on a national level would be interested in this gala. Would they? Ugh.

My breathing sped up and the edges of my vision dimmed. *No.* No way was I going to faint or hyperventilate on my way up to speak to everyone to this event. No freaking way.

I closed my eyes and took a slow, measured breath—counting to ten on the inhale and exhale. Once I repeated it a few times, I heard Maverick already halfway through welcoming everyone.

"I'd like to personally thank both Londa Flores and Dante Marian for taking this amazing program to the next chapter. We know with your leadership the kids of Marian House are in great hands."

Maverick went on to present Londa with a lifetime appreciation award for her years of service as the head of the shelter.

She refused to take the microphone but blew a teary kiss to the crowd before hugging her glass award to her chest and disappearing back into the crowd.

"Londa will be transitioning into her chosen role of house director while the new executive director and head of programming position is officially filled by the man who managed the expansion this year and wound up bringing the project in two months ahead of schedule and noticeably under budget. I am extremely proud to introduce my brother, Dante Marian."

The crowd applauded while I chanted in my head that I was cool, calm, and collected. I was zen. I was the most chill speaker who ever spoke in public. I could do this. I could... do... this?

I climbed onto the stage and approached my brother. His familiar friendly smile washed over me and he grabbed me into a tight hug.

"You got this. Just be yourself. I love you," he whispered into my ear.

When I stepped to the podium I blew out a breath. My damp hands slipped into my pockets to curl the worn edges of the notecards I'd spent ten days meticulously preparing and practicing with. *I should probably pull them out of my pocket and refer to them.*

My eyes looked out over the room. I couldn't do this. How in the world did I let Mav talk me into this? My eyes searched for a way out. An escape route that would lead me...

And there he was. The man from the line at the bar. Mr. Gorgeous.

His eyes focused intently on me, and I noticed concerned creases in his forehead. A lovely face like his shouldn't ever crease with worry. As my brain frantically searched a million directions for what to say next, my gaze settled on that one face. I would tell that one person, that nice-looking man, why everything was going to be okay and he could stop worrying. I wouldn't need notecards after all. I'd talk to this one guy.

"My name is Dante Marian," I told the man. "And I'm here to tell you my story."

His eyes widened in surprise and the light picked up golden flecks in their hazel depths. They were exquisite, and I felt myself relax into them with a smile.

"When people ask me about my past, I tell them my life began at age fifteen. Obviously, it didn't really. But I don't ever talk to anyone about the years that came before. Correction," I said with a small smile, "I do talk to a therapist about it. And now that I think of it, I'm sure she's here tonight, silently chuckling into her wineglass. She's probably also rubbing her eyes in disbelief that I'm up here speaking in front of such a large crowd."

There was a murmur of sympathetic laughter from the crowd and I noticed that even Mr. Gorgeous's lips twitched into an encouraging smile.

"The first fifteen years of my life were... hard. Confusing, stifling, abusive. I was the homeschooled son of a powerful man. My father took it very personally when I began to express interest in other boys.

He'd always believed strongly in corporal punishment and tried in vain to beat the gay out of me."

I noticed I'd balled my hands into fists in my pockets, and I forced myself to uncurl my fingers and relax my shoulders.

"We lived in a small Midwestern town. The police, the school principal, and even the town doctor were all friends of my father. In my scared fifteen-year-old mind, I had absolutely nowhere to turn for help.

"One night the entire school football team caught me kissing one of their teammates, and I wound up seriously injured. Did the police take me to the hospital when they found me bleeding and alone in the school parking lot? Nope. Took me to *my father*. Who turned around and beat me some more."

I paused a moment to let that sink in. Many people there in the high-end ballroom of the beautiful historic hotel in our liberal, gay-friendly city didn't realize stories like mine were really true. But I could see in the stranger's eyes that he somehow understood. I felt like he could see my old pain. That if he tried, he could actually touch it.

It made my throat tighten and I looked down at the podium and swallowed. Somehow the stranger's expression had made the old memories feel too real, and I squeezed my eyes against them. I could hear the silence in the ballroom and knew that any minute someone from my family was likely to leap to the stage to rescue me.

But this was my story to tell and I needed to do it. For Marian House. For myself. And for my angel who rescued me all those years ago.

The thought of my angel caused the band around my lungs to loosen and brought a smile to my lips. Opening my eyes, I found the stranger staring up at me, his expression unreadable. I continued telling him my story.

"Luckily, someone found me and delivered me to safety—to Londa, actually." I didn't mention the church or conversion therapy because it was too much. Too personal. Somehow that part of it was mine and mine alone, and I wasn't ready to share it.

"When Londa took me to the shelter, I didn't even get through the front doors before I panicked. I was terrified. I didn't know who Londa was, and when I found out I was going to a homeless shelter, I thought I'd go into the foster system and my father would find me. I panicked and ran.

"Clearly, I didn't have any idea where to go or what to do for food. So I didn't get very far before I lost my cool and sat down on a bench to have a good cry," I said with a smile, remembering how small I'd felt in the big city.

"While I sat there sobbing, a homeless guy walked up and held out this nasty old coffee cup asking me for money. I looked up at him in shock. Didn't he know I was homeless and alone just like he was?

"I stood up and walked farther away. I didn't know at the time that an older kid from the shelter program followed me, waiting for the right time to approach and offer to take me back to Marian House. That time didn't come until I stood at the railing of the Bay Bridge trying to figure out if I should take my shoes off before jumping or not."

The handsome man whose eyes I held in the audience raised his hand to his mouth, his eyes going wide. I had the ridiculous desire to reassure him. As if *he* was that scared kid on the bridge. But it wasn't his story. It was mine, so I shifted my gaze to my brother Griff and smiled to him.

"The older kid walked up and asked if I liked pizza," I said, then laughed. "Who the heck doesn't like pizza? I was a fifteen-year-old boy, for god's sake."

People in the ballroom chuckled in agreement, and I saw Griff's eyes were wet.

"So I said I did, and then he asked what I liked on my pizza. I said I liked sausage mostly, but pepperoni was fine too. Then he went on to ask what kind of soda I preferred and whether or not I liked basketball. I kept answering politely, as I'd always been raised to do. Even though that kid was five years older than I was, he was still kind of scrawny and young looking with a mop of curly hair."

Griff's husband Sam pulled Griff against him and kissed his forehead in a tight hug of support. He knew who I was talking about.

"He just kept talking my ears off and distracting me until I realized I was halfway back to the shelter with him. He'd somehow managed to lure me away in tiny, microscopic steps so subtle I didn't even notice I'd walked off the bridge. When I realized it, I confronted him, and I'll never forget what he said."

I paused.

"He smiled at me and shrugged. 'Just not today, okay? Just don't do anything like that *today*.'"

"So I didn't. And then I met the people of Marian House. And they showed up day after day with hands that didn't hit, voices that didn't rise in anger, and healthy meals that came at predictable intervals. They proved themselves as caretakers and friends over and over until I trusted again, and they finally became my family."

I looked around the ballroom at the faces of the people there and realized they were all allies to the cause. That thought emboldened me and helped me continue.

"I arrived at the shelter broken and hopeless. And I'm standing here today patched up and hopeful."

I noticed the stranger's eyes catch the light, and I could have sworn they were wet. And he wasn't the only one. As I scanned the room, I saw tears in the eyes of potential donors, and I reminded myself why I'd forced myself to stand up and share my story: so that other kids could have the same chance I did.

"I want you to know this program works. It saves lives. I could spend all night here telling you other stories of friends who've found the safe haven they needed just in the nick of time. When LGBTQ youth wind up on the streets, their chances of avoiding drugs and prostitution are miniscule, unless they have somewhere else to go or someone to help them. Often, their homelessness is not by choice."

I could hear the passion coming through my voice as I continued. "When a child has nowhere to go because of homophobic parents, when a teen needs a fresh set of friends because of school bullying, when a transgender child needs counseling to avoid an otherwise staggering suicide rate—Marian House provides all of those things."

"Our goal is for no LGBTQ child to be in need or face these difficult decisions. For no LGBTQ child to feel alone."

I gripped the edge of the podium tightly. "Tonight, I'm not asking you to donate money to Marian House. I'm asking you to donate hope." I paused, smiling before adding. "Okay, I am asking you to donate money as well." The crowd laughed. "Thanks to people like you, San Francisco is raising a generation of confident, well-educated LGBTQ leaders who will help our city thrive in the years to come."

My heart bumped a little faster in my chest. "Somewhere out there is a stranger who deserves my eternal gratitude for delivering me out of danger and into safety." I glanced toward my brother, placing a hand against my chest over my heart. "I'd also like to extend my most fervent thanks to Griffin Marian for asking me if I liked pizza. And my forever thanks to Londa and the Marian family for taking me in, loving me, and giving me a chance to pay it forward. I hope you will join me in this effort tonight and in the future. Please enjoy your evening."

I kept the public persona smile on my face until after I'd walked off the stage and exited the nearest door to the corridor. I knew I was likely leaving behind friends and family members waiting to give me a hug or show of support, but I was running out of time before losing my composure.

My legs carried me as quickly as they could to the one place I knew every venue could be counted on to have and everyone could be counted on to stay well away.

The dumpsters.

3

———————

AJ

s I stood listening to Dante's speech, I wanted to both cry
and cheer. My heart thumped with various emotions from
sadness at the implication he'd been through more than
I'd thought, to relief and happiness he sounded so confident and
strong.

I'd never known about the bridge. Londa either hadn't known or
had kept it to herself. The idea of him leaving me to end up on the
bridge was enough to cause me to shake.

I wanted to go up to him, congratulate him on his speech and tell
him how strong he was, but the minute he was off the stage, he disappeared out a side door.

Before I knew what I was doing, I followed him. My legs were
longer, but he walked so fast I had to hustle to keep track of him. He
finally pushed through the exit doors and I found myself getting
ready to follow him out to a loading dock area where the hotel dumpsters were.

As I reached to stop the door from closing, someone brushed past
me with a muttered, "Scuse me." I recognized the curly hair of
Dante's brother, Griffin Marian.

Griff grabbed Dante by one shoulder to turn him around and

Dante practically fell into Griff's arms, burying his face in his brother's neck with the sound of a muffled cry of relief.

My heart leapt into my throat and I stood there, frozen, feeling like a voyeur but not able to tear my eyes away from the man who'd fooled a thousand people into thinking he had everything together.

"AJ," a low voice called out behind me. "Is that you?"

I turned to see Griff's husband, Sam, approaching. "Yeah, it's me."

"They out there?" Sam asked, pointing through the open crack in the doorway.

I nodded. "Is Dante okay, do you think?" I asked. "He's upset, but he seemed so put together on stage."

Sam gave me a small smile. "He'll be fine. It's probably just an adrenaline crash from all the nerves leading up to the speech. He's terrified of crowds."

"Wow. You'd never know from the way he presented himself in there," I admitted.

"I've never seen him like that," Sam said. "Honestly, I expected him to bail or faint or stare down at prepared notecards. You know how he is."

The statement caught me off guard. "No, actually. I don't. We've never been introduced."

"What? You're kidding," Sam asked. "How is that possible? I met you like a year and a half ago, right?"

"Yeah. I guess the times I've visited, we just haven't run across each other." I shrugged. No sense in telling him I'd avoided running into Dante for fear he'd recognize me. Only, tonight, I'd gotten the sense he hadn't. At most, maybe he'd been wracking his brain to figure out why I looked familiar.

His eyes had locked onto mine while he spoke, but I hadn't seen any hints of recognition. I should have been relieved, but why had it left me feeling empty somehow?

Then again, he'd been so out of it that night long ago, and I'd had a super-short buzz cut instead of my regular dark brown mop of unruly thick hair. We'd both changed a lot over the last eight years. I'd been awkward and baby-faced until half-way through college when I began to hit the gym. And he'd been a broken, scared kid at the end of his rope.

I realized I was still staring out the opening in the doorway at Dante's head resting on his brother's shoulder while they talked quietly.

"I'd better, ah, get back into the ballroom and find my aunt. She'll expect me to dance with her once the band starts playing again, and I said I'd get her a drink, which I never got," I babbled.

What the fuck was wrong with me? I was never a babbler. I was rarely unsure of myself.

Sam shot me an inquisitive glance, but I waggled my fingers in a stupid goodbye wave before making my way back to the ballroom to get that drink and find Londa for a dance.

Sometime later that night, I saw Dante sitting around a table with several of his Marian siblings laughing. He had a drink in his hand, and I was struck again by how grown up he was compared to the scrawny teen I'd rescued that night so long ago. That kid was gone, and in his place was a complex man who could change his face like a chameleon changed color.

Dante the adult intrigued me, and I wanted to know more of him. Now that I was sure he didn't recognize me, I felt an intense desire to meet him and spend time with him. Hell, who was I kidding? Everything inside of me told me that man was *mine*.

I could either stand in that ballroom wishing and hoping he'd notice me or I could get some fucking balls and go get what I wanted.

I strode over to where he sat between two of his brothers. Before I had a chance to introduce myself to Dante, Griff's face split into a big grin.

"AJ Flores, come join us," he said. "Do you know everyone here?"

"No," I admitted with a smile. "Besides you and Simone, I only know... wait, what did you call him when you introduced us? Ah, that's right. Sam, your cookie-wookie."

The entire table laughed and gave Griff a hard time. Sam's face turned red and he punched his husband on the shoulder.

"Asshole," Sam said with affection.

"Well, I guess I should amend that," Griff admitted. "Now he's my old ball and chain."

The group groaned and Griff pulled Sam in for a kiss on the mouth. I was pretty sure I overheard him tell Sam he meant chains in a sexy way.

I waved to Simone, the only sister, and she continued to introduce several other Marian siblings until getting around to Dante, who sat in front of where I stood.

"And that's Dante, but you probably already know that from his speech," she finished.

I had waved or smiled at each person around the table, but when it was Dante's turn, I reached out a hand to shake. He turned his head to look up at me, and I felt my skin prickle before he even touched me.

"Hi, AJ," he said, and it was all I could do to swallow the moan I felt at the sound of my name on his tongue.

"Dante, it's so nice to meet you. Your speech was wonderful. Thank you for all your hard work with Marian House. I know your family is extremely proud of you, as is my aunt Londa."

As I spoke, Dante's face flushed until his cheeks were a delicious pink and his neck was mottled.

"Th-thanks," he stammered.

Oh dear god. He was adorable as fuck.

"Can I buy you a drink?" I asked him. Out of the corner of my eye, I saw his sister suppress a giggle.

He looked away, seemingly embarrassed by the attention. A mumble came out of his mouth but went straight down into his chest.

"I'm sorry, I couldn't hear you," I said softly. "Hopefully that was a yes?"

"I said, it's an open bar. The drinks are free," he said without looking back up at me. I put a hand on his shoulder and leaned my lips down near his ear.

"Then is there another cheesy pickup line that would work better for you?" I asked so softly only he could hear.

I could have sworn he shivered.

4

———————

DANTE

Hypothetically speaking, what would happen if someone came in their tuxedo pants in the middle of a formal gala at the Palace Hotel? Because that was about to happen if the man didn't get his sexy fucking lips away from my ear.

"Ahhaha," I gasped as I felt the warm breath from his exhale tingle the hairs by my ear. "Yes, please. A drink. Yes. A drink. Would be good. I mean, a drink. Please. Good be would. I mean, would be good. Please," I stammered. "A drink." I blew out a breath and put my face down in my hands. "*Jesusfuckingchrist.*"

The entire table burst out laughing, and I wanted to kill them all. Luckily, at least one asshole went down for the count, and that was my traitorous dick.

AJ lifted the corner of his mouth in a smirk. "A please drink good be would?" he asked.

"Goddammit," I muttered, standing up. "Let's go."

I stalked over to one of the bar areas and turned back to AJ, who followed closely behind. He smiled at me and raised an eyebrow. Shit, he was just as hot up close as I'd thought he was. I'd tried not to look at him since he'd approached our table, but there was no use. He was hot as a freaking space shuttle re-entry in a sci-fi movie, the kind the astronauts are never prepared for. That causes the thermal protection tiles to vibrate and peel off and the humans inside to wonder whether they'll survive it. Yeah, that kind of hot. Spoiler alert: they're probably not going to survive it.

"Well?" I blurted.

"Well, what?" he asked.

"What do you want to drink?" I asked, realizing belatedly my voice sounded snappish. I sighed. "Sorry. I mean, what would you like to drink, AJ? Since I'm in charge of this thing, I'm kind of buying." I forced my nervous lips into a grin and AJ's eyes widened in surprise.

"Well, shit. If you're kind of buying, then I'm going all out." He turned to the bartender. "I'll take a glass of ice water, please. On the rocks, with a twist."

AJ winked. I might as well get used to my face being beet red around the man.

"You're just getting water?" I asked.

"I'll let you keep the money for this one in the Marian House coffers," he explained.

Oh no. No, no. I needed this cutie not to be sweet or philanthropic. That was going to result in one thing, and one thing only.

"Do you want to get out of here?" I blurted. And honestly? I wasn't sure who was more surprised—him or me.

WE WEREN'T EVEN out of the hotel yet and I wondered what the fuck I'd done. When I'd asked him to leave with me, he'd grabbed my hand and yanked me toward the door. The move was so decisive and demanding, it nearly made my cock fling off my cumberbund.

I was in over my head.

"W-wait," I said, pulling back against his hand. "Maybe we should figure out where we're going first?"

He tilted his head and seemed to study me for a moment before I noticed his eyes soften. "Why don't we find a quiet place to grab a drink and we can just talk for a little while without all the other people around?"

I let out a silent breath of relief and smiled. "Yeah. That sounds good. I'd really like that."

AJ squeezed my hand and led me out the front door of the hotel where he had someone hail us a cab. When the doorman held the car door for us, AJ took his place and ushered me in first before turning to ask the doorman for a recommendation for a quiet place to get a drink. After slipping him a tip, AJ got into the car beside me and gave the address to the driver.

I held my hands together in my lap and looked down at them, realizing my fingers were white from gripping each other so tightly. Before I had a chance to relax them, AJ reached a hand over to take the one closest to him and pull it back over to his lap.

I looked up at him, heart racing. He smiled down at me sweetly. "Relax, Dante. It's just one drink, and you can leave at any time."

The low rumble of his sexy voice made me swallow thickly. "Sorry. I just don't... I don't usually do this kind of thing."

"You don't usually drink?" he teased.

I rolled my eyes. "I don't usually leave a place with a guy." When my words hit my brain, I wanted to kick myself. Could I possibly sound more pathetic?

AJ reached over and tilted my chin up with his free hand. "What made you do it this time?"

The lights from the street and passing cars flickered in through the window, lighting up his face in alternating bands of light and dark. His eyes gazed intently on mine, but it didn't make me feel uncomfortable at all. In fact, something about him soothed me in a way that felt familiar.

"I have absolutely no idea," I said with a laugh.

"Well, I'm glad you did."

The cab pulled up to a small pub and we made our way inside, finding a high-top table for two. Once we ordered a couple of beers from a server, AJ slid off his tuxedo jacket and hung it over the back of his stool.

"Good idea," I said, sliding mine off as well and untying my bow tie. After flicking open the top button of my shirt, I did the same to my cuffs before rolling up my sleeves. All the while, AJ watched me like I was a cold swimming pool he was desperate to dive into on a hot day.

I swallowed and looked away, noticing a different server approaching our table with our beer. As he came closer, I realized he was a guy I went to grad school with.

"Dante," the man said with a smile. "Thought that was you. I asked Emily to switch with me so I could have your table."

"Hi, Zane," I said. "Good to see you. How've you been?"

He set the bottles on the table and glanced at AJ before looking back at me. "Meh, can't complain. I'm working as a grant writer for a hunger program, but you know it pays peanuts. So I'm trying to make up for it by busting my ass here," he said with a wink. "What about you? Still at the shelter? Have they bumped up their dress code since I volunteered there with you?"

He gestured to my tux and I laughed. "Yeah. All the Bay Area nonprofits are going in this direction, so you'd better save up. It's nice to see you," I said, in hopes he'd leave us in peace. There was really only one man in the bar I wanted to talk to.

Zane's eyes flicked back over to AJ. "Yeah, sorry about that. I'll leave you to it then. Let me know if you need anything, okay? It's really good to see you, Dante. Don't be a stranger." Before he left, he reached out to squeeze my shoulder and give me a final smile.

When I looked back at AJ, he was studying me with those mesmerizing hazel eyes. The kind of eyes that seemed to look right past my defenses and straight into my soul. Every time those eyes were trained on me, I felt exposed. And I wasn't sure if that was good or bad.

What do you see? I wanted to ask him. *What do you see when you look at me?*

5

AJ

Why was Dante all wound up and twisted in knots with me, but he seemed to flirt just fine with his waiter friend? The stupid, immature part of me was instantly jealous when the cute guy approached our table with smiles for Dante.

When he squeezed Dante's shoulder, it was all I could do to shove my hands under my legs on the stool to keep from reaching out to fling the man's hands away. What in the world was wrong with me? I'd never before felt such a sense of possession about another person. Ever.

"He seems nice," I said, taking a sip of my beer and leaning back in my chair. I had years of experience in personal security, extractions, and undercover operations, and I could act nonchalant when the situation demanded it.

"Who?" Dante asked.

I blinked at him, trying to figure out if he was messing with me. It didn't seem like it. It seemed like he truly didn't know what I was talking about.

"Your friend Zane," I said with a smile.

"Huh? Oh. Yeah, Zane. Nice guy."

I couldn't help but chuckle. Dante Marian was seriously the cutest freaking thing in the entire world. And I wanted him with a singular focus that began to drive my every move.

"Why are you laughing?" he asked with a blush.

"You didn't even realize he was flirting with you, did you?"

"Who? Zane? No, he wasn't."

"He absolutely was," I teased.

"Whatever." Dante took a sip of his beer.

"I can't blame the guy," I admitted. "You seem like the total package."

His eyes snapped up and his mouth opened in an "O" before he let out a nervous laugh. "Oh, you're messing with me."

I'd like *to be messing with you*, I thought.

"No, Dante, I'm not. You're sweet and kind. And absolutely gorgeous."

As I spoke, his face got redder, which kind of made me want to keep talking.

"I'm not sleeping with you," he blurted.

I barked out a laugh. "Well, damn. That was unexpected. But okay. I guess. Even though I don't exactly remember asking you to."

"Oh my god," he stammered. "I have to go."

He slipped off the stool and grabbed his jacket. I dropped some money on the table and followed him out.

"Dante, wait."

"No. Must go home and die of embarrassment. Can't be late for that," he mumbled. We stood on the sidewalk in front of the bar when I snagged his elbow, turning him around as gently as I could.

"Just hang on for a minute and then I'll let you go," I said.

He spun to face me and I could see how miserable he felt. My heart went out to him and part of me wanted to wrap him up in my arms and whisper reassurances that it was okay. There was no reason for him to be embarrassed when I already liked him and wanted him.

"I'm sorry," Dante whispered.

"What for?"

"For being so unbelievably awkward and weird."

"Dante Marian, has it ever occurred to you I might *like* awkward and weird?" I said with a grin, bringing my hands up to cup both sides of his face. "I don't want to make you uncomfortable, but I'd like to see you again."

"Why in the world would you want to see me again?" he asked.

I dropped my hands and shrugged. "Meh, you seem like a nice enough guy, I guess. Might as well."

He stood staring at me as if trying to decide how serious to take me.

I reached out to squeeze his arm. "I'm kidding. I'd like to take you to dinner tomorrow night if that's okay with you. Can I pick you up at Marian House at seven?"

"Yeah, okay. I'd like that," he said. That he answered so quickly surprised me. Maybe he was as interested in me as I was in him. I decided to let him go before he let nerves take over again.

"Good night, Dante. Congratulations again for the success of the project and the fundraiser tonight. Your speech was amazing, and I was very impressed. I'll see you tomorrow night."

Before I allowed myself to grab him and crush my lips onto his, I turned and walked away.

THE FOLLOWING night I took him to a quiet Italian restaurant. We sat in a secluded booth and ordered a bottle of wine. Once the first glass was down, he finally started to relax. The guy was even more gorgeous than I'd remembered from the night before. He wore well-fitting dark denim jeans and an aqua-colored shirt that set off his olive skin. He looked healthy and alive, and I had trouble taking my eyes off him.

I asked him open-ended questions about the expansion project at the shelter and about his studies in nonprofit management. He asked me what I did and I explained a little about my new job, only saying I had a background in a certain type of personal security logistics I'd been hired for at Joel's company. I had about two weeks to find a place to live and settle in before I'd have to start the new job.

We spoke about our families and exchanged complaints about being the youngest sibling. As the dinner wore on, things became easier between us until I caught our waitress shooting moony eyes in our direction for being so flirty with each other.

It wasn't until we walked outside things became weird again.

"So..." he said. "I should probably go since I'm supposed to be at my parents' really early tomorrow to help them with something. Thank you so much for dinner, AJ. I had a really nice time." He glanced away and then back at me. "Ah, would you like to do it again some time?"

"Absolutely," I said with a grin. "The sooner, the better."

"Really?" he asked, and he truly looked surprised.

Instead of answering him with words, I leaned in to kiss him good night. Our lips barely brushed each other, but the sensation of his mouth against mine made my stomach flip over.

I started to pull away, but Dante grabbed a fistful of my shirt and yanked me back toward him. This time the kiss was raw and fevered; our tongues came out to find each other and our beard scruff scratched together. Noses bumped and teeth clacked. I moaned into him and he whimpered in response.

My hands moved down to wind around his back and pull him in closer. God, I wanted him. Wanted him in so many ways. There, in my arms on the street, kissing. Naked in my bed, underneath me, coming apart. I couldn't catch my breath from wanting him.

Our bodies were pressed so tightly together I could feel the hard push of his cock against my hip. The realization of it made me groan and arch my hips farther into him. He responded in kind, shoving his cock harder against my hipbone and then rolling his hips two or three times, mimicking thrusts.

Holyfuckingshit, we were grinding on the street. Not okay. Not what I wanted for him. I'd wanted to go slow, to earn his trust. Knowing his past meant making sure he felt in control at all times.

I pulled away with a gasp, holding out an open palm in a stop gesture while my other hand covered my mouth. "No," I breathed.

Just then, the door to the bar opened and out came our waitress. "One of you guys left your phone on the table," she said, holding up my phone.

"Oh shit," I said, patting my pants pocket even though I could tell by looking at it the phone was mine. "Thanks so much." I stepped forward to grab it and thank her again.

When I turned back to Dante, he was gone.

AFTER OUR DATE, I couldn't get in touch with Dante to ask him out again or even just talk to him. I wracked my brain to figure out how we'd gone from agreeing to another date to him avoiding me. The only thing that happened was me pushing him away during our public humping. Could he have somehow thought I was rebuffing him?

I spent the next few days shadowing Aunt Londa at the shelter in the hopes of running into him. When the third night of no Dante approached, I went from being disappointed to being concerned. I worried something was wrong, but Londa told me he was fine and working from home.

My brain could make all the arguments it wanted about how he might just be nervous or intimidated. But the truth remained he was actively avoiding me. There wasn't really a way to spin that without realizing I needed to back off.

I'd finished wiping down the last of the tables in the dining hall after dinner one night when Dante's brother Griff approached me.

"Hey, man, Sam and I are meeting some friends at a club later tonight. Come with us," Griff said. I'd always liked Griffin Marian. He was laid back and friendly, a very easy guy to be around.

"Nah, I don't think so. I'll probably just head back to Londa's and watch a movie," I said.

"Are you sure? Dante's going to be there," he said with a grin.

"Even more reason for me not to go. He definitely wouldn't want you bringing me."

His smile dropped. "What do you mean? Why not?"

I shrugged. "Don't know exactly. He's avoided me for several days."

"Shit, AJ. He's just shy and doesn't have much experience yet. Probably doesn't know what to do or say around you," Griff said. "We'll go to the club and you can ask him to dance. No need for small talk." He winked.

Was I really going to turn down the opportunity to dance with Dante Marian at a club? Hell fucking no.

"Okay. When and where?"

6

DANTE

When I'd stood out front of that restaurant in AJ's arms, I'd wanted to throw myself bodily on the man and beg him to fuck me right there on the street. The desire terrified me. Never in my life had I wanted someone like that. And I'd sure as hell never considered being fucked by someone I'd only just met.

So I got scared and ran. No big surprise. But once I'd made it back to my apartment, I fell down a spiral of second-guessing every move I'd made that night. Every word I'd said, every word he'd said.

When I finally had the nerve to grab him back into a real kiss to show him how much I wanted him, he'd stopped me. That's when I realized almost every stupidly forward gesture that had happened between us had been initiated by me.

Granted, he'd asked if he could buy me a drink and he'd been the one to lean in for the sweet good night kiss, but I'd been the one to ask him to leave the gala the night before. And I'd been the one to yank his shirt and shove my tongue down his throat.

Clearly that hadn't been well received. Wait. That wasn't quite right. He definitely seemed interested, but then when I jumped him, he pushed me off.

Whatever. I could think myself in circles all night like that. Wondering why he pulled away, barking out a *no*. Instead, I'd get over it. It wasn't like I was his type anyway. The guy was hot-shit alpha male all the way. And I was a dorky pipsqueak. Maybe I needed to get back in my own lane. But at least the experience served as a reminder I needed to put myself out there.

I was in my twenties, for god's sake, and I was horny as hell. I wanted someone to kiss. I wanted someone to make me feel the way AJ had made me feel that night. And I desperately wanted someone to run hands all over my naked body and touch my dick. Preferably with their mouth.

Ugghhhh. Just the thought of AJ's mouth on my cock made me fucking crazy.

That night I slept fitfully, having the same dream I'd had a hundred times about being in the middle of a crowd like Times Square on New Year's Eve. I was trapped between bodies and wasn't strong enough to shoulder my way to the edge of the mob to escape. The difference this time was being rescued by a hot-as-shit beefcake and waking up to massive, rock-hard morning wood.

I reached down to run my hand up and down my cock, rolling my eyes at myself for being so fucking predictable the morning after kissing a gorgeous man. Images of AJ flowed into my mind. His tanned skin set off against the starched white tuxedo shirt. The warm golden flecks in his hazel eyes. His large, masculine hand reaching over for mine in the taxi that first night.

My cock throbbed in my fist and precum leaked from the tip. *What the fuck?* Was I really going to rub one out to the thought of AJ Flores? Apparently I was.

After a few more tugs, I caved and reached over to my bedside table drawer for some lotion. I pumped a generous amount in my palm and warmed it between both hands before reaching back down to my raging hard-on.

Fucckkk, that felt good. Jacking off to thoughts of kissing and humping AJ was ten times better than jacking off to generic thoughts of strangers.

I bent my legs and brought my feet flat on the mattress, spreading my legs farther apart until I could reach one hand down to play with my sac while the other pumped my cock.

I remembered the feel of AJ's stiff length outlined against my belly, and I wanted so badly to touch it. Why hadn't I at least reached down to run my hand over his pants and feel it? It was probably fat and long like it had felt against my stomach.

A tingle built in my spine as my balls tightened. I imagined what it would feel like to have AJ's thick cock push into my ass and fill me up. My hand lowered from my sac to play with my hole.

Yessss.

My breathing sped up as my hips got into the action, pumping my entire pelvis up into my jacking fist.

My stomach was tight and my cock felt like it skated the line between good-hard and painful-hard. I fucked my hand over and over while my other hand began to press first one then two slick fingers into my ass.

Cum shot out of me in a sudden, shuddering rhythm. White fluid landed on my chest and abs as my eyes rolled back, and I did my best to swallow my cries. "*Oh g-godd,*" I breathed. "*Fffuck.*"

The orgasm didn't stop. It seemed to go on forever and as pictures of AJ flashed through my mind, more cum spat from the tip until I felt my eyebrows rise in surprise at the sheer intensity and duration of my orgasm.

Once I floated back down to earth, I realized there was no way I could face AJ at the shelter that day or even my family first thing that morning. I lay there holding the evidence in my sticky hand of what that man did to me, and I'd be damned if I would lose my composure in front of others.

No. I was better off staying home.

～

ONE DAY of being a chickenshit easily turned into three, and my roommates must have lost patience with my moping around. They decided to go dancing at a club and drag me along with them.

Robbie and Jason were friends of my brother-in-law Sam. When Sam and Griff moved to Napa, I took his place in the apartment with Robbie, Jason, and Sam's mostly absent sister, Lacey. It was nice to finally move out of Mom and Dad's house and feel more like an adult. But I also loved living with other people so I wasn't lonely all the time. I wasn't sure how I'd feel living alone.

"Come with us," they said when I entered the place. "Robbie's hoping to run into that kid he hooked up with last weekend, so I need you to keep me company," Jason said with a big grin.

"Nah, I think I'm—"

"Not taking no for an answer, Dante," Jason said, grabbing my hand and turning me toward the door. "You look like you need some cheering up. Nothing says 'feel better' quite like a little bump and grind on the dance floor. Let's go find you some fun. Plus, Griff and Sam are still in town and going to meet us there. I just texted them."

I couldn't disagree with his point and if there was one thing that could make me feel better, it was some positive attention from cute boys and a night out with my favorite brother.

"Fine," I said with a sigh. "Let's go."

7

———

AJ

When we got to the club, it was already late enough that the place hopped and the music blared. Bodies packed the dancefloor and bar areas, and the vibe was electric. After getting a round of drinks at the bar, Sam spotted a friend of his and led us over to a high-topped table against a wall.

Dante stood there with a few other men I didn't recognize, but it didn't matter. I only had eyes for him anyway. He was gorgeous as usual. As he watched the dancers on the floor his body moved slightly to the beat of the music.

Just before I had a chance to reach out for his elbow to get his attention, a hot guy on the dance floor caught his eye and crooked a finger with a sexy grin. My heart thrummed with nerves and jealousy as I saw Dante join him.

When Griff and Sam introduced me to their other friends, I had one eye on Dante and one eye on the men at the table just enough to be polite. Dante danced with his arms above his head, and the man dancing with him had his hands all over Dante's body. How long was I going to be able to watch without committing felony assault?

I took a deep breath and tried to pay attention to the conversation Griff and Sam were having next to me.

"So then they did the anal probe and told me they'd return me to my home planet just as soon as I danced the Macarena for them," Griff said loudly over the music.

"What?" I asked, wondering what part of the conversation I'd missed.

All four of them burst out laughing. "Go dance with him, AJ. Clearly you're not any good to us anyway."

I rolled my eyes and looked back at Dante. The man's hands were on Dante's ass, and they moved up under Dante's shirt and began to travel under his waistband. I saw Dante stiffen in response. He wasn't okay with the man's hands on him, but he didn't seem to make a move to stop it either.

Oh hell no.

I lurched up from the stool I'd been leaning on and strode to where Dante and the man danced. After rudely stepping between them, I told the stranger to beat it, and then I put my arms around Dante.

Oh my fucking god. He felt so good I wanted to cry. I wanted to bury my nose in his neck and hold him for the rest of my life. That's how good he felt against me.

He somehow smelled clean at the end of a long day and among all the sweaty men surrounding us. I wanted to inhale him, taste him, and feel him. Even though he was noticeably smaller than I was, he fit against me perfectly.

"What the fuck?" he barked at me, snapping me out of my reverie.

"I need to talk to you," I replied into his ear. He wore a small metal stud that brushed coolly against my lip.

His head turned slightly to rub his scruff against my own.

"Why have you been avoiding me?" I asked.

My hands splayed across his back, and I could feel his muscles move as he continued to sway to the music.

He tilted his head back to study me, but he stayed there in my arms, wrapping his own around my waist.

Dante leaned in closer again until his mouth was next to my ear, causing me to shiver.

"You pushed me away the other night," he said. "I thought that meant I'd fucked up or something."

I turned my face toward his ear and nuzzled my nose against it without realizing what I was doing. "Jesus, Dante. I pushed you away because if I hadn't, I would have taken you right there on the street and you deserve bet—"

He cut me off with a kiss. It was sweet and almost chaste before his lips moved down to my throat, sending shivers skating along my skin. As his mouth made its way back up the side of my neck to my earlobe, the beat of the music was replaced with the banging of my heart in my chest and the pulsing of my cock in my jeans.

I felt a groan escape me and my fingers got itchy. I moved my hands up under the hem of his shirt. The warm skin of his back made me crazy. Dante's hands grabbed my ass and squeezed. Fuck, *fuck*, I wanted him so badly.

"*Dante*," I breathed against his hair. I shouldn't do this. His brothers were right there and we were in public.

Just as he moved his mouth to mine, a hand pulled my shoulder back to separate us. It was Griff.

"We have to go," he said to Dante in a rush. "Aunt Tilly just texted me."

"What?" Dante asked in a daze. "What happened?"

It was almost impossible to hear over the music so Griff gestured to the entrance of the club. I leaned in to Dante's ear. "I'm coming with you."

He nodded and took my hand, pulling me with him as we followed Griff and Sam to the door.

Once we squeezed together into a taxi, Griff explained more. "She didn't say. Just that she needed help ASAP at her place."

I sat in the middle between Griff and Dante, and Sam sat up front. Dante leaned across me to talk to Griff, one of his hands planted on my thigh for balance. I tried to think of anything I could to avoid letting the sensation on my leg travel up to my crotch.

"I thought she and Granny and Irene were going to Vegas," he said.

The mention of the little old ladies helped my burgeoning boner situation.

"I thought so too," Griff said with a worried expression on his face.

"Shit," Dante muttered. "Should we call Mom and Dad? What else did she say?"

"She's not answering the phone. We're almost there. Let's just wait and see when we get there before we worry anyone else. You know how she is."

We pulled up in front of a stunning Wedgewood blue Edwardian home in Nob Hill. The place screamed San Francisco upper crust, and I almost laughed at how perfect it was for the Tilly Marian I'd met several times before through my aunt.

Sam paid the driver, and we all shuffled out of the car to the front steps of the house. Griff tried the door in case it happened to be unlocked before ringing the doorbell.

A moment later, a gentleman in a burgundy satin bathrobe opened the door. I wondered if he could be a butler.

"Hey, Carl, what's wrong with Aunt Tilly?" Griff asked the man.

You could tell Carl wanted to roll his eyes, but he remained stoic. "Nothing I'm aware of, Griffin. Why do you ask?"

"She texted me SOS," he said, taking us past Carl to the staircase leading up to what I assumed was the living area of Tilly's home.

We could hear big band music coming from somewhere and the sound of women laughing. It didn't feel like an emergency situation.

I followed the Marian men up the stairs and heard Griff cry out when he reached the top.

"Holy mother of god, Tilly! *Jesusfuckingchrist,*" he gasped before turning around to shield his eyes from whatever he'd seen.

Sam grabbed him and pulled him against his chest while he peered around him to see what the deal was. He, too, quickly covered his eyes, causing Dante to run up the last few steps to see what the hell was going on. I bounded up after him, passing Sam and Griff before accidentally almost bowling Dante over when he got to the top and froze.

There, in the living room, were at least eight older ladies holding various dildos. And it appeared they were, ah, trying to ... pleasure them.

Orally.

"There you are," Tilly said with a grin, placing her giant black cock on the coffee table with a thump. "We need your help."

8

DANTE

I wasn't 100 percent sure, but I thought maybe bringing a guy you had a crush on to your great-aunt's Blow Job Bonanza wasn't really the polite thing to do. The poor guy. It's not as if he was used to Tilly's usual antics. I wasn't even sure if he'd met her before.

I turned to look at him with what I hoped was a look of desperate apology written on my face but was more likely a mask of absolute horror mixed with embarrassment.

AJ burst out laughing and leaned toward me. "Your family is a little bit strange," he said only loud enough for me to hear.

"You don't even know. This is par for the course," I admitted.

"I kinda like it." He laughed some more before I felt him drop a kiss on the top of my head and move us farther into the room. I kept my eyes on the floor.

"Ladies, if you don't mind lowering your weapons, please. Thanks," AJ said.

I heard them titter and balk at his request, but the sound was accompanied by the recognizable thud of heavy silicone dongs hitting the table.

My brother still stood at the top of the stairs seemingly undecided about coming all the way into the room.

"What the hell, Tilly?" Griff asked. "What's the emergency you texted me about?"

Aunt Tilly looked over at him and clapped her hands together. "We need your help. Sally here has brought us all of these wonderful toys to try from some company called Love Junk, but none of us can remember how to use them. I told everyone I could get some BJ experts here in a jiff. Come on in and have a seat."

I felt more than heard AJ chuckling next to me. Sam stood next to his husband in abject shock. He turned to Griff and begged, "Fox, make it stop."

Griff continued into the room and leaned over to kiss Aunt Tilly on the cheek. "So, you ladies are okay?" he asked in a calmer voice than before.

Granny piped up from her seat in a large wingback chair. "We will be when you show us how to give these puppies some lovin'," she said.

Irene sat on an ottoman next to Granny and giggled.

Griff looked around the room at the women all staring at him with expectant looks on their faces. "Ah, what makes you think I would be able to—?"

At that, I couldn't help but bark out a laugh, earning me a glare from my brother and a chuckle from Sam and AJ.

"All right, little brother, why don't you give them a demonstration since you're such an *experienced* know-it-all?" he suggested with a glare.

Oh shit.

I felt my face heat up and tried not to look at AJ standing next to me. "N-no, thanks. N-never mind," I stammered. A reassuring hand landed on my lower back, and I wanted to turn and hide my face in AJ's shirt. But I refrained. No reason to give him a better angle from which to see how red my tomato face was.

Griff turned to his husband. "Why don't you do the honors, sunshine?"

Sam stood there in horror, wide eyes peering back at Griff. "Are you crazy?"

"Babe, you're the only one who can. Dante and I are brothers, poor AJ is practically a stranger, so that leaves you. Plus, I'm assuming you're the expert among the four of us anyway. You're really good at it," he said with a teasing grin. The ladies in the room chuckled and swooned.

I thought Sam was going to faint and fall backward down the stairs. "Grab him, Griff," I said. "You're scaring the poor guy to death."

"No," Sam said, shaking his head and taking a deep breath. "I got this. I can do it." He seemed to be talking more to himself than anyone else in the room. "I've been a member of this crazy family long enough. It's time for me to act like one."

Griff rubbed his hands together in excitement before beginning to unbuckle his belt. I felt AJ grab me and turn my face into his shirt again before stammering, "What the hell, Griff?"

"Surely Sam would rather demonstrate on a live model than one of those things. Right, babe?" Griff asked. I could tell from the sound of his voice he was teasing. The ladies were all a-titter anyway.

"*Glck*," Sam choked. "Dammit, Griffin. Don't make this more difficult than it already is."

AJ loosened his grip on me so I could turn back around. It was like watching a car accident. I felt guilty for wanting to watch, but my eyes stayed glued to it anyway.

Sam looked down at the various collection of phalli on the table and back up at the ladies assembled. "Is there one that hasn't already been… sampled?" he asked politely.

Sally the Love Junk saleslady produced a new one in a package from her tote bag.

"Here you go. It's the newest—Widow Wrecker. Go for it. This baby can take a pounding," she said sweetly, handing Sam a gargantuan veiny thing that looked a bit… gummy for my taste.

Sam took it with two fingers as if it had cooties. He cleared his throat and gathered his courage. "Okay. First, let's talk about some of the important parts of the anatomy," he began.

"Hang on," I interrupted. "Granny and Irene, why are you here? You don't even like the D."

"Wash your mouth out with soap, Dante Marian," Granny snapped. "Just because I prefer tacos doesn't mean I don't want a nice pickle every once in a while, right, Reenie?" she asked, nudging her wife.

Irene nodded. "Plus, every time we have that nice man from the apartment next door over, he always seems so disappointed in us. What's his name again?"

"Boris?" Tilly guessed.

"No, not that one. I wouldn't touch Boris's thundersword if it was coated in caviar. I'm talking about that other fellow. The one to the right of us," Irene said.

A woman I didn't recognize chimed in. "Is it Richard? The one with the toupee?"

Irene laughed. "Pfft. That man likes anything you do to his little Dick."

"Little dick?" I squeaked.

"His mini-me. You know, his tiny Richard," Tilly clarified. "But I think you're talking about Gerald. The one who thinks you two are sisters."

"Oh right," Irene said with a wistful smile. "I *do* like it when Gerald comes over."

"I don't know why since he does more watching than performing. He's a lazy ass if you want to know the truth," Granny said. "But Irene is talking about Martin. He's the one we need to step up our game for. Man's a goddamned tiger in bed."

That was it. I couldn't take any more. I turned my face to AJ and didn't even need to get the words out before he said, "Come on, let's get you home."

Before we had a chance to escape, Sally jumped up from her spot on the sofa and pressed a box into my hands. "Thanks for coming by on such short notice and bringing your beautiful boyfriend."

She fluttered her eyelashes at AJ until he was the one with a tomato face.

"No problem. Good luck with your lesson," I said before looking down at the box in my hand. "And, um, thanks for the... ah... Turgid Love Hammer," I stammered.

AJ put his arm around my shoulder and led me toward the stairs. I could hear him laughing behind me the whole way down to the entry hall. Before we reached the door, I saw Carl step out and gesture for me to wait.

"Dante, I hate to ask you to do this, but I'm not dressed. Some of your aunt's shopping bags are in the RV out back in the alley, and she might want them before she goes to sleep tonight. Would you mind retrieving them for her before you go?"

"No problem. I'll be happy to. When you say RV..." I said.

He chuckled. "She calls it the party bus. She bought it about six months ago for their road trips. She thinks it saves on hotel costs. When they go gambling, they overnight in Bakersfield and then park it at Brad and Miles' house in Vegas."

"How the hell did the woman end up so cheap? She's a multimillionaire, for god's sake," I muttered.

Carl rolled his eyes. "Good question. The party bus cost over eighty grand. I keep trying to tell her that's quite a bit of hotel stays, but you know how she is."

I sighed. "I certainly do. Thanks, Carl. Go on to bed. We'll handle the bags."

"Thanks again."

We turned around to make our way out the back door to the alley behind the house. There, in all its shiny splendor was a Zeus Navigator twenty-four-foot recreational vehicle. The sight of the cheesy road trip wet dream was so out of place in my great-aunt's Nob Hill neighborhood, I barked out a laugh.

I heard AJ chuckling beside me. "Now that's a fancy set of wheels."

"Let's check it out," I suggested, opening the door. "Knowing Tilly, there are cold drinks in here somewhere."

There were, indeed, cold drinks in the fridge. We couldn't find the right light switches so we worked together in the semi-darkness making cocktails.

"This is nice. Beats the hell out of the phallus party upstairs," AJ said.

"Oh my god, don't remind me. I apologize yet again for—"

AJ put a finger over my lips and smiled. "Don't. Please. You've already apologized several times, and you didn't even do anything."

The feel of his finger on my lips sent tingles across my face, and I felt my eyes widen. He must have noticed because his pupils began changing right in front of me. Without breaking eye contact I opened my mouth slightly, letting his finger fall in.

My tongue reached out to wrap itself around his warm finger and draw it into my mouth. His pupils shot and the entire atmosphere of the small camper space around us became charged with sexual tension.

I saw his lips part and his own tongue come out to run along the bottom edge of his top lip. His eyes were glued to my mouth now as I sucked his finger in farther. I brought a hand up to hold his wrist to keep him from pulling away.

I wanted to kiss him so badly, but I was terrified of coming off as the complete horndog I was. My head felt dizzy and my heart slammed in my chest. He was right there. Right in front of me, and mine for the taking. What did I have to lose?

I leaned closer until we were almost nose to nose. AJ was breathing heavily enough to make the rise and fall of his chest visible. I put a hand there to feel his heart. He brought his own hand from my mouth down to clasp mine on his chest instead of flinging it away like I'd feared.

"Dante," he said in a husky voice. A warning? A plea?

"*Please*," I whispered as I brought my other hand up to his cheek to pull his face down to mine. I brushed my lips across his before going back for more.

The next step with AJ was like the time my brothers took me cliff diving in Hawaii. I was terrified on the way there. Frozen with panic and nerves rather than excited anticipation like everyone else. And when I stood on that cliff with my toes hanging off the edge, I had to make a decision. Leap forward into the unknown or walk away to safety.

Once I jumped, the panic vanished, leaving nothing in its place except sheer joy, adrenaline, and a complete sense of freedom.

Kissing AJ was the best thing in the world. It was exhilaration coupled with the absolute knowledge I wanted do it again and again as long as I lived. I'd been an idiot to have ever hesitated in the first place. Fearing it was like fearing the very air around me.

His tongue was sweet and gentle. One of his large hands came up to cup my face and the other continued holding my hand to his chest. I heard a low moan reverberate through him and I pressed closer to feel more of him. That one movement ignited a spark of events.

Suddenly we were kissing feverishly, hands in each other's hair and lips all over one another. The only sounds were frantic intakes of breaths and light smacking sounds as our mouths tried devouring each other. My cock throbbed against my fly, and I wanted so badly to shove it up against something.

"Dante," AJ growled. "Are you sure? I don't want to go too fast."

"You're not going fast enough," I complained.

"Then move."

"Huh?" I breathed, pulling away far enough to look at him in confusion.

"Bed," he said, nodding behind him. "Go."

I was up like a shot, grabbing his hand and pulling him with me. We tumbled onto the bed in a tangle of arms and legs, trying desperately to find our way back to each other's mouths. With tongues reengaged, we each grabbed for the other's clothes—unbuckling belts, shucking off shirts, toeing off shoes, and shimmying out of blue jeans.

Finally we were blessedly naked and I thought I might come out of my skin if I didn't get my hands or my mouth on AJ's cock.

I reached down to grab it and his hand stopped me as I was about to wrap my fingers around his wide shaft.

"What?" I gasped, pulling my mouth off his.

"Gonna come if you so much as touch me right now," he said with a ragged voice, breaths coming in rough draws between his words.

"Isn't that the point?" I asked. "Just let me—" I leaned down to run the flat of my tongue along the smooth, hot skin stretched tight along the length of his cock. I relished the taste of him and the knowledge I was going to drive him over the edge with my mouth.

As soon as I took his tip into my mouth and moved my lips down to the base of his cock, he blew.

"Oh fuck, Dante, baby, *fuck*," he stammered, going off like a shot. I tried to swallow around him as his orgasm subsided but had a hard time keeping up. As soon as I pulled my mouth off him, he grabbed me under the arms and yanked me up his body before rolling us both over until I was on my back.

The look on his face was so intense, my heart jolted almost like how it felt when I was scared—tripping and fast. But I definitely wasn't scared around him.

"AJ?" I breathed.

His hands came up to cup my face and he leaned in to kiss me on my lips as softly and gently as the barest touch of a feather. The kiss was reverent and unexpected. A sweet, exquisite reward for a job well done. I felt so cherished by that kiss, I almost wanted to cry in relief and gratitude.

My knees bent and I brought my legs around his waist to lock his body against mine. I felt my cock hard and straining between us, and I couldn't help but arch up to rub into his belly. It was almost like the satisfied stretch of a cat in a delicious sun patch, except without the satisfied part.

I was naked in bed with AJ Flores and there was nowhere else on earth I'd rather be.

9

AJ

I was torn between wanting to fuck Dante's brains out like a sex-obsessed lunatic and wanting to worship him slowly and thoroughly, savoring every moment of his pleasure and lavishing him with the attention he deserved.

My body must have made the decision while my brain still suffered from blood loss because I found myself dropping tiny, light kisses along his lips, his chin, his neck, and down his chest to the tight flat plane of his stomach.

At the sight of his ab muscles contracting in response to my kisses, I felt my cock stir to life again. My hands roamed over his warm skin, and I sensed him shiver when they got down to his hips.

"Your body is out of this world, Dante," I murmured between kisses to his stomach. I felt his cock throbbing hot against my breastbone; it made my heart race. "I want to run my hands over every inch of you, kiss every part of you."

I nuzzled his cock with my face before running my tongue in the crevice between his thigh and the thatch of dark hair between his legs. I felt his hands resting gently on my head and I had an errant thought about what a damned sweetheart he was. I couldn't in a million years imagine him hurting me, and I hoped like hell I never hurt him either.

No wonder my body wanted to treat him like a beloved treasure. In a way, he'd always been a beloved treasure to me—someone I wanted to hold and keep safe.

I moved to run my tongue over his cock before taking it into my mouth. He whimpered, and I kept flicking my eyes up to reassure myself they were whimpers of pleasure instead of discomfort. He moved his hands down to clutch the bedding beneath him.

I cradled his balls in my hand and sucked my way up and down his length until he shouted my name and spilled into my throat. His beautiful, lean body flushed and arched beneath me, and I was torn yet again between wanting to slide my hard cock inside him and just holding him while he slept. *What the fuck was wrong with me?*

When I looked up at his face, he seemed frozen in a trance. "Dante? You okay?" I asked.

"Are you fucking crazy?" he answered in a hoarse voice, shaking his head and tilting his mouth up in a satisfied grin. He closed his eyes and rested a bent arm over his face. "Of course I am. How can you even ask me that right now?"

I couldn't help but laugh as I leaned down to press a kiss to the inside of his thigh. I realized we were both naked inside of an unlocked vehicle parked on a city street, so I stood and pulled the little door to the bedroom closed before closing the privacy blinds on the windows too. Now the only light coming in was dim streetlight glow through a skylight. I gathered our clothes and laid them on the tiny table surface next to the bed for when we were ready to go.

I crawled back onto the bed and wrestled us under the covers. "Just for a little while," I murmured when he opened his eyes to look at me. "Want to hold you."

He settled in next to me and let me put my arm around his shoulders to pull him in close. I ran my fingers lightly up and down his arm for a while until I realized he'd fallen asleep.

Considering he'd been the one in charge of the entire Marian House expansion project for the past year, culminating in the grand opening gala two nights before, I wasn't surprised he was so quick to pass out. I decided to let him sleep a little longer because, who was I kidding? I was in no hurry to let him go.

SOMETIME DURING THE night I felt vibrations in the bed and wondered if it was an earthquake. I wasn't really awake enough to worry about it and fell back asleep. At another point, I remember thinking Dante moved around a lot in his sleep because the bed kept jostling.

It wasn't until I heard him gasp right next to my ear that I realized the vehicle was moving.

"What the fuck is happening?" Dante said in a strangled voice. I opened my eyes to see the gorgeous man in bed beside me. His hair stuck up in a crazy, spiky halo of fucking cute-as-shit Dante hair. And his eyes were a cross between crazed and dazed.

My brain couldn't make sense of what was happening either though. "Why are we moving? Are you driving?" I asked before realizing how stupid that was. He looked at me and raised an eyebrow.

"Yes, AJ. I'm driving. And I'm very, very good at it. We're in stealth mode right now, so it probably looks like I'm just sitting here in bed."

"Shit," I muttered, twisting around to grab the clothes from the spot where I'd left them. I handed Dante's to him and threw on my own as quickly as I could before carefully opening the slider door from the bedroom to look forward toward the cab of the vehicle.

We were barreling down the interstate in broad daylight with absolutely no one at the wheel.

This was a nightmare. It was a bad dream. I turned around to tell Dante this was just a dream when he must have caught sight of the view through the front windshield.

"Holy shit!" he screeched. The vehicle swerved and then overcorrected, tossing me off my feet into the refrigerator before I crumpled to the floor. Dante banged his shoulder into a protruding doorjamb and yelped in pain.

Rubbing his shoulder, he climbed over me, stumbling forward

with his hands reaching out to brace him as he made his way through the narrow passage.

I heard a familiar voice from the front. "Dante, is that you back there?"

"Aunt Tilly?" he gasped.

"Oh god," I groaned.

"What the hell are you doing here?" she asked.

Please let this be a dream. Or a head injury. Or—

"Who's with you?" Tilly called out.

"Just concentrate on the road, please, and pull off when you see the next exit," Dante responded, more calmly than I would have expected.

"She can still drive?" I asked. "At her age?"

"Just how old do you think I am?" she barked. "Is that AJ?"

Dante glared at me. "Do you mind maybe ceasing the distractions until she gets us safely to a complete stop?"

He had a point.

I struggled to stand just enough to slide onto the sofa against one wall and buckle a seatbelt around my waist. Dante climbed up to take a seat in the passenger chair as I tried to get my bearings. We seemed to be heading south on Interstate 5 and from the directional signs, I suspected we were pretty far out of San Francisco.

"Dante," I hissed. "Does that sign say Bakersfield in *eighty-three miles?*"

His head whipped around to look out the window and then over at Tilly, who couldn't be seen from where I sat on the sofa. The large captain's chair hid her from view.

"Yes, Bakersfield," she said. "There's agents after me, and I've got to see a man about a thing."

I couldn't help but laugh at the absurdity of the statement and reached out to touch Dante's arm.

He turned his head and raised an eyebrow in my direction. I made the hand signal for drinking and raised a brow back at him. *Is she drunk?*

He rolled his eyes and shook his head before twirling an index finger in a circle over his temple to indicate she was crazy.

Good to know.

She finally pulled off the interstate and into a gas station before turning off the ignition and swiveling around in her chair. She pinned Dante with a glare.

"What the hell are you two doing in my party bus?"

I could handle this. I was an adult, for god's sake. And it wasn't like Aunt Tilly was a prude. Quite the opposite, in fact.

"Uh," I said.

She narrowed her eyes at me. "Out with it."

"Ah, well. We, ah…"

"Carl sent us out to fetch your bags and we accidentally fell asleep in the back," AJ said matter-of-factly.

Tilly tilted her head at him as her mouth opened in a wide smirk. "Riiigghhhttt. And did you accidentally get naked first?"

My mouth dropped open and I flashed a look at AJ. How did she know?

He looked over at me with an amused look on his face. "Your shirt is on inside out."

"Goddammit," I muttered, shucking it off to remedy the situation. I heard AJ's breath hitch and then felt my skin flush in response.

"Well, well, what have we here?" Tilly mused. "Is there something going on between you two?"

"No," I said at the same time AJ blurted, "Kind of."

Shit. I felt my ears burn as my embarrassment grew. My family had never really seen me with someone and I sure as hell had never been in anything resembling a relationship.

"That's not the point. What the hell are we doing halfway to Vegas?" I asked.

Tilly's eyes veered off to the side and her lips tightened. "Never mind."

"What did you mean when you said agents were after you?" AJ asked. "What kind of agents?"

"Secret Service," she said, still not looking at us.

"*The Secret Service of the United States?*" I shouted, causing her to jump in her seat and glare at me.

"No, smart-ass, the Secret Service of The Cheesecake Factory," she snapped.

"Why would the Secret Service be interested in you, Tilly?" AJ asked, reaching out a hand to squeeze my shoulder in a *calm down* gesture.

"I may or may not have had an intimate interlude with someone under their protection."

"I'm sorry, *what*?" I spluttered. I looked over to AJ in hopes he was about to give me a cheeky smile and a pair of finger guns with a cute, "Haha, we got you so badly, LOL."

His forehead was creased with concern and he turned to face me. "Dante, why don't you go fill up the gas tank while I talk to Tilly for a minute, okay?"

Oh, no he didn't.

"Sure, AJ. I'll just run along and play toys while you grown-ups handle the important stuff," I snapped.

AJ's eyes widened in surprise at my response.

"That's not what I meant," he said.

"Then what did you mean?" I asked, still glaring at him.

"I guess I was just worried you might hear something that would upset you," he said, looking concerned. The man had a point, but I didn't appreciate being treated like a child who needed to be protected. "Tilly, what happened?"

"It's a long story. But right now the Secret Service is knocking on my door and I'd prefer to head to Vegas, if you don't mind. Now, someone go fill up the damned gas tank so we can get this show on the road."

"Why Vegas?" I asked.

"Because I need to see a man about a thing. Stop asking so many questions. Feel free to get the hell out of the party bus if you don't want to come along."

It was clear she wasn't going to say anything else for the time being, so I took the opportunity to duck out and fill the tank.

It wasn't until the nozzle stopped pumping that I realized I should have made Tilly pay for the gas. *Motherfucking RVs.*

I went inside the gas station to use the bathroom and pick up a drink and a pack of gum before returning to the vehicle.

"Everyone all set in here?" I asked cheerily as I got back in. AJ was in the driver's seat, and Tilly was nowhere to be found.

"Tilly decided to take a nap," he said in a low voice. "I think that's a good idea."

"Are we heading back?" I asked.

"No. We're going to continue heading to Vegas."

"I don't understand. Why?"

"What do you think is going to happen if we try to go against her wishes?" he asked, focusing on the road as he pulled the vehicle back onto the interstate.

"Oh," I said.

He snorted and looked over at me. "Also, it's actually illegal for us to take her somewhere against her will. It's called kidnapping. Trust me, I know. That means we have two choices: join her or leave her and let her go alone. I'm not sending her off on her own."

I looked over at AJ and was struck, not for the first time, by how attractive he was. His warm brown hair stood up on top in an adorable messy pile and his beard scruff did all kinds of things to my nuts. The sun coming in through the window gave his skin a warm glow, and his lips looked full and tasty. I wanted to reach out and touch him. Run my fingers through his hair or put my hand on his leg. What would he think if I rubbed the back of his neck or leaned over and rested my forehead against his shoulder?

Instead, I turned away and stared out the window for a few minutes until a warm hand landed on mine where it rested in my lap.

"Hey, you okay? Did you have plans you need to cancel? I'm sorry I didn't even ask," he said, squeezing my hand but not letting it go. "Once we get to Vegas, you can rent a car or fly home."

I turned my hand around in his to thread our fingers together before I looked over at him. "Well, I was supposed to teach a tae kwon do class at Marian House this morning, but I've already missed that. I should probably call Londa and explain, but what the hell do I tell her? And won't she be worried about you since you never came home last night?"

My brain flashed the idea that maybe it wasn't unusual for him to spend the night out while he was in San Francisco. Maybe he made a habit of picking up one-night-stands in clubs and sleeping over at a strange man's place. Just the idea of it made my stomach lurch; I looked away again.

AJ lifted our joined hands to his lips and dropped a warm kiss on the back of mine. "When I didn't come home last night, she would have assumed I was with you."

My heart felt like it had been zapped with tiny tingling volts of electricity. "Really? Why?" I asked.

He laughed. "Because I haven't stopped talking about you for two days, and she finally told me to put up or shut up."

Now my heart lurched up into my throat. "What do you mean?" I croaked.

He laughed and looked over at me. *Was AJ Flores blushing?*

"Why are you so surprised, Dante? You know I'm interested in you, right?"

"Well, yeah, but—"

"But what?"

"Well, I couldn't tell if maybe you changed your mind," I said.

AJ chuckled.

"Now you know."

"So you're interested and not changing your mind?"

We came up on a slow-moving car and he needed to change lanes. AJ carefully set my hand down on his thigh with a press to make sure I knew to keep it there. As if I'd ever voluntarily take my hands off him.

He used both hands to steer us into the passing lane, and when we returned to the cruising lane, he grabbed my hand again.

"I can't deny being concerned about some things. Namely, me settling into a new city. I'm just moving to the Bay Area from Chicago," he said quietly. "Starting a new job and all that. I don't really know what my life is going to be like."

Oh. Right.

"Yeah" was all I said. It occurred to me such a detail would only matter in terms of a relationship. The idea that AJ thought of whatever this was as something more than just fooling around made excitement twist in my stomach.

"And in Chicago, did you... have a boyfriend? Or whatever?" I asked.

He glanced over at me, eyebrows drawn together. "Do you think I would have been with you last night if I had a boyfriend, Dante?"

"I guess not."

"Do *you* have a boyfriend?" he asked.

He dropped my hand again and put both of his on the wheel. Shit.

"No, NO. I don't. Of course not. I'm sorry. I just—"

AJ glanced at me. "Just what?"

"Just don't get why you'd—" I stopped before I came out with some self-deprecating bullshit no one wanted to hear. After taking a breath, I tried again. "You seem like a good catch. So why hasn't anyone hooked you already?"

I felt heat bloom in my cheeks.

"Maybe none of the bait attracted me until now," he said with a big flirty grin.

Something tumbled in my stomach. The man was god's gift to the world and he was flirting with *me*.

"And now?" I asked with what I hoped was a flirty grin instead of a constipated grimace.

"Now the one I want is dangling right in front of me."

11

———————

AJ

Was Dante Marian flirting with me?

The sweet, quiet man who preferred standing off to the side over being noticed? The kid who probably spent the first fifteen years of his life being treated like he was worse than nothing? The person who had seemed to want to believe he wasn't good enough for me?

I picked his hand back up and held it to my chest. God, he was so kind and gentle. Just the man my gut told me he'd grow up to be.

We changed the subject and spent the next hour chatting about benign topics like recent movies and what kind of music we liked. When we got to Bakersfield, Tilly convinced us to stop at a place called Golden West for lunch. Surprise—it was a casino.

"You ever eaten at a free casino buffet?" Tilly asked.

"No," Dante said, swiveling his chair so he could see her on the sofa behind me.

"I have vouchers. All you can eat. It only makes sense to try it, don't you think? I mean, we're here anyway. Might as well," she declared. "Come on. It's happening."

After I parked the monstrosity in a nearby parking lot we

confronted her. She tried to get up to open the side door of the vehicle.

"Not so fast," Dante said. "We need to talk some more before lunch."

I followed him to the back and sat down on the sofa next to Tilly. Instead of sitting, Dante began to pace in front of me until I grabbed his forearm and pulled him down next to me.

His skin was warm and smooth, reminding me of the night before when his entire body was bare and within arm's reach. When could I get him alone again?

I heard Dante clear his throat and looked up to meet his eyes.

"Ahem," he said, pointing significant eyeballs at his forearm where I still held it. My fingers idly stroked across his skin, and I realized I'd pretty much been caressing him while thinking about him. *Jesus.* I withdrew my hand and stood up.

"Ah, we need to talk about what's going on here," I said, propping my ass against the little kitchen counter opposite the sofa.

He snorted. "Understatement of the year."

I looked over at his great-aunt where she sat hugging her giant purse to her chest like someone was trying to pry it from her cold, dead hands.

"Tilly, what's this about?" I asked again. "Why would Secret Service agents be looking for you?"

"Pfft," she scoffed.

Dante tilted his head at her and burst out laughing. "Uh, try again, Aunt Tilly. Out with it. In case you haven't noticed, we're on the lam in some kind of happy camper bus. Tell us what the heck is going on."

Tilly just glared at him with narrowed, slitty eyes. "Mind your business, Dante Marian."

"Dude, my business is practically across state lines right about now, and I'd like to know why. Why did you come home early from Vegas? I thought you, Granny, and Irene were there visiting Brad and Miles this week."

"We were."

"So then why were you back so soon?"

"I forgot I told Sally I'd host the Pecker Party," she admitted. "So we had Carl race us back in the pleasure bus and didn't have time to stop at the garage and pick up the car."

"How did you get mixed up with the Secret Service?" Dante asked.

"Dammit," she muttered, looking away. "You know what it's like in Vegas. It was just supposed to be a joke. Don't know why that cocksucker, no offense, took it so seriously."

Dante looked at me, red faced. "Can you just, maybe, put your ears on mute for a minute? There's really zero chance she's going to be able to explain this without insulting large swaths of people in general and possibly you in particular."

"It's okay. I just want to keep you both safe, and I can't do that if I don't know what we're dealing with," I explained.

"We're not in any danger. Don't get your jock in a twist," Tilly warned. "You're being overly dramatic."

"What happened in Vegas, dammit?" Dante repeated. "You're starting to freak me out."

Tilly let out a huff and set her giant purse on the floor next her. She began to twist her hands together until Dante moved to kneel on the floor in front of her and rub her hands with his own.

"Please, Aunt Tilly. Tell us so we can help."

"I may or may not have hooked up with Harold Cannon while I was in Vegas," Tilly began.

"What?" he croaked. "Harold Cannon as in *Senator* Cannon, father of the *president of the United States*?"

"Cut the crap, Dante. You heard me. Don't act so surprised," Tilly said, rolling her eyes.

"Define 'hooked up with,'" I interjected, hoping like hell she was using the term wrong.

"I went all the way with him, okay? We did it. He plucked my flower petals and I played his pan flute. There, now stop asking stupid questions or I'll answer them, and I don't think any of us want that, now, do we?"

The three of us sat there in stunned silence while the words "petals," "pluck," and "pan flute" assaulted our ears and carved horrific scars in our psyches. Poor Dante looked like he was going to choke and vomit.

After a moment, Tilly stood up with her regal posture, slipped her giant purse onto her shoulder and waltzed out of the van.

"Come find me when you pick your jaws up off the ground."

ALL I COULD THINK of was the freaked out look on Dante's face and how much I wanted to make it go away.

"C'mere," I said, pulling him in for a hug but veering off at the last minute and taking advantage of his open mouth. He stayed frozen for a brief moment until he melted against me and relaxed his mouth into mine.

"Mmm," he hummed against my lips. We kissed for a few moments, my hands holding him around the back and his pressed against my chest. Only half of me was present for the kiss, the other half of me frantically flipped through options to figure out when and where I could get him naked again. But then the rational adult in me kicked into gear and booted the horny teen to the curb.

This was a situation, and one thing was for sure, there was no way we could allow Tilly to go into another casino unchaperoned.

Fuck. I pulled away from the kiss. "We need to go find her," I told him.

"Uh-huh," he agreed in a daze.

We shifted where we sat, rearranging unhappy cocks and standing to exit the camper.

"Did she seriously say Harold Cannon?" Dante asked.

"She did," I confirmed.

12

—————

DANTE

No. *NO*. This wasn't happening. None of this was happening. Someone had clearly slipped an acid tablet into my drink at the bar the night before and all this was some kind of sick trip.

After I came out of the kissing haze, the truth of the Tilly situation slammed into me. I stumbled to my feet and lurched to the door of the bus to escape into the fresh air. Maybe it would help me sober up and come down from this flippy, trippy hellscape.

Once in the brightly lit parking lot, I closed my eyes so I could think for a minute. I idly tested the spot where I'd banged my shoulder earlier that morning and felt a big bruised knot there. If I hadn't seen the slight look of truth in Tilly's eyes, I might actually think this was all some elaborate prank orchestrated by my crazy brothers. But I *had* seen the look, and my heart was banging drums trying to convince me how *not* funny it all was if it was true.

A water bottle appeared in front of me, and I looked up to see AJ's concerned face.

"How's your shoulder?" he asked.

"Hurts like a bitch," I admitted.

"You okay otherwise?" he asked. I shook my head but took the water.

"No. Jesus, no. Of course I'm not okay. This is ridiculous. I just wanted a little nookie in the back of a camper van, for god's sake."

"It's kinda funny, if you think about it," AJ said with a smile. I couldn't help but smile back.

"Is this... really happening?" I sighed. "Secret Service? For real? Please tell me I'm high or have a head injury or something, AJ. "

He rested a warm hand on my good shoulder. "I wish I could, Dante, but it seems to be real. We need to figure out what to do about this."

"I don't even know what 'this' is," I said. "And whatever happened to shit *staying in Vegas*, for god's sake?"

AJ laughed and squeezed my shoulder before letting go. I felt the loss of his hand on me like a punch to the gut.

I opened the water bottle to take a big sip and spit the entire mouthful out in a giant spray, liquid running down my face, my neck, and all over my T-shirt.

"*Ueaghk!*" I sputtered. "It's straight vodka."

He grabbed the bottle from me and looked at it. It looked like a normal bottle of water. After sniffing it and tasting it, he winced. "Tilly."

Sometimes that one word said it all.

I PULLED the hem of my T-shirt out from my body to keep the cold, wet fabric from touching my skin as we walked into the air-conditioned casino.

"I'm going to grab you a new shirt. That one's soaked," AJ said.

I headed to the men's room while AJ visited the gift shop. Once he joined me in the restroom, I slipped off the wet garment and placed it on the edge of the sink while I reached into the bag for the new one.

AJ's eyes stared at my chest. "What?" I asked. "Is the bruise that bad?" I twisted to look at my shoulder but couldn't get the right angle.

"Uh, yeah. But also, the tattoo. Tell me about it."

"It's an angel. Had it done when I turned twenty-one," I explained, pulling the tag off the new shirt.

"Why an angel?" he asked, reaching out to run his fingers across it. Goosebumps flared to the surface of every inch of skin he touched.

I thought of the man who'd saved me. The one the doctor had called Angel. I felt my lips curve up in a smile. "It's my guardian angel. Someone to watch over me, I guess. Sounds silly, I know."

I looked over to see why AJ had gone quiet.

"It's nice," he said. "I'm glad you have someone to watch over you."

"I'm lucky to have him," I said. "He's gotten me through some tough times." What I didn't tell him was the guardian angel was a real person—my touchstone.

AJ leaned in to kiss me again; I lost myself in his mouth.

"You're so fucking beautiful, Dante," he murmured against my lips. "I can't help but want you every time I look at you." His hands roamed down to cup my ass, and I let out a whimper.

It was unbelievable a man so put together, so hot and commanding, was interested in little Dante Marian.

I stepped closer in and ran my hands up to his neck. His skin was warm even though it was scratchy from his beard scruff.

AJ pulled away with a groan. "Not here. I'm not going to make out with you in some men's room in a Bakersfield casino, for god's sake. You deserve better."

"Did you hear me complain?" I replied with a grin. I brought the new T-shirt over my head and smoothed it down.

AJ smiled back at me before shaking his head as if to clear it. "Let's go find Tilly before she meets another man and gets into more trouble," AJ said, changing the subject.

I blew out a breath. "Shit."

"Does everyone in your family have crazy stories like this? It seems like the Marians are always up to something," The words were said with the slightest curl of his lips in a teasing grin and I couldn't help but think it was cute as hell.

I sighed. "It seems like it. But not me, thankfully."

"You're aiding an octogenarian in evading federal agents."

He had a point.

"AJ, what did you mean earlier about keeping us *safe*?" I asked as we approached the hostess stand of the restaurant and got seated at a table. We gave the hostess Tilly's description and hoped like hell she was in the ladies' room.

"I didn't say that, did I?" AJ asked, scooting his chair a little closer to mine.

"You did."

"Huh, dunno. Side effect from working in personal security, I guess. Hey, did you even look at the shirt I got you?"

I looked down, trying to read it upside down.

I blew my load in Bakersfield.

I looked up at him in shock. He tried so hard not to crack up, but he could hardly contain himself. Finally, the dam burst and we both started laughing.

"I'm going to hold you to that, asshole," I said, pointing at him.

"Already done, but I can help you do it again if you want. Just give me five minutes in a supply closet somewhere. Shall we look for one right now?" he asked hopefully.

I smiled at him but shook my head. "Tempting, but I think I'll go look for Aunt Tilly instead," I said, standing up from the table.

Within minutes I'd found her at a slot machine on the closest edge of the casino.

"Maybe you can play a few minutes after lunch," I told her. "But if you want to get to Vegas tonight we can't stay too long."

Tilly came willingly and even chatted us up through the meal, telling AJ crazy stories that had become classic Marian lore over the years. The familiar tales were soothing, and I felt myself relaxing again. She started to tell him about the Alaskan cruise she, Granny, and Irene had been on the summer before, but I tried to stop her.

"God, no. Not that one. Let the poor guy eat without choking," I said.

"Oh hush, he'll love it."

"Maybe, but he'll choke, and I'm not sure I remember CPR," I warned her.

"Now I have to hear it," AJ said with an encouraging smile.

"It all started when Granny and I decided we wanted to see some bears," Tilly said.

I looked over at AJ. "This is how Tilly learned never to let her gay friends book the cruise."

He snorted. "Go on."

"We were going to spend a week cruising from Seattle to Alaska. What could possibly go wrong, right?" she said.

"Lots of things," I said.

"So we boarded the ship and I noticed at least 95 percent of the people on board were men. And they were very... I want to say *colorful*."

"Gay. They were gay," I clarified.

"Of course they were gay, Dante. Stop messing with the pace of my storytelling. There's an art to this," she warned before looking back at AJ. "Suuuuuper gay. So anyway, there we were—me and two married lesbians on board a ship for a week with thousands of horny gays. It was eventful to say the least. And goddamned impossible for me to get lucky."

AJ laughed. "I guess so. I can't even picture you on a gay cruise."

"Can't you though?" I asked before breaking down and laughing too. The image of her on that ship cracked me up every time she told the story.

AJ winked at me. "I guess she saw her fair share of bears at least."

We both laughed harder and even Tilly started giggling so much she had a hard time telling him the other funny parts of her trip.

After lunch, we told Tilly she could spend an hour at the slots while we took a nap in the camper. We hadn't gotten much sleep the night before and were eager to pretend to nap while we really humped each other. At least that was my plan. I wasn't completely sure AJ felt the same way, but if the looks he gave me while we paid the bill were any indication, I wasn't far off. The part of my brain that should have kept an eye on Tilly got sidetracked by the cute man standing next to me.

I made sure Tilly had her cell phone before following AJ out to the parking lot. He reached over and held my hand as we walked, brushing the back of it with his thumb in a way that made my chest feel tight.

I'd never really had a boyfriend, and this holding-hands thing was something people did with a boyfriend, not a hookup. My head spun with the ridiculous crap young teens thought of when falling for their first crush. *What does he think about me? Does he like me? Like, like me, like me? Where is this going? Don't think about it; just enjoy the moment. But I want to think about it, because I really like him.*

Like, like him, like him, you know? UGH.

That's what went through my mind when I followed him inside the RV before being body-slammed against the door. I never even saw it coming.

13

AJ

I couldn't wait one more goddamned minute to get my fucking hands on Dante Marian. Since kissing him, sucking him off, and sleeping against his hot body the night before, all I wanted was *more*.

The minute the door to the vehicle closed behind us, I turned around and shoved him against it, crushing my lips against his as if his mouth was the source of the only air I could breathe. Part of me felt like it was. It must be. Otherwise why couldn't I stop obsessing over how to get my mouth back on his?

I ran my hands down his arms until I reached his fingers, threading them together and raising them high above his head on the door. He panted and moaned into my mouth, but his eyes were huge.

"I'm sorry, did I scare you?" I gasped, pulling away just far enough to see his expression.

"Yes, scared the shit out of me, but don't stop. *Jesus.*"

I smiled before leaning in again and tasting his mouth. My hands roamed down his arms and around his back before lowering to his perfect, full ass.

"You have the kind of butt I can't stop wanting to grab," I mumbled against his neck as I moved my kisses farther down.

"Hell, AJ. Grab it all you want. No one's stopping you."

I moved my fingers up to his waistband to slide down inside his pants so I could grab his cheeks without the bulky blue jeans in the way. He arched his cock up into me, and I felt its hardness against my upper thigh.

We started making our way back toward the bed, Dante stumbling against me while kissing a trail under my chin. Just before I tossed him down onto the bed, his phone rang in his pocket.

"Shit," he said. "It might be Tilly."

He stretched his legs down to stand in front of me as he pulled his phone out to answer it. I turned around to close the bedroom door before turning back to Dante.

"Carl?" he asked when he answered the phone.

I couldn't hear the other side of the conversation, but I could tell it was about the Tilly situation. When Dante finally hung up, he looked over at me and pulled me down to sit next to him on the end of the bed.

"He said the agents came back this morning looking for Tilly."

"What did they want? What did they say?" I asked.

"They wouldn't talk to him at first, so he told them he was her husband."

"He's not though, is he?" I asked.

Dante shook his head. "No. She calls him her pool boy, but he's more like a house manager who also drives her sometimes. He used to be one of Jude's drivers until Tilly stole him."

"Were they more forthcoming after he said he was her husband?"

"No. That's the weird part. According to Carl, they lost their collective shit. Apparently, whatever is going on with Tilly and Senator Cannon is not conducive to her being married."

"Uh-oh," I said. "They must know she slept with him. But he's not married, so what does it matter? Oh wait. He'd be caught by the press sleeping with a married woman."

"Right. And now poor Carl is upset because he's afraid he's screwed things up with his lie."

"He couldn't have known. I mean, I assume he didn't know."

Dante blew out a breath. "Carl said there are news vans from all the major networks parked outside the house."

"We'll figure it out when we get to Vegas," I said. My brain wasn't working properly with Dante's close proximity to me. I was horny and hot for him, so no amount of Tilly turmoil would distract me from my singular desire to put grabby hands all over the man. "Take your clothes off."

Dante's eyes opened wide and he looked startled by my commanding tone. I decided to take the bull by the horns.

"Dante, I want to touch you, stroke your cock, suck you off, and feel your hands on my body. Do you want that too?"

As I spoke, his chest heaved up and down with rapid breaths and his hand automatically pressed into the crotch of his jeans.

"Holy fuck," he whispered.

"Not yet," I said with a grin. "But hopefully soon. Maybe when we have more than an hour to ourselves."

I reached over my shoulder to grab a handful of shirt and pull it off. Next, my hands dropped to my waistband and flicked open the button of my fly. All the while I kept my eyes locked on Dante, who sat mesmerized on the foot of the bed.

My fingers lowered my zipper as I kicked my shoes off.

"Dante?" I growled. "Yes or no? I don't want to pressure you, but I *will* be having an orgasm in about sixty seconds with or without you. If you want to join me, get your damned clothes off. If not, you might want to go sit out there on the sofa and leave me in peace."

His Adam's apple bobbed as he swallowed and pressed his cock again.

"I want to join you," he said, his voice breathy and strained.

"Then strip."

I tried so hard not to laugh as he stood up fast enough to trip over his own feet. My hands reached out to grab him, and I wound up caught in the crazy vortex of a horny Dante. Hands and elbows were everywhere, grabbing at clothes and shucking off socks. I heard the sounds of shifting fabric as we finished getting naked and landed side by side on the bed.

My hands reached for him, yanking him in for a hard kiss. "Your mouth, *Jesus*," I mumbled against his lips. He tasted so fucking sweet. I wanted to dive into him and never leave.

"*Mpfh*," he moaned back, not taking his lips off mine even long enough to form words. His tongue came out to find mine and he ended up nipping at my lower lip, *oh god*, that felt good.

I moved a hand down to grab his bare ass cheek and squeeze. That fucking ass was perfection. Thick and firm and begging to be fucked. I pulled at his ass, wanting to sink my teeth into it but not wanting to scare the poor guy any more than I already probably was.

Dante's hands cupped my face and he moved his lips off mine to kiss across my chin and down onto my neck to my collarbone. I wanted to roll over on top of him and devour him, but I was scared of overwhelming him. Instead, I rolled onto my back, pulling him on top of me so he could set the pace.

His legs fell to the bed on either side of my hips and his cock landed next to mine, causing a guttural noise to escape my throat. I tilted my hips up into him and saw his eyes squeeze shut for a moment before he seemed to make a decision. He opened his eyes and grinned down at me.

I stared at him, reaching out to run my fingers through his shiny dark hair. He kept his eyes focused on mine as he dropped kisses onto the center of my chest, my diaphragm, my navel, and the dark fuzz leading down to my groin.

Once his tongue landed in my happy trail, his eyes twinkled and I felt like drool might just start leaking out of my lips.

"Dante, please put your mouth on me," I begged, arching up into him gently but suggestively. "*Please*."

"Patience, AJ," he teased. "I'm not sure your sixty seconds is up yet."

I didn't know what the hell he was talking about because my brain no longer functioned other than to chant, *Suck me, please suck me, please.*

My hands stayed in Dante's hair, but I held back from guiding his head. The muscles of my arms trembled from the effort not to pull his hair and force my cock deep in his throat. Little garbled noises came out of my throat as the tip of his tongue came out to tease the slit of my cock.

"Mmmm," he hummed after tasting the precum there. "Mm-hmm."

"Oh fuck, yes."

Dante looked up at me through his thick, dark lashes and I swore to fucking god, he put on puppy eyes to drive me batshit fucking crazy. "What do I do now, AJ?" he asked in an innocent voice, as if he hadn't already made me come with his tongue once already in that very camper van.

My dick bucked so hard, it flicked him under the chin, causing his eyes to twinkle mischievously and his grin to come out.

"Ooooh, someone likes being teased, huh?"

I groaned and threw my head back, pulling my hands out of his hair and squeezing fists over my eyes. What the hell happened to me bossing *him* around?

"Dante," I begged again. Well, it may have sounded more like a whine.

"Hmm?" he said before leaning down to take one of my balls into his mouth. He sucked the entire thing in with his wet tongue, and I couldn't handle any more. I flipped him onto his side and swiveled around to take his cock into my mouth to show him how it was done.

Without thinking of much more than punishing him with the blow job of his life, I ended up sucking him off while he took my own cock like a champ.

Wait... punishing? By giving him head? Whatever.

The sixty-nine was fast and dirty at that point. Desperation took over, and I went to town on his steely length, sucking, licking, stroking. My fingers fondled his balls and moved lower to rub gently across his tight little hole. Fuck, but I wanted in that hole. It was right there in front of me. I wanted to lick it, eat his ass out, and then shove my cock inside and lay claim to him like some kind of animal marking his turf.

What the hell had gotten into me?

"Fuck, fuck, AJ, I'm gonna—" Hot fluid caught me in the face, and I took his cock back down my throat while he finished coming. His warning had turned into a roar as his climax intensified and just the sound of him coming threw me over the edge. I moved off his face and wound up thrusting my cock at an angle across his chest for the final pushes of my own orgasm. I felt his hands wide and grasping on my ass, and my hands were wrapped around the backs of Dante's thighs.

The smell of sex and man swirled around the small room, and the sounds of our panting filled the air. I carefully swiveled back around to face him, wiping my face and mouth with the back of my arm. I noticed a box of tissues on a shelf by the bed and reached out to clean Dante's chest off. His eyes were half lidded and there was a sexy smile of satisfaction across his lips.

"Okay?" I asked.

"Guess so," he replied with a cheeky smile. His nose was red, and I couldn't help but land a kiss on it.

"Did my performance let you down in some way, Dante Marian?" I asked, handing him some clothes so we could cover up in case Tilly came back.

He continued to grin up at me and shrugged. "It was all a blur actually. I'll let you try again sometime soon to see if I can get a better assessment."

"Sounds prudent," I agreed. "Give me the opportunity to practice and improve. I promise I can do it, coach." After we slid our boxers back on, I maneuvered us under the covers and pulled him in against my side.

"Shouldn't we go find Tilly?" he suggested halfheartedly.

"Yes, but let's just lie here for a minute first." He curled into me and dozed off within seconds, with me not far behind. I guess I'd assumed we'd be woken up by Tilly's return to the vehicle or by a phone call from her asking for more time.

When we woke up, the light was dimmer than before and I realized it was much later than we'd expected. Dante snuggled in closer to me; I ran my fingers lightly up and down his back under his shirt.

"I think it's late. The sun is going down," I murmured against his hair. "Where's Tilly?"

"Dunno. Keep doing that. Feels good," he said.

"Should we call her?"

"Ugh. I don't want to move yet."

"Then don't," I said. Dante dozed off again while my brain began working overtime. Was it okay to be pursuing something with Dante? What did I hope would happen?

A relationship? Hell yeah, I wanted a relationship with Dante. And I had the feeling he'd be interested in one too. Then why did I feel a tiny tremor of unease about the whole thing?

Was it because I was essentially lying to him about who I was? What the hell would he think when or if he ever realized I was the guy who'd kidnapped him that night? How could I be intimate with him with such a huge secret between us?

Dante shifted beside me and I instinctively turned to place a kiss on his head again. God, the man was everything I'd ever wanted: sweet, kind, committed to his work. Adorable. Loved by his family and generous to others. Just the thought of him with anyone else made my stomach lurch.

I saw the angel over his heart and felt a tightening in my own.

My head spun and I felt like my heart would fly out of my chest as I recalled his words from earlier in the day about his tattoo. I wanted to tell him it was me. That I was his angel. But how could I ever live up to his false vision of who I was?

I wasn't some kind of knight in shining armor. I was just a regular guy who'd been doing his job.

What would he say if he ever learned I was the one who'd delivered him to safety? I couldn't imagine how the conversation would go. Would he ever trust me after that? After never telling him who I really was?

I tried not to think about it because it wasn't going to get me anywhere. The goal was to help Tilly, but I knew I needed to tell Dante the truth. He deserved it. Unfortunately, I was turning out to be chickenshit.

If I told him sooner rather than later, I stood a better chance of him forgiving me. So I'd tell him. For sure. Soon. But... maybe not right this minute. Because he felt amazing in my arms, and I didn't want to say something that might take away my ability to touch him some more.

After a while, it was my bladder that forced me up. I gently peeled myself off Dante, slipped on the rest of my clothes, and made my way to the tiny bathroom.

There was still no sign of Tilly, so I sat on the bed next to Dante to wake him.

He woke up quickly and tried to call Tilly's phone. It went straight to voicemail.

"Damn," he muttered, picking his jeans up to put them back on. "Her battery must be dead. Let's go see if we can track her down."

An hour and two cups of coffee later, we finally found her holding court at the center of a roulette table.

"Time to go, Aunt Tilly," Dante said, wrapping his arm around her and guiding her off her stool.

"But we just got here," she scoffed.

"Yes, we just got here about six hours ago. The last place you need to be right now is in another casino. Let's get back on the road."

When we got back to the RV, I took the driver's seat and Dante offered Tilly the passenger seat.

"No, thanks. All that winning wore me out. I'm going to go lie down for a bit unless you two messed up the bed with man juice." She narrowed her eyes at me.

"Ah, no, ma'am. There's no man juice on the bed," I said carefully.

"That's a shame," she muttered, turning to walk to the back. "Poor Dante. Always the bridesmaid, never the bride."

14

DANTE

Sometimes I wanted to melt into the woodwork and disappear. Had my great-aunt just called me out as sexually inexperienced in front of the guy I was desperately trying to get some experience with?

I decided to ignore her comment in hopes it, too, would disappear into the woodwork.

Once we were rolling, I pulled out my phone to look up some options for a campground along our route in case we decided to stop before we got to Vegas. AJ turned on the radio and we listened to some soft music while we drove. After a little while, a familiar song came on.

"Hey, isn't that your brother's song?" AJ asked.

I smiled and looked over at him. "Yeah. They don't play it very often anymore, but it's a fun one. Everyone calls it 'Cold Sheets.'"

"I dated a guy a couple of years ago and I remember hearing this on the radio right after we broke up. It was so perfect, you know? One of those moments where you go from feeling down about being alone to feeling empowered by your own independence."

He looked over at me with a wistful smile illuminated by the dash lights. "I don't know. Maybe it's silly, but it seemed to make a difference," he said.

"I know what you mean. Well, I haven't had a relationship like that, but I know there's a difference between feeling lonely and feeling independent."

AJ glanced over to study my face as if he was going to ask a question, but he didn't.

"Tell me about the guy," I pressed. "The one you broke up with. What happened?"

Just the idea of him in a relationship made me feel strange. Like it somehow didn't work for me, didn't fit. I couldn't picture it at all.

AJ ran a hand through his hair, making it even messier than it already was, which was boner-worthy messy. "His name is Chris. Nice guy. He's a professor at Northwestern, in the political science department. Anyway, we met through friends out at a birthday dinner one night at a restaurant. We ended up sitting next to each other and discovered we liked some of the same things."

"How long were you together?" I asked, trying to be polite and pretend to be a normal human being who didn't have murderous thoughts about a complete stranger named Chris.

"Just over two years."

"And what happened?"

He shrugged. "Unfortunately, by the time I got up the nerve to tell him I didn't see it going anywhere, it was too late to avoid hurting him."

"What do you mean?"

"He proposed."

I felt my jaw drop. "Marriage?" I asked stupidly.

He glanced at me with a smirk. "Yes, Dante. He proposed marriage. A ring, big production, flowers, the whole deal."

"You're kidding?" Was it my imagination, or was my voice way higher and squeakier than I originally thought?

"I wish I was."

"And you said *no*?"

"You're not helping ease the guilt, Dante," he said with a chuckle.

"How did he ask you? What did you say?" I wracked my brain and couldn't think of a single time I'd heard of someone turning down a proposal in real life.

"He took me to the Ledge at the Skydeck in Sears Tower. Do you know it?"

"No."

"Well, Sears Tower is called something else now, but it's one of the tallest buildings in the world and on the hundred-and-third floor is the Skydeck. It's like a viewing area to see everything from that vantage point around the city. The Ledge is a four-foot glass extension box you can step out on, and it's like you're standing on an invisible balcony fourteen hundred feet in the air. It's one of those places in Chicago where people propose."

"Sounds scary as shit," I muttered, stressed out just by thinking about it.

"*Thank you!*" AJ blurted, causing me to jump in my seat. "Sorry, I didn't mean to startle you." He laughed. "But that's exactly how I felt. I *despise* high places. I'm terrified of heights, Dante."

"And that's the place he chose to propose to you? Jeez. That would be like someone proposing to me in a giant crowd or with a flash mob. The guy sounds like an insensitive douche."

AJ glanced over with a grin on his face. "Right? At the time I just felt so guilty about saying no, but when the dust settled, I realized the location of the proposal alone should have been enough of a hint to both of us we weren't right together."

"How'd you tell him no?" I asked.

"Well, it was pretty bad since everyone watched us and waited for my big excited acceptance. My face must have registered the right kind of shock because I saw his face go from excited anticipation to confusion pretty quickly. Then I leaned in and asked if we could go somewhere else to talk about it."

I winced. "Oh god, AJ. I'm so sorry for both of you. How awful."

"It really was. And then he was so embarrassed that he went apeshit and swung a wrecking ball through our entire lives on the way out. Trashing me to all of our friends, even tried some bullshit on my sisters. Took stuff from my apartment even though we never lived together officially. It was nasty. But it helped me realize I did the right thing."

"I guess so."

"What about you? You said you've never really had a serious relationship?" AJ asked.

And there it was.

"No, I haven't."

"Why not?"

I shrugged. "No one beating down my door, I guess."

"Bullshit," he said.

My eyes widened as I looked over at him. "Okay, fine. Then I guess the men beating down my door were mute and invisible. In which case, I don't go for that kind of dumb transparency."

AJ barked out a laugh. "Oh my god. Did you really just say that?"

I couldn't help but snort a little. "I didn't mean to. That was stupid and rude. I'm sorry."

"Seriously, no *visible* men wanted you? I find that impossible to believe."

"Why?" I asked.

"Dude, look at yourself. You're fucking adorable. You're... Wait a minute. You're fishing is what you're doing."

"No, I'm not. I really don't think I'm anything special."

"Not possible. I'll bet you ten bucks if I took you back to that club from last night, you could pick up twenty different men who would want you," AJ said with a flirty tone.

"Okay," I challenged with a smirk. "Turn this bus around and let's go there now. You'll see."

"No fucking way am I taking you somewhere other men can get their hands on you," AJ said in a rough voice. And holy fuck did that make me hot. Deep, rumbly possessiveness from the alpha male sitting next to me? Yes, please.

∼

SINCE AJ and I had napped all afternoon, we were able to stay awake and drive well into the night. At one point we stopped for some groceries and coaxed Tilly out of the back room to eat a late snack.

She still wasn't ready to tell us more about her Vegas adventure, but she was content to gossip about the family and wound up spilling some beans she was supposed to keep to herself.

"I saw Simone out on a date recently," she said with glittering eyes. I knew that look. That was the look of someone with some grade-A dirt on someone.

"Spill," I said.

We sat around the little table in the RV eating a salad and bread and cheese. Tilly had a jug of cheap wine she'd pulled out of somewhere and kept refilling her travel tumbler.

"Wait, I thought my aunt said she was dating someone?" AJ asked.

"She was," I said. "Dillon broke up with her a while ago. Last year sometime."

"Why? She's adorable," AJ said.

"Pfft," Tilly scoffed. "She's been burned in the past and can't get over herself. At this rate, she's going to die alone."

I turned to AJ to explain. "She was left at the altar a couple of years ago. Kind of did a number on her ability to trust a guy."

"Shit. I guess so," AJ said. "She didn't trust Dillon?"

"I think it's more that she was so gun shy she wouldn't let him get close enough to take the relationship to the next level," I said.

"Anyway, guess who she was out with?" Tilly asked.

"Oh wait, was it Thad's friend Bell? He's tried to set those two up for years."

"No, but that guy is definitely a looker. I saw her out with that sleazy singer from the coffee shop by the clinic. You know, the one with the greasy hair and jeans so tight you can see his giant cock head?"

I glanced at AJ to see his reaction. Not fazed at all. The man was getting used to her, and I wasn't sure if that was a good thing or bad.

"His name is Mitchell," I said. "He's a nice guy. And as for his cock head, he—" AJ's hand came down on my arm.

"Whoa there. Am I getting ready to hear about how you have intimate knowledge of some guy's package?" he asked. "I'm not sure I want to hear this."

"Jealousy?" I teased. "Go on."

AJ grumbled before taking a bite of his food.

"I was going to say Mitchell takes great pride in sharing that cock head with anyone who wants a piece of it. I hope Simone uses protection."

AJ's eyebrows went up. "Does Simone know he's a player?"

Tilly piped up. "She probably does by now. The guy was all over her." Tilly's face was alight with mischief. "What if that's not really his cock? What if he's wearing a strap-on or a pecker packer or something?"

"Tilly, Jesus," I warned. "It's real. I've heard stories. He's bisexual and my friend Jacob has had some Mitchell action."

"Tilly, how the hell do you know what a packer is?" AJ asked.

"We called them falsies back in my day. And they were made out of tube socks," she said.

"Simone deserves love. I hope she finds it," I said.

Tilly took another sip of her wine and smiled to herself. "She'll find it. Something just right is out there for her. She just hasn't found it yet. She's a bit like Goldilocks right now and none of the beds fit."

"Maybe Mitchell's bed is the one she's waited for all along," AJ suggested.

Tilly and I both shook our heads. "No," I said. "The guy might be a good singer, but he can't play guitar for shit. Jude would kill her."

15

AJ

We got back on the road and drove a few more hours before finally pulling into a campground in the middle of the night.

I turned to Dante, who was responding to a text on his phone. "I never asked if you told your family where you were."

"I texted my mom and Griff. Told them I met the man of my dreams and took off for a little wedding chapel in Vegas," he said with a straight face, not bothering to look up from the screen.

"We'll be there in a few hours, lover boy. Just say the word and we can be hitched by lunchtime," I replied just as seriously.

He didn't look up but his skin bloomed dark pink, and I saw him trying to hide a smirk.

"I'm going to try and figure out how to hook up this bad boy and then hopefully find the magical switch that makes a bed appear somewhere in here. It seems like Tilly's down for the count in the back."

"I know how to do everything. This is just a smaller version of the tour bus Jude uses. I stayed in his last summer in South Carolina."

We worked together to hook up the outside cables and hoses before returning inside to convert the sofa into a double bed. Luckily, we were able to find blankets and pillows without having to disturb Tilly.

I stripped down to a T-shirt and boxer briefs and got into the bed. Dante followed my lead and began to peel off his jeans.

Goddammit. I wanted him again, but I wasn't about to mess around with him when Tilly could come prancing right out to ask for detailed demonstrations.

Despite my best efforts to ignore him while he undressed, I couldn't stop myself from stealing glances. He was no longer the frail, skinny teen I carried out of his father's church. Despite his small frame, he was fit as hell. I'd heard about him teaching martial arts to some of the kids in the shelter and asked Aunt Londa about it. She told me he'd gotten into it very early on during his time in San Francisco and achieved his black belt rapidly. Whatever it was he did for exercise, he wore his clothes well.

I'd tried hard not to think of Dante that way right before I was supposed to sleep platonically next to him, but I couldn't help it. He was hot as hell and set all my senses on high alert even more now than he had when I first saw him at the gala. Something about him just plain did it for me, and I had to admit my feelings for him weren't casual.

I felt the warmth of his body as he got in bed next to me, and I noticed all my muscles stiffening in an attempt not to hump him to death.

"What's with the plywood board imitation?" he whispered, sending warm puffs of breath against my neck. I couldn't hold back a groan.

"You're so hot; I can't lie here and not want to do naughty things to you, Dante," I admitted.

"Then do naughty things to me," he purred into my ear.

Oh fuck.

My dick was hard as steel, but I refused to have an orgasm within feet of Tilly Marian.

"No way," I ground out between my teeth.

"Fine, then let me tell you a story about the time I accidentally walked in on your aunt Londa making out with some guy in the supply closet at the shelter," he teased.

I heaved out a breath of resignation as the pressure in my dick eased. "Done. Thanks. It's probably only a temporary fix though."

"Go to sleep, AJ," he said. "Big day ahead of us tomorrow." Dante leaned over and placed a sweet kiss on my lips and all thoughts of my aunt flew out of my head.

The only thing left in my brain was Dante Marian. The sweet taste of him, the gentle feel of him.

"*Baby*," I breathed.

I knew I shouldn't have called him that. It wasn't like we were an item, but I couldn't help it. It was how I thought of him. Dante's entire body shivered at the word.

My fingers slid into his hair as I deepened the kiss. Within moments, our tongues were engaged and our breaths came faster.

"We can't," I murmured.

"I know," he said, moving a hand down to cup my erection.

"*Fuck*. Don't stop," I groaned as quietly as I could.

His hand slipped into my underwear until he gripped my cock. *Christ*, his fingers on me felt amazing. Warm and strong, giving me the perfect kind of caress followed by a tug.

"*Unngh*," I grunted into his mouth. "Want you so badly."

Dante moved his mouth over to my ear and blew the words into it, "Let me suck you off."

My cock jumped in his hand and I arched my head back. There was no blood left in my brain to keep me from doing something stupid. I kicked off the blanket and shoved my underwear down my thighs as he swiveled around to take my cock into his mouth.

I reached my hands up to where his hips were next to my head and shucked his own briefs down, positioning his body so I could return the favor. My tongue stroked and sucked until he had to take his mouth off me to suck in breaths.

Even though it went down in history as the quietest orgasm I'd had in a very long time, possibly ever, it was spectacular. Coming into Dante's hot mouth was *unfuckingbelievable*. Luckily, he came first, so by the time I came, I was able to bite my fist to keep from screaming. I felt like my chest was going to implode as my body shuddered against his.

After a few moments of collecting ourselves and pulling underwear back on, we lay back down side by side, only close enough to hold hands since we'd worked up some heat in the small space. Once our breathing slowed, I realized Dante had fallen asleep. I wasn't far behind.

I came awake later to the sounds of soft whimpering. It took me a minute to remember where I was and get my bearings. *Dante*. I was in a small bed with Dante Marian, and he was scared.

I shifted over to put my hand on his back. His body was curled up in a tight ball with his back to me.

"Dante," I whispered. "Wake up. You're having a nightmare."

"*No*," he said in a small voice.

"Yes. It's okay, it's just a bad dream. Wake up. You're safe."

"*No*."

I leaned up to try and get a look at his face. His eyes were closed and deep lines broke the planes of his forehead. My chest felt tight and a lump formed in my throat. Fuck, this wasn't okay. None of this was okay. I never wanted Dante Marian to be scared again.

"Dante," I said, shaking him a little more forcefully. I felt him trembling under my touch and I gave up trying to shake him awake. I scooted closer to him and wrapped my arms around him, curling against his back and sliding my face next to his to whisper words of reassurance and calm.

Gradually the trembling stopped and he seemed to sleep peacefully again. I could smell the light scent of soap from the bathroom and it coupled with the warm scent of his body to create an intoxicating blend. I turned my nose into his neck to seek it out and must have fallen asleep like that.

Several hours later, I awoke to the amazing feeling of my cock nestled against Dante's ass. Just as I was about to arch into it, I heard a familiar voice above me.

"Well, I'll be damned," Tilly said. "Is it hump day already?"

16

DANTE

I awoke with the feeling of having been in a delicious dream. I snuggled back into the warm body behind me and let out a sigh of contentment. There was a glorious hard cock pressing into me, giving me all kinds of ideas.

Before I had a chance to back even farther into it, the unexpected combination of hard cock and Tilly's voice made me lose my ever-loving shit.

"What the fuck?!" I blurted, scrambling away from the warm body and practically falling off the bed in the process.

Large hands came out to grab me before I went ass over end off the edge, and I found myself right back where I started again—in AJ's arms.

I turned my head to look at him in surprise and noticed his raised eyebrow and upturned mouth.

"Is my morning breath really that bad?" he said in a sexy-as-hell gravelly morning voice that went straight to my balls.

"Yes," I said without thinking. "It is."

I stood up and tried like hell to point my massive morning wood away from both Tilly and AJ as I shuffled to the tiny toilet cubicle in the back of the camper. If the place hadn't been such a tiny box, I might have actually considered rubbing one out. I'd slept pressed up against a fucking gorgeous man whose arms were wrapped around me and whose face nuzzled my neck. Just the memory of it sent shivers all over me.

I vowed never to think of it again while Aunt Tilly was around.

Much.

Okay, more than, like, once per hour. Or once per fifteen minutes. Or once per...

There was a knock on the bathroom door. "Dante, you want your pants?" Tilly called out through the door. "Might help tame the raging bull if you know what I mean."

And there went the morning wood. Gone in an instant.

WE GRABBED breakfast and made a quick Walmart run for some clean clothes before preparing to get back on the road.

After stowing our bags in a cubby, I turned to him. "Why don't you let me take a turn driving?"

AJ nodded. "Okay, that would be good actually. If you don't mind."

"Not at all. Maybe it'll give you a chance to get some details out of Patty Hearst back there."

I heard Tilly mutter something about Vienna sausages not being worth the trouble but giant salamis necessitating a repeat trip. I tried not to dissect what she meant.

After a while, I pulled over at a gas station in teeny-tiny Baker, California, to fill up the RV's large tank. I made Tilly pay for it that time with her credit card since all this was her fault to begin with. It didn't hurt she was richer than Midas.

Once we switched seats and I turned on the ignition, I called back to make sure Tilly didn't need anything else before we got back on the road.

There was no answer, so I turned to AJ. "Where is she?"

"Hell if I know."

"Shit," I muttered, unbuckling my seatbelt.

I found her in the gas station buying a bag of ice. "What's that for?" I asked.

"Margaritas."

Of course. Because nothing said running from the law like a good cocktail.

"Get in the camper, Aunt Tilly. AJ is waiting for us."

"Why? For all we know, this AJ guy is an ax murderer. Did you ever think of that? Huh?"

"No," I said, rolling my eyes. "Of course not. He's not an ax murderer. He's trying to help us."

"How? By driving the pleasure palace to some godforsaken rundown shit shack in the middle of nowhere California?"

A local man filling up his truck lifted his head to scowl at us.

"Beg your pardon," I called out to him. "Dementia, you know."

Tilly rolled her eyes. "Like that man's in a position to disagree. This town's biggest bragging rights are linked to a big-ass thermometer, for Christ's sake. Anyway, at least ask your boyfriend what he does for a living."

"He's not my boyfriend. I barely know the guy."

"Oh, you barely know him yet you know for a fact he's not a serial killer? What are you, some kind of psycho?"

"I think you mean psychic. And I see what you're doing. You're trying to distract me from asking you more about Vegas. It's not going to work. Get in."

While I drove, AJ sat in the back and talked to Tilly for a while. I couldn't hear them over the noise of the road and eventually gave up trying and turned on the radio.

We finally made it to Vegas and stopped for lunch at a place Tilly swore was great. It turned out to be Hooters.

"Really, Tilly?" I asked. "I'm not eating at Hooters." I saw AJ laugh and shake his head out of the corner of my eye. As if someone could tell the woman what was or was not going to happen.

Once we were seated at Hooters, I had to admit, the burgers were good and after having a beer, Tilly seemed to finally loosen her lips.

"It wasn't my fault," she began. "Ask Granny and Irene. I was minding my own business at the Wheel of Fortune slots when someone bumped my elbow and spilled my drink."

While she spoke, she gestured with the hand holding her beer glass and I couldn't take my eyes off it for fear she would accidentally fling it somewhere. She continued.

"I threw a hissy fit at the asshole who did it, and he got in my face. Some young pissant hotshot type. Probably works for one of those dot-com deals. Anyway, he pissed me off, so I got right back in his. He called me a name I'm not repeating, *senior citizen*, so I hauled my purse back to deck him one."

My lips were pursed as tight as possible in an effort to hold in my giggle at the image in my head.

"Then what happened?" AJ asked with a barely suppressed grin.

"I was well and truly into a decent backswing, you know, the windup, when a big strong arm grabbed me from behind to stop my forward motion. The whole thing took me by surprise, and I went ass over teakettle onto the casino carpet. That shit is nasty. Have you ever seen those colors? Jesus, they clash like an ABBA concert in the Mormon Temple. Anyway, that's beside the point."

"What *is* the point, Tilly? You tripped and fell on the senator's penis?" I asked.

At this point AJ couldn't hold it back any longer and neither could I, quite frankly. We burst out laughing and couldn't catch our breaths. Patrons around the restaurant looked over to see what all the fuss was about, so we tried to calm down as quickly as we could. As if saying the word *penis* in a room full of giant boobsicles was taboo.

"I was so grateful to the man who helped me up, I decided to give him a pity blow. Actually, now you mention it, that's where you guys came in."

The laughter died in a vacuum hiss of silence around the table.

"Wh-what?" AJ asked.

"No! Don't ask her to repeat it. God, AJ. Haven't you learned a single thing about Aunt Tilly? Never, ever ask her to repeat shit like that. I swear she mumbles it on purpose just for that very reason. She gets Sam with that trick every time."

I heard Tilly giggle beside me. "He's so easy. Even Beau has caught on quicker than Sam. Just the prospect of doing the beej made me realize how rusty I was. I need to learn the new tricks. Maybe you guys can show me while we're here."

"That's *so* not going to happen," AJ said. "Let's refocus on Vegas. So the senator helped you up and you ended up sleeping with him," AJ clarified in a voice too low for passersby to hear.

"No, I don't know the name of the man who helped me up," she said.

"Oh god," I muttered. "Here we go."

"That guy was quite handsome, don't get me wrong. But only in a 'middle management' kind of way. I figured a quickie wouldn't hurt anyone, so I followed him to his room anyway. On the way there, I saw a total beefcake doing some kind of pole dance in a club off the hotel lobby."

If there was a god, he would make sure the pole dancer was not the president's father. *Please, oh please.*

"So I ditched Middle Manager and veered into the club to watch Pole Dancer. If I'm not mistaken, he and I shared an intimate moment of eye contact. The bachelorette girls next to me swore he was eye-fucking me during his dance, and they weren't wrong. Unfortunately I'd lost track of my eyeglasses at that point and figured out later I was tipping him with free buffet vouchers. Thanks to me, that boy's gonna eat free for years."

I bit my knuckle to keep from laughing loudly enough to draw attention to the table again.

"And then what happened?" AJ prompted.

"Then the bachelorette ladies invited me to a private room with them in the back of the club.

"When I got back there, I was expecting another hottie pole dancer, but the guy on the private pole was like an old lounge lizard. You know the type. The ones who work the crowds off-off-strip in some seedy bar wearing polyester suits and a look of grim desperation? Yeah, *his* name I remember. *Ringo.* And before you ask, no, not the good Ringo."

As if, for a minute there, we thought she'd met Ringo Starr in the back room of a strip joint in Vegas.

I sighed.

"So there I was, wondering if I would have to waste more buffet vouchers on this piece of crap, when up walks a gorgeous young woman."

I was going to die of old age before she finished telling the story.

"I wanna say she was about my height and had bleach-blonde hair—"

"Tilly, no offense, but is her physical description necessary?" AJ asked. I closed my eyes and shook my head before opening them up to look at him again. Yup. He'd gone pale.

Being on the receiving end of the Tilly Death Glare was no joke.

"Never mind, jackass," she snapped. "Maybe you can let me know when you regain your patience and want to hear the whole story. I've got all the time in the world. I'm going to take a walk."

"Wait, no. Tilly, I'm sorry. Please forgive—"

I put my hand on his forearm where it rested between us on the table. "Leave her be. We'll let her have a few minutes to herself and then loosen her lips when she comes back for her beer. There's no way she's leaving it here untouched."

17

AJ

Dante was right. Twenty minutes later she was back, sucking her lukewarm beer down and asking for a refill while Dante and I finished dessert. Her powdery skin looked soft and worn, and I wondered how she was handling the stress of the situation.

"Aunt Tilly, now that we're here in Vegas, we really need to know what we're dealing with. We can't just keep pretending this isn't serious," Dante said.

"Don't you think I know that, Dante? It's very strange is all. I don't understand what the big deal is."

"Why don't you finish telling us what happened? So you were in the back room with the Lounge Lizard and the Pretty Woman. Then what?"

"The Pretty Woman invited me to a high stakes poker game in one of the fancy suites. So I followed her, not realizing she was the prize, not one of the players. Well, at first I thought *I* was the prize but... anyway—"

I started to open my mouth but Dante placed a hand on my knee under the table and squeezed so hard I thought I might yelp. I placed my hand over his and squeezed in acknowledgement before threading my fingers through his to keep it there.

"Once I got up to the suite, there was only one man there. The winner of the game," she said.

"The senator?" Dante asked.

Tilly shook her head. "No, he came later. This guy's name was Lionel."

"Lionel Valetti, the old mobster?" I couldn't help but ask, hoping to god it wasn't.

"That sounds right. Anyway, Lionel wanted to take us to the suite where a bunch of his buddies were partying, but I didn't get a good vibe off the guy so I said no."

"He's probably not the kind of guy to take no for an answer, Tilly. How'd you get out of there?" I asked.

"That's when I met Harold. I was just getting ready to open my mouth to give Valetti a piece of my mind when a nice-looking gentleman appeared and pretended he knew who I was. I didn't recognize him because I'd lost track of my glasses. I think I told you that part. He gave me a big ole bear hug and everything, like we were school chums from way back. Then he suggested we get out of there so we could go somewhere private to catch up. After that, the weirdo let me go. It was probably because the new guy had bodyguards with him."

"Secret Service," I said.

"Well, I know that now, but I didn't at the time. Harold just introduced them as his friends, and he introduced himself as Harry. He asked if he could buy me a drink downstairs, so we headed to one of the bars off the lobby. We drank and talked for a couple of hours until we were drunk enough to get our karaoke on."

"Dear god," Dante muttered under his breath.

"Did anyone recognize him at that point?" I asked. "The man's on television all the time."

"Maybe? I remember people taking pictures, but I didn't think much of it at the time. I was heavily, ah, soused and busy concentrating on my Beyonce number—the one about putting a ring on it.

Then this couple said *they* were going to put a ring on it at the wedding chapel, so a bunch of us decided to go with them...." She got lost in thought for a minute. "I'd forgotten that part. We were *really* drunk by then."

"And you still didn't realize you were with Harold Cannon?" Dante asked.

"Were you not listening when I mentioned I'd lost track of my glasses?" she snapped, shooting daggers at Dante.

"So, Tilly, if you were drunk when you slept with him, there might be a consent issue the Secret Service is worried about," I suggested as gently as I could.

"No. I didn't sleep with him till the next morning."

I felt Dante's hand squeeze mine as if he sought patience from an external source.

"Without any salacious details, please explain what happened between the wedding chapel and sleeping together," Dante requested.

"That part is fuzzy. I remember leaning over at one point and telling Harry his two buddies were awfully creepy. They were always staring at us and kept asking me personal details, like what my full name was and where I lived. They were friendly, don't get me wrong. I just thought it was none of their business."

"So you wound up in his room or your room?" I asked.

"His room. When we woke up, we were still fully dressed and on top of the comforter. He asked me to stay for room service, we ate breakfast, yada yada yada, we had sex."

Dante shuddered and looked down at his lap.

"And then you left? Did you exchange contact information?" I asked.

"I left. He asked for my number and I politely declined. I didn't need some man swooning all over me just because of a one-night stand. No, thanks. It wasn't until later that day in the lobby I saw him again with my glasses on. Granny elbowed me and asked if that was who she thought it was."

"Did you talk to him again?" Dante asked.

"No, are you kidding? I don't want to get mixed up in that crap. The man's a media whore. I don't need that mess. Which is a shame, because the man slurps a good oyster if you know what I mean."

"I'm out," Dante said, standing up and walking off.

I sighed. "Okay. So you two met while in the company of a known criminal, you immediately left with him to drink and sing in the hotel bar, you met a couple tying the knot and were, what, legal wedding witnesses do you think?"

"I remember signing papers, so we must have been," she said hesitantly. "Although I wish I could remember the poor woman's name because I think I somehow ended up wearing her ring."

The blood slowed in my veins. "What ring? Where is it? Were you wearing a ring when you woke up *after visiting a wedding chapel with Senator Cannon*?"

From somewhere behind me I heard Dante squeak.

"Well, yes, I woke up with a ring on and... oh shit. Harry might have had one on too. Do you think he's married? He's not married, is he?" she asked. "I thought his wife was dead."

I let out a deep breath. "Actually, yeah, Tilly. I think he just might be married after all."

18

DANTE

Hearing that your great-aunt might have accidentally become the president's stepmother while on a drunken karaoke ramble in Vegas didn't pair well with a nice key lime pie. My stomach started rolling. I scrambled to find my phone as I stepped out of the restaurant into the hot summer sun.

When my brother picked up I began talking a mile a minute and my breathing took a lower priority until I practically hyperventilated.

"Griff, holy hell I need your help, we're in trouble, there's some major shit going on—you're not going to believe this, it's about Tilly, and I think I might—"

Strong arms came around me and plucked the phone out of my hand, pulling me into a large, warm chest. My face went into the vee of his shirt, my nose landing in the sparse hair there. *Mmmm.* I tried to inhale the scent of him and use the deep breaths to relax.

"Griff, it's AJ... yes, everything's okay. He's fine, I have him right here. Just needs to catch his breath. Let me tell you what's going on so you can try and help us from your end. Are you still in the city? Good."

He continued to calmly relay what we thought happened and asked if Griff could go over to Tilly's house and speak to the Secret

Service to give them AJ's phone number. I heard Tilly mutter something about meeting us at the RV.

"I'll try to get this sorted out, Griff. In the meantime, though, we're in Vegas. Apparently Tilly's hoping to find the senator and confront him directly to find out what this is all about."

I couldn't make out Griff's exact words, but I could hear the familiar cadence and rhythm, which helped calm me down. As long as Griff knew what was going on, I no longer had to be the Marian in charge.

AJ's free arm rubbed up and down my spine as he talked.

"Yeah, okay. We'll give you a call tonight if we don't hear from you sooner. Take care," AJ finished before hanging up.

He kissed the top of my head. "He'll handle it."

"Thanks, AJ. I appreciate it," I said, looking up at him.

A swarm of tourists came out of nowhere and surrounded us on their way down the sidewalk where we stood. There must have been four busloads of people walking shoulder to shoulder, all talking at full voice and jostling us as they walked along. AJ tightened his hold on me to keep us from being separated and I winced and pulled away, bumping into an older gentleman who turned to smile and apologize. He was too close. They were all too close. I got bumped again from behind.

My entire body stiffened and I felt the blood rush from my head to my feet. A loud buzzing sound began in my ears and I looked up at AJ. "I can't," I said, turning to flee even as the crowd thinned again.

AJ reached out and grabbed me around the waist to stop me. "Whoa. What just happened?"

"Nothing, I just need to go." The words felt like an automated response pushed through teeth that took up too much space in my mouth. Memories of my childhood began clanging like the giant roar of a storm siren. "Let me go."

My heart hammered, clashing with the buzzing in my ears, and the memories blared until my entire being felt like a cacophony I couldn't get away from.

AJ looked at me with wide eyes. "I got you. Let me help," he said slowly and carefully, like I was a wild animal he meant to lure into a cage.

"No," I breathed.

He tried to draw me into his arms. While my brain knew he was trying to help me, my body only felt more touching, and that was not okay.

I gave him a desperate look and asked in a small, strangled voice. "P-please let me go?"

He let go of me and I stumbled back, almost falling with the momentum. AJ tried reaching out to steady me, but I was off like a rocket, running for all I was worth through the crowd, past the parking lot, and around the building until I found the dumpsters and could calm down.

BY THE TIME he found me, I'd stopped and sat on a cinder-block wall next to the loading dock behind the restaurant, far enough away from the dumpsters not to smell them. It was plenty hot out and the sun burned down on my skin, a somewhat welcome relief from the chill of the restaurant air-conditioning.

When AJ sat next to me on the wall, he handed me a bottle of water he must have grabbed from the RV. "It's actually water. Don't worry, I checked," he said with a wink.

I gave him a feeble smile of thanks and took it. After taking a long drink, I offered it to him.

I took a sip of water before asking him, "AJ, do you have phobias besides heights?"

He studied me. "Yes. I'm scared of something happening to the people I love."

We sat together in easy silence.

"Does it give you nightmares?" I asked.

"Sometimes."

I took another drink of water and began to stand up. AJ reached out for me.

"Dante, do you want to talk about it?"

I opened my mouth to tell him I didn't, but I stopped myself. I was so used to keeping my past a secret, I'd automatically assumed it would scare him off. But I remembered he'd heard my speech already at the gala and hadn't freaked out.

"My biological father was a minister who tried to pray the gay away. During special church services, he would gather all of the congregation around me in a big circle and lead everyone in prayer chants. Almost like an exorcism or something. The chants would get louder and people would start to reach out and put their hands on me like they were trying to heal me. I couldn't get away because everyone was packed so tightly around me. I hated it so much," I said, my voice coming out raw and quiet.

"Fuck, Dante," he breathed.

"It was awful. I hated being the center of attention. I hated that he'd told the entire town my business. And I hated there wasn't a single person in the entire church who stood up for me."

"No wonder crowds bother you."

"Yeah. I can't stand it when strangers brush up against me. I don't usually talk about my past, but... I guess I just felt like telling you so you'd know it wasn't you."

"Thank you for trusting me," he said. I looked over at him and was relieved to see nothing but tender concern for me in his eyes.

I quirked up the side of my mouth in a tiny smile. "And that ends today's episode of Dante's Demons. Check back with us tomorrow to find out more about spiders and that weird rind you find around some fancy cheeses." I shot him a wink.

"I hate those things too, so you're in good company. Why don't we head back?" He grinned, standing up and reaching for my hand as we began to follow the road back to the parking lot.

"So, how does it feel to be related to the president?" AJ teased.

I barked out a laugh. "What's funny is how *not* surprising this all is, really. It's such a Tilly thing, it's not even funny."

AJ laughed too. "Yeah, Griff didn't sound all that surprised."

"What did he say?"

"That he'd get your brother Pete to handle it."

"Shit, why didn't I think of that? Pete's an attorney," I said.

"He's flying here to help. I told him we'd be at the Bellagio since that's apparently where all this started."

I let out a deep breath. "Fuck, this shit is exhausting. I think I'm going to take a long shower and a nap when we get to the hotel." I peeked up at him, trying to ignore the heat rushing to my face. "Care to join?"

19

———

AJ

Once we got to our room at the Bellagio, I held him long after he'd fallen asleep. My teeth ground together until my jaw ached, and I couldn't stop thinking about what had happened to him as a kid. Why did he have to end up in such a perverted upbringing? Why couldn't he have been the son of a loving father instead of the asshole who'd raised him?

All I ever wanted was for Dante to feel safe. To forget his awful past and move forward. I wanted to scream. Or beat someone up. Or just plain motherfucking murder his jackass father.

After leaning down to kiss his forehead, I carefully moved out from under him and climbed off the bed. I found his phone and took it into the bathroom to call Griff.

"Hey, Dante," Griff answered.

"Griff, it's me, AJ," I said quietly.

"Is Dante okay?" he asked.

"Kind of. That's why I'm calling. I wonder if it's too late for you to hitch a ride here with Pete? I think Dante could use your company."

It made my heart hurt to think I wasn't the person who could bring the most comfort to Dante, but I knew I couldn't possibly be. He barely knew me, yet he'd been close to Griff for eight years.

"I'm already on my way, AJ. I met Pete at the airport."

I breathed a sigh of relief and dropped my face in my hand. "Good. We're in room forty-three twelve, so call or come knock when you get here. Who's coming with you?"

I heard him hesitate on the line for a moment before answering with a smile in his voice.

"You want the good news or the bad news?"

A WHILE later I came awake to the sound of knocking at the door. My nose rested behind Dante's ear and I pressed a kiss there.

"That's your family. Apparently the Marians were running a buy-one-get-twenty special," I rumbled into his ear.

"Huh? What do you mean?" he said in a groggy voice.

"They're all here, I'm afraid."

The knocking on the door got louder and he jerked. "What the fuck?"

"I think they somehow got the idea the Bellagio would make a great spot for a Marian get-together. Your entire family came with Pete," I repeated.

"Oh god," he groaned, sitting up and rubbing his hands over his face. "I don't know if I can handle this right now."

"Why don't I tell them we'll meet them downstairs in a few minutes?"

"Yeah, you wouldn't mind?" he asked.

"Course not."

I threw on the rest of my clothes and opened the door to see Griff and Sam standing in the hallway with Simone right behind them.

"Give us a few minutes and we'll—" I began before Simone stepped between the two men and slipped past me into the room.

"Think again, AJ," she said with a smile. "We're not the most patient people."

Griff shot me an apologetic look. "And by that, she means, *she's* not the most patient person. But we're coming in too."

By the time I closed the door, Simone was hugging Dante on the bed and Griff sat against the headboard on the other side of him. Dante gave me an eye roll.

"Remind me never to hire you as a bodyguard," he said.

"Dude, your sister is pushy as hell," I admitted.

"True. Did you guys even check on Aunt Tilly before you came here?"

Griff ruffled his hair. "No, Granny and Irene told us we had to wait in line. Apparently the senator is still in town and Tilly's already reconnected with him. Granny and Irene called dibs on meeting him first, so we decided to come see you instead." He looked at me and winked, letting me know he had come straight to us first but played it off for Dante's benefit.

"Maybe I should leave you guys—" I began.

"What? No," Dante blurted. "Stay."

Something warm bloomed in my chest and I nodded, giving Dante a reassuring smile to let him know he had me as long as he wanted me there.

"So tell us all about it, baby brother," Simone encouraged.

"Apparently Aunt Tilly is now the First Stepmother," he groaned.

"Yes, but how did you end up in Vegas? And no offense, AJ—how did Londa's nephew end up with you two?" she asked.

I held my breath while he contemplated how to answer.

"Ah, well, AJ and I were in the RV when Tilly began her escape across state lines," he said carefully.

"And you didn't stop her?"

"By the time we realized what was happening, we were almost to Bakersfield," Dante explained, not making eye contact with her. His entire face and neck had flushed with embarrassment and I had a hard time not having a physical reaction to how fucking cute he was.

"Dude, Bakersfield is, like, five hours away. Were you unconscious?" she asked.

Silence. I saw Griff and Sam exchange a look, trying not to laugh. I knew the feeling.

More silence, more Dante blushing.

"Oh my fucking god, I'm an idiot," Simone exclaimed with a laugh. "You finally got your cherry popped."

The silence was deafening this time, and now it was my face that turned beet red. Dante was a *virgin*?

"Simone," he hissed. "You're a fucking jackass." He got up and made his way to the bathroom, locking the door behind him.

I wanted to throttle her for being so insensitive.

"Simone?" Griff chastised. "Really?" He tilted his head toward me and she followed it, realizing at last what the deal was.

"What, AJ didn't know?" She turned to me with a glare. "You took his virginity without realizing it?" she growled, standing up and moving toward me like she was going to rip me to shreds.

"What? No. *No*. We haven't done... that. I didn't take *anything*," I stammered.

Sam finally spoke up from his spot on the opposite bed. "So what if he did? It's about fucking time."

Griff nodded at his husband. "Seriously. He's twenty-three, for god's sake."

"I can hear you fuckers," a miserable muffled voice called out from the bathroom.

I walked to the bathroom door and knocked softly. "It's AJ, will you let me in, please?"

"Um, no, thanks. I'd rather die."

I couldn't help but laugh. "Don't die. Please let me in Dante."

The door opened, revealing a Dante who was even more pink with embarrassment than before. I slid through the crack and closed the door behind me, locking it just in case. He turned away from me and crossed his arms in front of his chest. I reached out to grab a handful of his T-shirt and yanked him back into me, catching him off guard so he had to scramble to grab hold of me to keep from slipping.

"What the—?"

My mouth crushed his before he could finish. I laid into him with the most searing, dick-plumping kiss I could give until our toes curled against the tile floor and desperate whimpers squeaked out of Dante. Finally I pulled back and locked eyes with him.

"If you think for one minute that finding out you're a virgin makes me want you any less, then you're an idiot," I said in a low growl. "I want you more with every minute I spend in your company, and I plan on being your first if and when you ever decide you're ready. But so help me god, if you spend one more minute being embarrassed or avoiding me because of this, I'm going to lose my shit. Do you honestly think hearing you've never been with another man that way would turn me *off*? You're fucking crazy. Knowing I could possibly be the first person you let into your body makes me want to take you right here, right now, your siblings be damned."

This time Dante's skin was flushed from the kiss, and his eyes widened with each word until his eyebrows disappeared into his hairline.

20

DANTE

I went from plotting my sister's murder to being overwhelmed by pure, aggressive lust.

"Okay, well, I think we should save it for later. I didn't imagine my first time happening next to a toilet."

AJ's face broke into a wide grin. "His sense of humor returns. We're making progress." He leaned in and kissed me softly on the lips before continuing. "I've heard stories about your family's love for revenge plots. If you ask me, Simone deserves some shit for opening her big fat mouth, don't you agree?"

"God, you're the best thing ever." I sighed dramatically. "Ideas?"

"Give me time. I'm on it," he said with a wink.

We rejoined the others in the room, and I slid my jeans back on. "Are Mom and Dad here?"

Simone nodded and looked sheepish. "Dante, I'm sorry about earlier."

"Don't worry. I'll get you back."

She started to laugh before she caught sight of AJ's serious face. "Oh shit," she muttered.

Sam threw his arm around me. "Griff and I are on board with whatever plan you come up with. Right, Foxy?" he asked his husband.

Griff leaned over and kissed him. "Absolutely. Now let's go find everyone downstairs for dinner."

We joined the rest of the family already seated around several outside tables at one of the hotel restaurants. I did the rounds of greeting and hugging everyone before introducing AJ to Mom and Dad and taking the two spots they'd saved for us at their table.

"Did you hear about the feature spread that came out yesterday in *Ask Out Magazine*?" Dad asked after we sat down. "We brought you a copy so you could see. Great coverage for Marian House and the grand opening, Dante. You should be very proud of yourself."

I felt my face flush and mumbled a thanks while my stomach flipped with nerves.

"What did it say?" AJ asked.

Rebecca shot me a smile. "Well, honestly, it was about the Marian men. You know, the *sensational pack of six gay brothers*. But it covered the philanthropy work too. It mentioned Maverick's large donation for the expansion, Jude and Derek's support for the upkeep endowment, and Dante's hard work executing the plans as well as directing the program moving forward. The article named Dante as one of San Francisco's up-and-coming philanthropy leaders. It was very flattering. Even had some photos of you boys playing in the shirts-and-skins basketball game at Marian House last week." She winked at me. "They're calling you the last eligible Marian man, Dante. The city's hot gay do-gooder, who also happens to be single."

"Ahh, the great white whale as it were," Griff teased.

"Oh god," I groaned. "That's all I need right now."

"So, AJ, tell us more about you," Mom said with an encouraging smile. She was so good at making new people feel welcome into our family and included.

"Let's see. I, ah, graduated high school in a small mountain town in Colorado but moved to Chicago after college. I've just relocated to San Francisco to consult with the security company your son-in-law Derek used to work for," he said.

"What will you be doing there?" she asked.

I saw AJ's eyes flick over to me, and he seemed to hesitate. "Well, it's confidential, actually. But it's basically helping them develop a new type of personal protection just like the other services they offer."

Mom looked at me and back at AJ. "I'm sure Londa will love having you close to her. Maybe you can find time to volunteer with Dante at the shelter."

"Subtle, Mom," I muttered. AJ's hand snuck into my lap under the table and squeezed my thigh.

"It's something to consider," he said with amusement in his voice. "I hear the people are really nice there." The hand squeezed again, and I felt my face heat up.

I cleared my throat. "What's Pete saying about the Tilly situation?"

Dad glanced over to where Tilly sat next to Senator Cannon, surrounded by Granny and Irene, who seemed to be talking a hundred miles an hour to make up for the two whole days they were apart from each other.

"Oh, sorry, Pete found out they didn't actually marry legally. No license. The wedding chapel took advantage of their inebriated state to perform a ceremony when they realized who the senator was," Dad said.

"You're kidding?" I asked. "It was all a media stunt or something? They're not actually married?" I couldn't believe it. After all that.

"Not married. But from the looks of things, she definitely has a new fan," Mom said with wink. "Oh, and it turns out he knew her growing up in Bakersfield."

"What?" I asked in surprise. "So he really was a chum from way back? Why didn't she say something?"

"She didn't remember him. I think it was the kind of thing where she was hot stuff and he was a smarty-pants," Mom said with a smile. "Anyway, it's kind of sweet if you ask me."

"Does the press have the story?" AJ chimed in.

"Not yet," Dad said. "It's only a matter of time before someone lets it slip."

"It's going to make national news when they find out," I said. "We need to make sure she's prepared for what that means to her privacy."

"Very good point, son," Dad said with a nod. "Pete is handling it with some people at his firm."

The word "son" hit me out of left field. It wasn't as though he'd never called me that before. He had. Many times. Had done it for years. I loved it when he claimed me like that. But hearing it now, here, tonight, hit me hard in a way I wasn't expecting.

I glanced over and caught AJ studying me. Could he see how much it meant to me to be the son of someone who loved me unconditionally? He slid a little closer and squeezed my hand.

Goddammit, I felt like my heart was painted in neon on my sleeve for all the world to see. I grabbed for my beer and took a large swig, enjoying the cold bite as it hit my taste buds. It was late enough at night that the warmth of the day had dissipated and the air moved a bit. Flowers were in baskets all over the place, and I looked around at all the happy couples and families enjoying the summer evening together. I was grateful the hotel had managed to give us some privacy.

I felt myself relax. There I was, holding the hand of potentially my first boyfriend (god, did that sound cheesy or what?), and surrounded by almost every human being on earth who'd ever loved me. How lucky could a man get?

I squeezed AJ's hand before letting it go. When he glanced at me, I gave him a reassuring smile. "Be right back."

After pushing back my seat, I wandered over to where the newest Marian lay asleep in his father's arms. "Hey, Jude, can I hold Wolfe?"

Jude looked up at me with a big smile. "Of course. He's probably going to stay asleep for a while, so just let me know when you get tired of holding him or if he starts to stink. Actually, if he starts to stink, let Derek know," he said with a wink.

Jude wore horn-rimmed eyeglasses, and I knew it was more from sleep-deprivation than a desire to disguise himself from nosey fans. As it was, he was careful to sit with his back to the public spaces. His husband kicked him under the table. "Next dirty diaper is all you, superstar. I got the last one."

The baby settled against my chest and burrowed his sleepy face into my neck. I turned to inhale the baby scent of his head and smiled at Jude and Derek before walking back to my spot.

"Who's this?" AJ asked with a smile.

I noticed Mom give Dad a sweet look. I thought about how happy they must be to sit there surrounded by this amazing family they'd created.

"This is my newest nephew, Wolfe Marian. Jude and Derek's baby."

"He doesn't look like a wolf. Poor kid needs a little more hair, doesn't he?" he said in the sweet voice people get when talking to babies.

"I love this age. They're not quite so fragile anymore, but they're still snuggly and easy to hold," I said. Mom and Dad nodded, but my brother Jamie shook his head.

"Nope. Babies of any age freak me out," he said.

"Well, that explains the lack of grandchildren from you two," Mom scoffed.

Teddy put his arm around Jamie. "We've thought about it, but we both love to travel so much; we're not sure it would be the right decision for us. It's awfully fun to have nieces and nephews though. It's like the best of both worlds, isn't it, Jamie?"

"Definitely. Every time Teddy travels for a photo shoot, I swear half his luggage coming back is filled with gifts for the kids."

"Just because I'm their favorite doesn't mean you have to be jealous," he teased. "You're just pissed because I brought an alpaca sweater back from Peru for Nimrod instead of you."

"His name is Tommy, you ass," Ginger yelled from another table.

Jamie leaned back in his seat to call back to her. "Hey, Ginge, send the girls over here, would you?"

When my nine-year-old twin nieces Hazel and Chloe came running over from their table, Jamie threw an arm around each of them. "Now tell the truth, girls. Who's your favorite uncle?"

The girls looked at Jamie and Teddy before turning to look at me and grinning widely.

"Uncle Dante for sure," Chloe said.

"Or maybe Uncle Tristan," Hazel added.

They knew exactly what they were doing, and I gave them each a high-five.

"I heard that," Tristan called from the table next to ours. "Remind me to give you five bucks later, Ladybug," he said to Hazel.

The girls laughed and hung around our table for a few more minutes, fawning over Wolfe and asking us if they could check out Aunt Tilly's camper van later.

"Sure. We can do it tomorrow. I think it'll be way past your bedtime when we're done with dinner," I told them.

They went back to their own table and waited for their food. AJ draped his arm around the back of my chair and leaned over to rub Wolfe's back.

"He's a good sleeper, huh? To stay down even with all this noise," he said.

"Babies just zonk out anywhere. Especially when they're milk drunk," I said softly.

"He's lucky to have so much family around him all the time. They all are," he said, looking around at my other nieces and nephew.

"Do you get to see your parents and sisters very often?" I asked, reaching for my beer to take a sip.

"Definitely at the holidays. We all go to see my parents in Colorado either for Christmas or Thanksgiving, depending on what year it is. They live in a ski resort town called Aster Valley. Sometimes we try to meet up during the summer too, but that usually only works every few years."

Little Wolfe stayed asleep on my shoulder, which made it difficult to eat when the food arrived. AJ must have noticed me struggling, because at one point halfway through the meal, he leaned over and took him from me, sliding him onto his own shoulder while he was in the middle of telling Maverick about the youth shelter he'd volunteered with in Chicago.

When I lifted an eyebrow at his maneuver, he leaned over and said, "Eat."

My heart did a skippy-dippy pitter-pat at the combination of him looking out for me and him holding a fucking Marian baby on his shoulder like he was not only an old pro but also a member of the family.

~

It was late by the time we returned to the room, but I wasn't about to spend one more minute of that day, of that trip, without getting naked with AJ Flores again. He'd pulled the fucking ripcord and my parachute was deploying whether he liked it or not.

Before the room key was even out of his pocket, I slammed him up against the hotel room door and caged him in with my arms. "You're mine tonight, AJ," I growled into his ear before landing my lips on his.

I heard a moan escape him as I attacked his mouth. He tasted like summer nights with a hint of beer. He was so sexy. Fit and trim with muscles under his skin and the intoxicating scent of a man at the end of a long day. He practically growled his need into my mouth as I devoured him.

AJ seemed to want me with the same desperation I wanted him.

I stepped in closer to his body and felt his hips push into mine, the outline of his cock hard against my stomach. A grumble of want escaped me as I ran a hand down to feel him.

"Oh god," he gasped, pulling his lips from mine as my hand squeezed him through the fabric of his clothes. He twisted his body and fumbled to get the door open.

"Inside," I said. My lips traveled down to his neck as I walked him backward into the room.

"Dante, wait," AJ said through panting breaths.

"No. *Hell* no. Not waiting," I breathed against the join of his collarbone at the base of his throat. "I've waited long enough."

Another moan escaped, and I felt his cock move under my hand.

We stumbled the rest of the way into the room, letting the door swing closed behind us. The bed beckoned from the main room, and we made our way toward it while stripping each other with grabbing hands.

"Wait, wait," AJ gasped again between his bites to my bare shoulder. "Baby, wait."

That word almost made my heart explode. "What is it?" I asked, moving to snake my fingers into his hair.

"We don't have to... I mean, Dante, what do you want to do?" he asked, looking up at me.

"What the hell, AJ? I want to get naked and rub myself all over you. Is that unclear somehow?" I said with an exasperated puff of air. "Why are you putting the damned brakes on?"

He pulled me down to sit on the edge of the mattress next to him and tilted my chin up with his finger.

"Dante, but you haven't done this before, right?" he asked.

Ohdeargod. My face turned a thousand degrees and I tried to look anywhere but at his eyes.

"It's okay, I just don't want to hurt you or do something to—"

"No. Okay? I haven't had anal sex before, but I would like to. Does that help? Now can we stop talking about it and move on?" I begged.

AJ's smile was sweet and understanding. Goddammit.

I huffed in frustration. "Stop being so fucking nice. I don't want nice. I want your dick in my ass. And I most especially don't want to have a 'Kumbaya' moment about it ahead of time."

He barked out a laugh, and I couldn't help but smile.

"Well, at least that answers one question I had," he teased.

"AJ, please. Can you just take my word for it that I'm 100 percent ready and good and happy about this? Please?" I begged.

"Define ready," he teased, leaning in to press a kiss to my lips again and slide an exploratory finger down the crack of my ass.

21

I was afraid of hurting him or scaring him. I was afraid of disappointing him. In truth, I was afraid of so many things when it came to Dante Marian, but I was no longer afraid of whether or not I should act on my feelings toward him.

"Dante, I want you so badly. But will you please be patient and let me take it slowly?" I asked. "I want to savor you, and I want your first time to feel good."

His entire face opened up in a shit-eating grin. "If you insist." And then he stood up and shucked off the rest of his clothes before lying down on his back spread-eagle in the center of the bed.

He was so fucking hot; I wanted to consume him bit by bit.

Long, slender legs were covered in honeyed skin and dark, masculine hair. His thick cock stood rigid against his belly out of a nest of dark curls that fed into a luscious trail above. The bumpy muscles of his abdomen stood out as he tilted his head up to stare at me, and his rounded shoulders moved as he propped himself up on his elbows.

"Your body, Dante. *Jesus*," I murmured, crawling onto the bed between his outstretched feet and placing kisses along his ankle to his shin to the inside of his knee. "I want to lick every single inch of it."

I saw his cock jump at the sound of my voice. My lips turned up in a smile as I ran the tip of my tongue up the inside of one thigh.

"Holy shit," he breathed.

"Mmm-hmm," I agreed, lifting his balls with my nose and kissing him just below.

"Oh god," he groaned. "*Fuck.*"

It occurred to me I may have been a tad optimistic in thinking this wouldn't last long.

I lifted my head up to peek at him over his erection. "Dante?" I murmured in a low voice before dropping my wet lips onto his tip and sliding them over the head of his cock.

"*Glck,*" he squeaked. "I can't—what if I can't—?"

He came in a rush against my tongue, which caught me off guard. Part of me wanted to laugh, but I was terrified of actually choking, or worse, embarrassing him. I did my best to keep up with him, but it took concentration. And when I was done, I looked up to find him lying back with his hands over his face.

"*Oh. Dear. God,*" he moaned through his hands.

I wasn't 100 percent sure, but I thought his ears might have burned clean off from the blush on his skin.

"Babe," I began.

He held up an open palm but kept his eyes closed. "Do not say another word. We will never speak of this again. I'm going to throw myself in traffic later. It's the best I can do to achieve an honorable death without all the mess of a traditional seppuku."

My laugh finally bubbled out as I crawled up to rest my head on his chest.

"Oh good," he said. "The laughing. Glad we've moved on to Step Two of Dante's Humiliation."

I ran the tip of a finger down the center of his chest from the base of his throat to his sexy-as-shit happy trail. "Do you have any idea how hot and flattering it is that you just came the minute I put my mouth on you?" I admitted.

He peeked through one eye at me. "Are you crazy?"

I leaned in to press a kiss to Dante's nipple and heard him hiss. "Yes, but not about this. You just rocked my fucking world coming like that when I barely touched you. Made me feel like some kind of sex god."

Dante groaned and leaned back again. "You *are* some kind of sex god. You just look at me and I come all over myself."

"Do you know you're a couple of years younger than I am?" I asked.

He narrowed his eyes at me, probably expecting insult added to injury. "If you so much as hint at premature *anything*, I'm going to kick your ass."

I laughed again. "Quite the opposite actually. The younger you are, the quicker your recovery time."

After my words were out, I ran an inquisitive hand down to his spent cock and found it happily recovering.

"Take two?" I asked.

"Hell fucking yes," he breathed with a grin. "But this time I think I should be the one making the moves."

I gave him a playful shove so I could take his place in the center of the bed and lie back with my hands behind my head.

Dante's skin was still flushed pink from the orgasm and his embarrassment, and he looked adorable. I was already hard for him, and when his hand reached down to stroke me, I groaned and arched into him.

A devious smile widened his lips. "What if I could get you to come just as fast, old man?" he teased.

"I'd like to see you tr—ahhaahh!" I gasped as his mouth landed on me in one big engulfing suck. My hands flew to his hair and I bucked off the bed. "Oh fuck, fuck, Dante. *Fuck.*"

He laid into me with the most incredible, magical mouth I'd ever felt. Within moments my head spun out of control. His hands worked in tandem with his mouth, and my fingers scrabbled to hold on to the bed sheets, the headboard, the pillows behind me—anything to keep from fisting into his hair and hurting him.

"W-wait, *Jesusfuck* I'm going to come," I stammered as I felt my balls pull up and the warm swell of pleasure expand outward through my body. When I came, I felt like it lasted forever. He pulled off just in time and cum shot over my belly while he dropped kisses along my hip and kept one hand on my balls.

When I was done, he took me into his mouth again and I jack-knifed up into a sitting position from the sensation, yanking him up and slamming my mouth over his. We kissed feverishly until gradually slowing back down, Dante crawling up to straddle my lap and put his arms around me.

His ankles were crossed behind my back and I put my hands down on his bare thighs to stroke their muscled shape.

When Dante tilted his face back to look at me, his mischievous grin was back.

"What?" I asked with a smile.

"That didn't go down the way we planned, did it?"

THE NEXT MORNING we were walking back to the hotel from brunch with Tilly, Granny and Irene when my phone rang.

It was my dad.

"Hello?" I answered.

"AJ, I have some news about Dante," my dad said into the phone. "You know I normally call Londa about these things but she said to check with you. Do you know where he is?"

I noticed Dante look up at me with a curious glance so I quickly shifted the phone to press against my chest and told Dante to go ahead back to the hotel without me.

"Yeah, I do. It's a long story, but we're in Vegas," I explained.

"You and Dante?" Dad asked in surprise.

"Yes, Dad." I tried not to sound defensive but I knew how he would feel if he found out I was getting involved with Dante.

"Dante's biological father, Richard Lawton, has just announced his run for US Congress."

I heard the words but replayed them in hopes I'd heard wrong. "Oh shit."

"Yeah. Oh shit. I didn't see the details but the seat came open unexpectedly. I wanted to give Londa a heads-up and suggest she keep an eye on Dante in case he sees it on TV."

"He'll be devastated," I said, almost to myself. "Do you think I should tell him?"

"If you think it'll unsettle him then let's wait and see if it goes anywhere," he said.

"Yeah. I think that's a good idea. It would really upset him."

There was a pause before my father spoke up. "Angel, you know the policy is to keep a distance from the people you rescue, not just because of safety but there are emotional and moral issues around getting involved with someone you've rescued."

"I know that, Dad," I said. "It's been years. Dante is fine, and he doesn't even remember me."

Another pause. "Is this more than a friendship, Angel?"

I felt my jaw tighten as I ran shaky fingers through my hair.

Dad sighed. "Think this through, son. At the very least Dante has the right to go into a relationship with his eyes open. He needs to know the truth about you. And you need to decide if Dante is worth revealing that."

His voice was soothing and familiar, and it made my eyes sting.

"He's worth it."

"Then you need to tell him."

"Dad," I breathed. "He's never going to speak to me again after I do that."

"You're a good man, Angel. Hopefully he'll see that."

Goddammit. I didn't want to ruin what we had developed, but I knew my dad was right. It was only a matter of time before shit was going to blow up if I didn't tell him. I needed to.

I walked back to the hotel and straight into a shitstorm.

Before I could even see into the lobby, I heard the noise of a crowd. The paparazzi was there in droves. I wondered what was going on, who they were there for. Regardless, I didn't want any part of a mob, so I put my head down and tried to snake my way toward the elevator banks.

Cameras went off and shouts hit my ears. I winced but kept walking.

"Are you Matilda Marian?" A reporter asked and suddenly I knew who they were there for. Us.

"Mrs. Marian, is it true you and Senator Cannon were married several days ago?"

The crowd closed in around us, and I started to feel my heart rate pick up and my breath come faster. I wanted to turn tail and run, but Tilly needed my help to make it through the group of reporters.

Granny pushed me forward into the crowd. "Do something," she said.

"How the hell do you expect me to get us out of here?" I asked.

"Distract the fuckers so they stop hounding her," she said with a pointed look.

I tilted my head at her. "How the hell am I supposed to do that?"

Granny turned around and stepped on her tippy-toes, becoming all of four feet eight if anything. "Attention, everyone. Do you know who this guy is? This is Dante Marian, San Francisco's hottest gay bachelor from the Internet!" she shouted.

There was a microsecond of silence before the cameras and questions shifted to me. I stood there, unable to move, still trying to come to grips with the fact she'd set the media hounds on me with no compunction.

"Wh-why did you do that?" I asked Granny.

"So I can get Tilly back to her room. We've got to get her away from these vultures." She turned to exit the crowd, grabbing some random guy and using him as a body shield as she tried to pull Tilly and Irene behind her.

Reporters and photographers moved toward me, shouting questions about the Marian brothers, the Marian House shelter, and whether I was, indeed, single.

Certain questions stood out. "Is it true your brother is Jude from Jude and the Saints?"

"Where is Jude right now? Can you get him down here so we can interview you two together? Would all of your brothers be willing to do photos together? Have you ever modeled? Are you dating anyone? You were seen with someone last night—can you tell us who it was? Was it a man? Are you really gay? Aren't all of your brothers gay too? Do you have a boyfriend?"

The questions came at me one on top of the other. I didn't intend to answer them, but I couldn't think straight, and I started stammering.

"I... uh... I... need to... um..." My breaths came in shallower and shallower pulls until I felt dizzy and spots danced around my vision. Someone bumped my bruised shoulder and I jumped in surprise, knocking me sideways into someone else who pushed me to keep from falling.

From there it seemed bodies jostled me from all sides and I started repeating, "Excuse me, excuse me," in a shaky, breathy voice, looking around for a path out of there. I was turned around and couldn't see which way the elevators were. I thought about finding an exit door to wherever the hell their dumpsters were but knew it would be better to try and get to my room.

I spotted Griff trying to push his way through the crowd. He looked worried, which meant he knew what a big deal this was for me. I knew he was trying to get to me, but he had a hard time. A group of teen girls had come screaming into the lobby wearing some kind of sports uniforms—soccer, maybe—and they swarmed around the media and my brothers, pulling out cell phones and trying to video everything.

Someone reached out with a microphone until it bumped my cheek. My blood went cold, and I felt myself finally succumbing to my fear. I was going to pass out.

My clammy palms came up to push at the people in front of me when I felt big, strong arms grab me from behind. I screamed bloody murder, but it came out sounding like a broken sob.

The black spots grew in my vision until it was easier to give up than keep fighting.

23

AJ

When I got to him, he was already white as a ghost and looked out of it. I pulled him against me, turning him around so his face was hidden against my chest. One of my arms was wrapped around his back and another was wrapped around his head.

"Hey, hey, I have you. Shh, it's okay," I said in a low voice. "I'm going to get us out of here."

I wanted to shout for everyone to get back, but I didn't want to yell in his ear.

Luckily, Griff was able to grab Tilly and get her away while the media pressed against Dante and me.

I shuffled us through the throngs of reporters and teenagers to the elevator. Once we were there, I saw Jude's husband, Derek, running toward us from the stairwell. His presence was like magic. He had the people around us properly intimidated and moving away. He was a professional bodyguard who *looked* like a professional bodyguard.

When the elevator doors opened, he nudged us inside with his hip and stood guard until the doors slid closed. Once alone in the elevator I looked down at Dante. He trembled and breathed erratically.

"It's just us now," I repeated softly. "Deep breaths. We're away."

He nodded but couldn't speak through the breathing thing he was doing. His eyes were huge. "*AJ*," he breathed, looking like he was trying so hard not to lose his shit.

"I'm right here, baby. We're going back to the room so you can lie down."

As soon as we entered the room, he pulled away and crouched into the narrow space between the bed and the wall. He crammed himself into the corner on the floor and curled up in a tiny ball, reaching out one arm to pull the duvet from the bed over on top of him.

My heart broke watching him, and I wanted to kill those reporters. I had no idea what happened, but it didn't really matter at that point. One thing I knew for sure, he was nowhere near ready for me to tell him the truth about who I was.

I shuffled into the space and knelt down to peer under the blanket. Large brown eyes looked back at me, still terrified. His breaths came in desperate gulps.

"Help," he gasped. "Can't... breathe."

"You can. It will end soon, I promise. I know it doesn't feel like it right now, but it will. Hang on."

I found a paper bag on the TV stand and emptied some snacks out of it before bringing it over to Dante.

"Here, breathe into this," I said in my calmest voice.

He reached out a shaking hand to hold it; I was shocked at how cold his skin was. I managed to pull him out of the corner and onto the bed where I sat behind him and held him. Firmly letting him know I was there, but not impeding his breathing.

My mouth was by his ear. "That's it. Slooooow breath in... slooooow breath out."

His entire body shook and was cold, but he started to steady his breathing finally. I murmured into his ear as he slowed down. "Dante, it's okay to be scared or nervous. Just let those feelings wash over you so they can escape and leave you alone. You know this will end. You'll be tired, but you'll be okay."

I continued my reassurances until he seemed to be breathing better and put the bag down. He turned around in my arms and tried to crawl as close as he could get until his face was mashed into the space between my neck and shoulder. I began rubbing his back and spoke to him in what I hoped was a soothing voice.

"When I was a little boy, I was in a bank with my mom when it was robbed," I said.

He made a sound and began to pull away, but I put my hand on his head to let him know he could stay buried where he was. "Shh, it's okay. It was fine. No one was hurt. Two men entered the bank when Mom and I were in line to see the teller. It was a little branch with just a couple of tellers at the counter and one manager at a desk by the door. I remember a little old lady sat across from the manager's desk and her purse was on the floor by her feet. Now that I think of it," I chuckled, "Tilly would have grabbed up her purse and beat the robbers with it.

"But this woman was terrified, which made the manager terrified. I remember their eyes darting around. One of the robbers stayed by the door to keep an eye out and the other walked up to the counter and handed the teller a note before he started shouting. He ended up grabbing the other woman in line with us and putting a gun to her temple until all of the money was collected. We all assumed he was going to shoot her because he was acting so crazy."

I felt Dante's body trembling again and wanted to kick myself. Why the fuck did I decide to tell this story? Jesus.

"Anyway, he didn't. The point is, it was one of the scariest five minutes of my life. Until then, I lived with the knowledge a child has: that all is well and all will *be* well. But from that point on, I knew things could go bad in an instant when you least expected it. Mom and I had been at the park right before that, playing on the playground in the sunshine. Then we went to the bank, where the most excitement we'd expected was a lollipop from the teller."

Dante lifted his head up to look at me, his eyes exhausted and skin pale. I ran my thumbs along his face to get some color back in his cheeks. "I had panic attacks after that for a long time. Mostly it happened if a tall man entered a store or a room when I wasn't prepared for it, but it also happened sometimes when I least expected it. I was jumpy at the slightest thing, even though I wanted so badly to be braver than that.

"It took me a while, but I got over it. I don't have the attacks anymore, but I still remember them vividly."

"Did the robbers get caught?" he asked.

"Yes. They got caught. One accidentally set off the dye pack in the cash and ended up covered in neon pink with skin burns that needed an ER visit. And when he got picked up, he turned in his partner in exchange for a lesser sentence."

I pulled Dante back enough to cup his face in my hands. I kissed him gently before resting my forehead against his.

"The bottom line is: panic attacks are normal. You just have to learn to let them happen. I know it's much easier said than done, and if you're anything like me, they leave you feeling wiped out. So, I suggest hanging out in the room a little while. Maybe we can watch a movie or something."

Dante's lips turned up in a small smile.

"Or something."

24

DANTE

few minutes later my brother Griff brought us some food. Apparently, they wanted to warn AJ not to let me out of the room for a while since the media still hovered.

"I can't believe they swarmed you like that," AJ said. "I should have come down with you in the first place," he said.

I shook my head and frowned. "You couldn't have known."

"What hell was all that anyway? How did they find you?"

"They didn't find me. They found Tilly. I guess word got out about the Vegas wedding thing and the media was there going nuts. Granny freaked and used me as the sacrificial lamb, taking advantage of how I was named the...whatever it was...in that magazine. She bellowed it out to get them to focus on me so Tilly could escape."

"San Francisco's hottest single gay man, who also happens to help kids in need, has a gorgeous wealthy family, and sports a big teddy-bear heart?" he teased. "In other words, the world's first actual unicorn?"

I rolled my eyes. "Whatever. If we can't go out and enjoy Vegas, maybe we should go somewhere else. Take Tilly's camper and go to the Grand Canyon or something."

I saw the twinkle appear in his eyes as he stood up to throw away our lunch wrappers. I stood up to help. "Hmmm, a road trip with San Francisco's hottest eligible unicorn? How can I say no to that?" he teased.

I shrugged and smirked, stepping in front of him and putting my hands on his chest. "I gotta warn you... you might be really bored."

AJ barked out a laugh. "Ha, you think so? Explain."

I traced one of his eyebrows with a fingertip. "Well, let's see. We won't be able to spend much time in public around other people. Those places are full of tourists on social media."

His eyes melted into dark brown pools of heat. "You mean we'll have to stay in the camper and hide out?"

I shrugged and moved my fingertip down to trace his jaw. "Yup. Have any ideas of how we'll pass all that downtime?"

AJ's lips twitched up at the edges. "A few."

"If you're thinking about—" I looked around, pretending to be looking for eavesdroppers in our hotel room. "*Sexual things*," I whispered, "I don't know... I'm not very *experienced*. Might need some..."

I leaned forward and put my lips against his ear, tracing the edge with the tip of my tongue, causing him to shudder under me.

"*Practice.*"

AJ let out a shaky breath and slid his hands under my shirt to the skin of my back.

"Dante, dammit, don't tease me," he groaned in a rough voice.

"Who says I'm teasing?" I murmured, moving my finger to his mouth and feeling the plump curve of his pouty bottom lip.

"You just had a panic attack, for god's sake. I think you should take it easy or..." He sighed. "Or something."

I felt my cheeks stretch in a grin. "Okay. I pick *'or something'* first and *'take it easy'* second."

My lips landed on AJ's mouth, and I slid my finger away, moving both hands to the back of his neck to keep him from pulling away.

"Take off your clothes," I commanded. AJ's eyes widened in surprise at my tone.

"What do you have in mind?" he asked as I moved away from him to sit on the bed with my back to the headboard and crossed my arms in front of my chest.

"The hookups I've had in the past have been rushed or sneaky—in clubs or in college. I've never had the opportunity to study my partner's body, but I've always wanted to. We finally have time and privacy. I want you to strip for me. Slowly." My eyes bore into AJ's, and I saw his pupils widen.

He stood still for a beat before looking for his phone. He selected some music from an app and set the phone down on the bedside table. I quirked a brow at him, but he only answered with a wink.

"You want me to strip for you, baby?" he purred in a voice that might as well have been a hand on my cock. "Want me to take off all my clothes and let you watch? Would you like to see me naked, Dante Marian?"

Oh shit.

What happened next was the filthiest strip show I could ever imagine. If I'd had ten thousand dollars in small bills, they'd have been piled on the floor at his feet. He started by threading his fingers together on the back of his head, elbows thrown wide exposing a stretch of skin below the hem of his shirt. I wanted to crawl across the bed and beg him to let me lick it.

AJ rolled his hips to the beat of the music, sultry and slow. His dark happy trail led down into faded, low-hanging jeans and the sight of his ab muscles moving made my dick stiffen even more.

"AJ," I whispered.

"Mmm-hmm," he purred some more.

His hands came down to his crotch, where he framed his cock through the denim before sliding both palms up his abdomen, under his shirt, and over his chest. The hem of the shirt came up with his movements, exposing the ripped muscles below. My eyes were locked on his skin, and I felt my mouth water.

AJ made a small sound in his throat. I glanced up at his face. His eyes were closed and his head was tilted back. I had to put my mouth on his skin. Had to.

Before I could, he turned around, his hips moving in languid circles, his shirt still drawn up from where his hands remained on his chest. The back of the shirt stretched across his wide shoulders and his hair was messy from where his hands had been in it earlier. God, he was so fucking hot.

"AJ," I whispered again, feeling my desire for him growing with every swish of his hips.

"Mmm?" he asked, looking at me over his shoulder with an innocent look on his face. "What is it?" As if he had no care in the world. He knew exactly what he was doing to me.

"Take off some fucking clothes already," I said between clenched teeth.

Without turning around he began to lift the T-shirt slowly, exposing more of that glorious honey-colored skin inch by inch. The curve of his spine divided strong back muscles. As the shirt rode up, the width of him changed from narrow waist to wide shoulders until his entire back was uncovered.

Shoulder blades and arm muscles moved as he dropped the shirt on the floor and slowly turned back around to show me his bare chest and stomach.

My tongue was in my throat. His abs undulated as he rolled his hips, causing the waistband of his jeans to slip even lower. I didn't see any underwear. And that's when I began to feel dizzy with lust.

"You don't have any underwear on?" I squeaked.

He made a clicking sound with his tongue before putting a pout on his sexy lips. "Guess not. Must have forgotten. *Oops.*"

My cock jumped forward in my own briefs and I palmed it with a groan. Motherfucking teasing son of a bitch. The striptease was working. I wanted to lunge at him like a panther. My heart rate had kicked way up, and I felt my chest heaving with labored breaths.

AJ put his palms on his belly and slid them slowly down, locking his eyes with mine as he did so. I couldn't help but follow the movement of his hands until I saw his fingers move to flick open the button of his fly.

I whimpered a little bit. Okay, a lot bit.

AJ stuck out the tip of his tongue as if he was concentrating. How hard was it to pull down a zipper? *I mean, really.*

But I was mesmerized. My eyes flicked from his pink tongue to his fingers on the zipper and back again. The hand on the zipper stopped and moved to slide down into the front of his pants. He must have rubbed his cock because he made a shameless cry of pleasure that made me scramble for my own fly.

"Fuck this," I ground out. "Get your fucking clothes off right fucking now."

25

____

AJ

The look in Dante's eyes was desperate and feral, and it only turned me on more. I wanted to laugh, but I was too turned on to do anything other than will my shaking hands to work faster. Within moments my jeans were off and I was blessedly naked, helping Dante with his own clothes until he was naked too.

"What about you wanting to savor—?" I began.

"Shut up," Dante said, grabbing my ass and pulling me on top of him on the bed. "Fuck me right now, AJ, before I come out of my skin. Want you so badly."

When I landed against him, my dick pressed into the crease between his cock and his thigh and I groaned. I knew what I wanted.

After standing back up long enough to get some lube from my toiletries bag, I came back to kneel over him, pouring some of the cool liquid onto my hand and then coating both of our cocks with it. Dante's eyes were dark as night and his forehead creased in confusion.

"Condom?" he asked.

"Not yet," I said, shaking my head. "Don't want to hurt you."

"AJ, Jesus, I—"

I dropped my mouth on his to shut him up. No doubt he was

going to argue with me about wanting to have sex, but I didn't want to do that right after he'd had a damned panic attack.

I reached down and rubbed both of us together, grasping the two cocks in my hand as best I could. The minute I did, I felt and heard him moan into my mouth. I couldn't help but smile against his lips.

I thrust my hips and felt his slick length move against mine. *Yep, just like that.* I kept going, thrusting and squeezing and sliding. Dante moaned some more until I couldn't concentrate enough to keep kissing him. His hips pulsed while mine thrust. My hand jacked us in a slippery, tight tunnel. In and out, hot slick skin sliding against each other.

His hands were on my ass, squeezing and encouraging. "AJ, AJ," he panted. "God, don't stop. Oh my god."

The words spoken in his strangled voice tipped me over the edge. I'd already been hard for him for what seemed like hours. "Dante, baby, I'm—"

And there it was, hot cum shooting, electric pulses racing, loud blood rushing in my ears. Flashes of sensations imprinted on me. The sight of Dante's head thrown back and mouth wide open. The sound of his gasp and cry. The feel of his cock, hot and swollen in my fingers. The smell of sex on our skin. It was the sexiest damned combination I could imagine.

After we were both empty and spent, I fell onto the bed beside him on my back, reaching for a hand towel on the bedside table. Dante turned his head on the pillow to look at me.

"Whoa."

I coughed out a laugh. "Yeah. Whoa."

His mouth turned into a wide grin. "Go again?"

AFTER A LONG NAP, I woke up and looked over at Dante. His face was relaxed in sleep, midnight black lashes resting on his cheeks. I wanted to stroke his cheeks, run my fingers through his hair, and kiss his stubbled jaw. There were so many thoughts about Dante racing through my head. I was falling for him. I wanted to protect him. I wanted him to choose to stay with me, even when he discovered who I was.

My dad was right. If we were going to move forward in a relationship, he needed to know. And I just needed to come to grips with that fact that I would be risking losing his trust when he found out.

That evening, the Marians managed to rent out a nearby cafe so the family could go out to eat in peace.

As we stood around the bar area to have a few drinks before dinner, I enjoyed watching Dante get fussed over by his parents and siblings. They alternated between teasing him for his newfound fame and comforting him for being swarmed earlier. His face was red from all the attention, and I felt the now-familiar feeling of tenderness wash over me at the sight.

I chatted with his brother Blue about their plans to adopt another child when my phone rang. It was my dad again.

After excusing myself from Blue, I stepped to the edge of the bar area and answered.

"Hey Dad."

"Just wanted to give you a heads-up that Dante's picture is all over the news," Dad said. "I'm not sure how much he cares about his biological parents tracking him down, but if he does, it could be a problem. He looks just like his father."

"What?" I asked, head spinning.

"Apparently he was with his aunt earlier when the news broke about her and Senator Cannon. The story is about the senator but Dante is standing with her in all of the video clips.

I saw Dante look up at me suddenly from across the bar. His eyes didn't look right. I tilted my head to study him and caught sight of a television screen nearby showing video of the situation in the lobby earlier in the day.

Fuck.

"Gotta go Dad," I said.

"Bring him to Aster Valley, son. Just get away from the media for a little while until things die down."

After finishing the call and making my way across the room, I noticed Dante didn't seem to be focused on what Simone was talking to the group about. His wide eyes were still locked on me, and his arms were crossed in front of his stomach.

I put my arm around him and said something to the group asking for them to excuse us for a minute. Then I turned him and walked us out a side door onto the restaurant's enclosed courtyard.

I didn't say a word, only folded him into my arms and held him for a minute. He trembled, and I wondered if it was somehow residual exhaustion from what had happened earlier in the day.

"I want to leave," he said in a quiet voice.

"Okay, I'll tell your parents we're going back to the hotel."

"No, I mean leave Vegas."

I cupped his cheeks to tilt his face up to mine. "The thing on TV?"

"Yeah. It's too much, AJ. All this attention, my face all over the media," he said. "I… I don't talk about my past very much but I really don't want my biological family to find me. I feel like I'm in a fishbowl here."

Well, there was my opportunity, handed to me on a silver platter. I'd do as my dad said and take him home to Aster Valley. I could explain everything to him when we got there. I could show him Dad's files to help him understand how many kids like him we'd saved over the years. Surely when he saw the work we did, he'd understand. Wouldn't he?

"My dad called this morning and mentioned their house is available in Colorado. Would you let me take you there for a few days?" I asked. "They're on vacation, so you won't have to meet anyone. It's a secluded little mountain ski town. I think you'd really like it."

Dante looked up at me. "Yeah. That sounds nice, actually."

I felt Dante's hand sneak under my shirt to land on my lower back. "Do you want to go say goodbye to your family?" I asked.

He let out a long exhale. "What do I tell them? I don't want to explain this to them right now."

The door to the patio opened and Griff came out, followed closely by Sam. "What's going on?"

"We've decided to hit the road," I said with a sudden smile. "I want to take Dante up to Colorado to see my hometown before we both have to get back to the city for work."

Out of the corner of my eye I could see Dante glance up at me, and I felt his fingers clench the back of my shirt before he turned around.

"Yeah. Sorry, guys. But if we want to go before he starts his new job, we kind of need to leave sooner rather than later," he said.

My arm rested on his shoulder and his hand clutched my shirt tighter.

Griff's face fell. "Really? You're really going to stand there and bullshit me like that?"

Sam put a hand on his shoulder. "Griff, babe—"

"No, Sam," he said, shrugging the hand off. "It's not okay. Dante, you look like you've just seen a ghost or something. If you're in some kind of trouble, we can help."

I looked over at Dante. It was his decision what he wanted to tell his family, not mine.

"Please just leave it alone," he said.

"Hell no, I'm not going to leave it alone. Are you nuts? You're my baby brother. And if something is going on, I want to know."

Dante let go of my shirt and stepped forward, reaching out to put his hands on Griff's shoulders. "Griffin. I'm just overwhelmed, okay? And I don't want the media in my face."

Griff's eyes shifted to look at me over Dante's shoulder before looking back at Dante.

"Is this about you being on TV?" he asked.

"No," Dante said. "Well, yes. I mean, sort of. Not really. I guess so. *Fuck.*"

Part of me wanted to chuckle at how adorable he sounded if it hadn't freaked him out so much.

"Are you okay?" Griff asked in a softer tone.

"Yes, Griff, but I just don't want to be confronted with all this shit right now. The press is telling the whole world about me, and I don't like it. If AJ and I can sneak out of here, we'll get off the grid for a little while until the media attention dies down or I just get my head on straight about it. Maybe I'm just tired from all the work getting ready for the gala."

Griff pursed his lips and then huffed out a breath before grabbing Dante in a fierce hug. Dante made an *oof* sound before returning the hug and staying like that for a minute.

Sam looked over at me with a small smile, and Griff's eyes came up to meet mine.

"You better fucking stay with him, AJ," he warned at me over Dante's shoulder. "You hear me?"

I nodded. "Of course, Griff. I promise. There's nowhere else I'd rather be."

Griff pulled back and kissed Dante on the forehead. His hands clasped the sides of Dante's face and Griff stared at it. "Listen to AJ and don't do anything stupid. Call me if you need anything at all. I love you."

"I love you too," Dante said in a small, whispered voice that made my heart break. The guy had finally gotten the loving family he deserved and scars from his shitty past were tearing him away from it. It wasn't fair.

26

DANTE

In the end, we left the RV with Pete's family so they could take the kids to the Grand Canyon before heading home. After making our way to the airport, we lucked out and caught the next flight from Vegas to Denver, where we rented a car for the hour-long drive to Aster Valley. Eventually, we pulled off the main highway and headed into the town.

It looked like a quaint little alpine ski village with picturesque storefronts rimmed with heavy baskets of wildflowers. Even though it was late at night, I could tell the place was like a hidden gem, nestled in the Rocky Mountains but still seemingly within driving distance to Denver. How had I never heard of it?

After driving through the little town and out the other side, we made our way up smaller side roads until we turned down a wooded private driveway. We approached a huge sprawling log cabin set into the side of the mountain with warm light glowing through the many windows facing the driveway.

"You're being quiet," AJ said.

I laughed. "I'm a little nervous, AJ. Seeing where you grew up is a little strange, I guess."

"Just think of it as a cute resort town instead of the place I grew up."

"Why are there lights on if your parents are out of town?" I asked.

AJ's forehead crinkled. "Don't know."

I wanted to ask him what we were doing. Were we dating? Was he my boyfriend now? I wasn't sure. He'd implied he didn't let people get close, but did that include me? And what did I want?

Well, that was stupid. I wanted AJ. Now, and probably for a very long time to come.

Before AJ even had a chance to turn off the ignition, a man strode out the front door, and as he got closer to us, I could see he had similar coloring to AJ.

I turned to ask who it was when I heard him mutter, "Shit. My parents are back. They must have come home early. Sorry, Dante."

I felt my stomach flip a little in response as I realized I was about to meet AJ's parents.

Holy shit. Am I about to meet his parents? Like, what if they become my in-laws? Okay, too fast. But still. What if they don't like me? What if I say something stupid? They know he's gay, right? Fuck.

I realized I was still sitting in the passenger seat with the door open. I tried to step out of the car to introduce myself, but before I had a chance to say anything, he spoke.

"Angel, you're here," he said with a big smile. "We decided to catch an earlier flight home from our trip."

Angel.

The name brought with it a torrent of memories. My father's fists. His face, purple as he raged at me. The church bathroom. The bruises and the pain and then my Angel. His arms wrapped around me. The smell of safety and comfort. The warmth of his chest and his promise that I'd never hurt like that again.

I turned my head slowly, my eyes raking over AJ as he hugged his father. It had been dark the night he'd rescued me, and maybe because it was dark now, I could suddenly see what I'd missed before. His hair was shaggy rather than buzzed, his features were sharper, his body more muscles than angles. But the furrow of concern along his forehead was still there.

I couldn't believe I'd missed it. He must have thought I was a fucking idiot. For some reason, I wanted to laugh, but I couldn't find enough air in my lungs for anything other than a broken whimper.

AJ was my Angel.

Of course he was.

And he'd fucking lied to me.

His father came toward me, a grin on his face, and suddenly I was no longer worried about making a good impression on my potential father-in-law. All I cared about was making it through the introductions without turning and screaming at AJ.

That could wait until after the pleasantries. As if I could remember what pleasantries were at a time like this.

His father reached his hand out to me, and I stared at it a second too long before realizing I should do the same.

I know there was something I should say but all I could think was, "AJ Flores is my Angel. Angel is my AJ. Holy shit."

AJ looked at me strangely as he cleared his throat. "Dad, this is Dante Marian."

"It's nice to see you again, Dante," he said with an understanding smile.

I blinked. "What did he mean by "again"? I tilted my head at him and then looked at AJ, who looked decidedly uncomfortable.

"Uh, Dad, I think Dante and I need to talk for a few minutes. It's late. Why don't we see you guys in the morning?"

His dad looked from me to AJ and seemed to let out a sigh, as if he understood what was happening. He nodded and clapped a hand on AJ's shoulder. "Okay kiddo," he said before returning to the cabin.

And then it was just us and suddenly I couldn't find any of the words that had been swirling around my brain a moment before. So, instead, I turned and sagged against the side of the car, my arms clutched across my stomach.

AJ approached slowly, as though afraid I might bolt. Had I been holding the keys to the rental, I would have. He slid against the car beside me. "Dante," he began hesitantly.

"Please tell me you aren't who I think you are," I said in a low voice without looking over at him.

"*Dante*," he repeated. This time the tone was almost pleading.

"Goddammit, tell me you aren't him, AJ. *Please*," I begged, turning to confront him and seeing the truth I knew would be on his face when I looked.

"Baby—"

"Don't you dare call me that," I seethed. "Don't call me that ever again."

"Please let me explain."

My heart beat rapidly, and my head began to pound. Sarcasm came easily under these conditions. "Sure, *Angel*. Why don't you explain?"

"*Fuck*," he muttered. "Okay, here goes... Ah, I don't know where to start exactly."

"Start with how the hell you ended up in a church basement in Gordon, Indiana, eight years ago. That'd be a great place to start, I think." My words pushed out through gritted teeth and if I wasn't careful, my jaw was going to crack in half.

He swallowed and leaned forward, resting his hands on his knees.

"My father and I do personnel extractions," he began. "When I was seventeen, he let me do my first solo extraction because it was located in a small town where a strange man would look out of place but a teenage boy might not stand out as much."

"What's a personnel extraction?" I asked.

"It's when a team removes someone from a situation, usually a hostile or dangerous one. In your case, my dad had gotten a call from a client who wanted to hire him to pull you out."

Now I felt like I was in some spy thriller movie and I laughed. "Yeah, right," I scoffed. "I didn't peg you as the kind of guy who'd chase one lie with another, but maybe I should have."

"I'm telling the truth. We were hired to get you out," AJ said. And he sounded like he was telling the truth.

"That's ridiculous, AJ. By whom?"

He paused for a moment before replying in a gentle voice. "Janet Lawton. Your mother."

27

______

AJ

My hands clasped each other so tightly to keep from grabbing Dante, my fingers had turned white.

He sat there staring off into space as my words hit him.

"Where is my bedroom?" he asked. "I'd like to go to sleep now."

"Do you—?"

He let out a loud sigh before growling at me. "Just fucking show me to a bed, AJ. One that doesn't have you in it, okay?"

A pain sliced through my gut, but I wasn't exactly surprised. He needed some space while the news sank in. "Yeah, okay. Follow me."

I led him down the hallway to the guest room and pointed to the room next to it. "That's my room. Let me know if you—"

"Wait," Dante blurted. He seemed to think of something. Suddenly he grabbed me and pulled me against his body, crushing his lips to mine and running his hands up and down my sides like he couldn't get enough of me. His tongue was hot and aggressive, and I felt my breath hitch. What the hell was happening? Was this his way of forgiving me? Could that be possible? My hands threaded into his hair, and his hips tilted into mine. I could barely catch my breath and my cock was filling faster than the speed of light.

Then just like that, the kiss was over. Dante pushed me away abruptly, leaving me dizzy and confused, wondering if it had really happened.

"Good night," he said, stepping back into the guest bedroom.

After he closed the door in my face, I stood there, staring at it.

When I fell into my bed a little while later, I had a grin on my face. He'd kissed me. So maybe I hadn't fucked up as much as I thought, and he'd forgive me. Surely he realized it was a good thing that I'd been the one to get him out of such a horrible situation.

I slept fitfully, waking once to go to the bathroom. I could have sworn I heard Dante crying, and it was all I could do to keep from barging in there and demanding he let me comfort him. The very idea of that left me pissed at myself, and I beat the fuck out of my pillows in an effort to get comfortable.

When I finally awoke in the morning, his door was still closed. I made my way to the kitchen and greeted my mom, who was cooking breakfast.

"There you are," she said. "Sorry I didn't stay up last night to see you boys."

I hugged her and kissed her on the cheek. "No problem. It was late."

"Where's Dante? Did you leave him asleep in bed?" she asked with a wink.

"No. Actually, he's still asleep in the guest room with the door closed," I said, lifting an eyebrow at her in challenge.

"Oh."

"He's mad at me," I said, caving because I knew she was desperate for details when it came to my love life.

"Why is he mad at you?" she asked.

"I didn't tell him who I was until we got here last night," I admitted.

"Oh, Angel, honey. Why? That poor boy."

Leave it to my mother to twist the knife in my gut.

"Because I knew this would happen. I knew he'd hate me for keeping it from him," I said.

"Why didn't you tell him early on before things developed between you?"

"Because when I met him, he'd just finished giving a speech about his past and he said he'd never told anyone about it. That he'd kept it all in the past and I just... didn't want to be the one to bring it all back to the present, you know?"

She sighed and took a sip of coffee. "I guess there's no easy way to go about it, and what's done is done. Why don't you go knock on his door and see if he wants breakfast?"

I poured a cup of coffee for him and took it back down the hallway to the guest room door.

"Dante?" I called out as I knocked. "My mom is fixing breakfast and wants to know if you'd like some."

After a few moments of silence, I tried again. Still no answer. I slowly opened the door to see if I should go in and shake him awake when I noticed the made bed.

"Oh shit," I muttered, throwing the door open and walking in. In my gut I knew he was gone, but in my heart I didn't want to believe it.

"Dante?" I called out. I searched the bathroom and the rest of the house, not stopping until I noticed the rental car missing from the driveway.

Well, fuck. I'd had the keys in my pockets last night when he'd pulled me in for that monster kiss. I let out a breath and almost laughed. He'd kissed me just to fleece me for the car keys. I didn't know whether to be pissed at him for tricking me or proud of him for doing what he needed to do to protect himself.

I TRIED CALLING and texting but got no answer or response. I finally called Griff and had to admit to losing Dante.

"I've already talked to him, AJ," Griff said in a resigned voice.

"Did he tell you what happened?" I asked.

"He just said he found out you'd lied to him about something important and he couldn't stay there. What the hell?"

"First of all, is he okay? Where is he?"

"No, he's not okay," Griff said. "And it's none of your fucking business where he is."

"I fucked up," I said.

"No shit," Griff snapped. "That didn't take long. You've known him for, what, less than a fucking week? The guy was already half in love with you, asshole."

My heart was in my throat, and I could barely get the words out. "He wasn't the only one."

"Look, I'm on Dante's side. I don't have to know the details, I just have to know he's hurt and you're the guy who hurt him."

"I... I'm falling in love with him Griff," I admitted. My stomach was twisting in knots but I knew the words were true.

"Then prove it. Get back here and find a way to convince him you're not the person he thinks you are. He deserves better than this, AJ. And it's going to take a hell of a lot to convince me you're what he deserves."

"I know. Don't you think I know that? This isn't about some stupid little lie. This is all mixed up in his past, Griff. It's a long story, and I don't know if he wants anyone to know about it," I said, wishing I could tell him the details so he could support Dante better.

"I don't need to know it. I'll be there for him regardless. If you care about him, you'll get back home and fix this."

But after returning to San Francisco and trying my best to reach Dante, he wouldn't give me the time of day. When the following Monday rolled around, I was heartsick and exhausted, but I dragged my ass to work at On Your Six and threw myself into my new project.

Joel had high expectations of me helping him build the domestic personnel extraction arm of his security company. He already had some ex-military people who formed the extraction group for international contracts, specifically kidnap, ransom, and extortion insurance for high-level executives. My job was to run the kind of jobs I'd done for years with my dad—taking people out of cults, abusive situations, and the cycle of addiction. The majority of our clients would be teens and young adults whose families feared for their safety and maintained legal guardianship of them. But some would be off the books and required complete confidentiality that would not fall under the official arm of the company.

It was only a matter of time before I would be called out on a rescue job, and I had to work my ass off to get up to speed on the way Joel did things around there before it happened.

I worked eight days straight before a call came in from a client needing someone to recover her daughter who'd run away with an older boyfriend to New Orleans. Within hours I was on an airplane heading east, and I worked night and day until I found the young woman and returned her to her family in Massachusetts.

When I got home from the trip, it had been thirteen days since I'd seen or heard from Dante. Every down moment on my trip had been filled with thoughts of Dante. I tried again and again to reach him, but he made it very clear he wanted nothing to do with me. I couldn't say I blamed him, but I craved a chance to speak to him nonetheless. I wanted to plead my case or at the very least, apologize.

I finally heard back from him a week later in the form of a text.

Dante: *Please stop. I know this is frustrating for you and I'm sorry.*

AJ: *Just please let me explain. Please, Dante. I fucked up and I'm sorry, but I'll do anything to make it right.*

Dante: *No. I thought you were my future, but it turns out you're my past.*

The days after returning from Colorado felt like balancing on a narrow beam over dangerous waters. If I leaned one way, I'd drown, and if I leaned the other, I'd get eaten by sharks. One side meant giving AJ another chance, which meant throwing my heart to the wolves. The other side meant walking away from AJ, which meant freezing my heart into a block of ice.

At least with ice, I could go numb and stop feeling altogether.

I flew home from Denver and tried to put the whole damned thing behind me—AJ, the crazy Tilly fiasco, the media coverage, everything.

I threw myself into my job at Marian House and buried myself in paperwork when I wasn't dealing directly with the kids or the programming. If I wasn't working, I was lying low in my bedroom, sleeping or zoning out to mindless movies on my iPad. Once a week, on Sundays, I came out of my self-induced solitude long enough to fake it in front of my family at Marian family dinner.

Griff knew the truth, and I was sure all the others suspected it. I was heartbroken. I'd thought AJ was something special, but it turned out he was just another person from my past who betrayed me.

I'd been through enough therapy at that point to know relationships based on a lie didn't work. I deserved better than someone who wasn't honest with me. The problem was, I didn't expect it to hurt so fucking much.

Hell, I'd only really known the guy for, like, a week. Just because he'd rescued me years before didn't mean he was entitled to be a part of the life I'd built since. So why was I *that* torn up about it?

The whole thing made me feel like a moron. Like a kid pining after his first crush. And the funny thing about it was the realization the breakup was *my* fucking choice. I was the one who walked away, not AJ.

After three weeks of working way too many hours, I was exhausted. Wasn't this supposed to get easier as time moved on? It didn't fucking feel any easier. It felt lonelier. And a hell of a lot more pathetic.

Late one night after the millionth text from AJ begging me to let him explain, I finally responded. I felt so weak; I knew if I didn't put a stop to his calls and texts, I'd cave and crawl back to him.

After that, the calls and texts finally stopped. I thought that would make things easier, but it sure as shit didn't. It made things much worse. I ended up binge eating ice cream late one Friday night after getting home late from work. I was in my pajama pants and an old ratty T-shirt when Griff threw my bedroom door open with a bang, causing me to jump.

"Fuck this, Dante Marian," he barked. "Get dressed. We're going out."

I knew he was hanging out to keep an eye on me, but I refused to humor him and let his presence change my schedule of work and moping.

"Not going out," I said around the spoonful of chunky ice cream.

"You are. It's not optional. Nico is coming over and we're going dancing. Sam's here too."

I put the ice cream on my bedside table and rolled over, facing away from him. "Fuck you," I mumbled.

"Get up and get dressed or I'm getting Mom and Dad over here," he warned. "They're worried about you. Everyone is worried about you. The way you're acting, you'd think Dante Marian is the first human being to ever have his heart broken. Well, guess what? You're not. I know that's not easy to hear and it doesn't take the pain away. But life goes on. So we're going out, you're going to grind that cute ass of yours into some stranger's dick and get your Lady Gaga on while I make out with Sam on the dance floor. Got it?"

I heard a knock on the apartment door and groaned. "Fine, I'll go. Tell Nico to hold his horses while I get dressed."

After I put on jeans and a clean shirt, I walked out to see Nico wasn't alone. Tilly, Granny, and Irene all sat in a row on the sofa.

"What are you guys doing here?" I asked.

"We heard it was drag night at Harry Dicks. We want in," Granny said.

I looked up at Griff with an expression of, *Really?* He shrugged. "Okay, ladies, if you want a bathroom visit that doesn't involve glory holes, might as well take a leak here before we leave," Griff said.

ONCE WE GOT to the club, I threw back two shots as fast as I could. If I was going to survive a night out, I would need liquid courage.

Nico asked me to dance and we made our way out to the floor. I knew Nico was a safe choice since he saw me as a little brother just like I saw him as a big brother. He and Griff were best friends, and he'd always been there for me the same way Griff had. We danced without touching much or grinding, and I concentrated on letting the music take me away. The alcohol started hitting me enough to help me relax and stop taking myself so seriously.

After another couple of drinks, Nico and I danced together again and I noticed him staring over my shoulder as if he'd seen someone. I felt pretty damned good at that point and even thought about dancing with a cute stranger to get my grind on.

"You don't have to babysit me, you know," I shouted over the music. "I can dance with Tilly." I winked at him and smiled to let him know he was free to go pick someone up.

What he did next took me by surprise. He reached out and pulled me in close, sliding one of his legs between mine and grinding against me. His strong hand came around the back of my neck to hold me against his face. He whispered into my ear, "Humor me for a second."

I wanted to roll my eyes. So he was using me to make someone jealous. Okay, whatever. I was drunk enough to play along.

I ran my hands up into his hair and ground against him in return. He shook his ass like a champ and nuzzled into my neck with some kisses. I bit back a sigh. If someone was going to nibble on my neck that night, couldn't it at least be someone who didn't feel like my—?

Suddenly Nico was plucked away from me and a familiar man took his place against me with a growl. Before my brain could react, my body sank into him with a sigh of relief and prickling eyes.

It was AJ. AJ was holding me, and I wanted to cry my fucking eyes out it felt so good. His touch, his signature scent, the sound of his voice as he asked me what the hell I was doing making out with Nico.

"What?" I sputtered after his words sank in.

"You let him put his mouth on you, Dante," he snapped. "How do you think that makes me feel?"

"What the fuck?" I snapped back. "It's none of your goddamned business what I'm doing."

I struggled to get out of his grasp, but he wouldn't let me go.

"Please," he said, his tone changing from anger to pleading. "Please wait. Wait, Dante. I didn't mean to snap. Just hang on."

I stopped fighting him and stood still, looking up at him. He was the hottest man in the entire club by a healthy margin. Even with storm clouds in his eyes, he was drop-dead gorgeous.

"*Fuck me*," I muttered, causing his eyes to widen. "Why can't you be ugly and gross?" I shouted over the music. "That would be better, I think."

His brows furrowed. "Are you drunk?"

Yes. "No," I said. "Are you?"

"No."

"Glad we had this little chat. I was just about to find someone cute to dance with so I'm just gonna—" I started to pull out of his embrace but, again, he wouldn't let me go.

"There's no fucking way I'm letting you go dance with some random stranger, Dante," he said in a low rumble that gave me a whole-body shudder.

"I'm horny and there's gotta be at least one guy in this place who wants to fuck me," I said defiantly.

"Oh, I can guaran-damn-tee you there most certainly is," he said, pinning me with those hazel eyes. *Shit.*

"Then let's go."

We both stood there, shocked by the words that had come out of my mouth.

29

AJ

When Griff told me to show up at Harry Dicks that night, I didn't even hesitate. Any chance to see Dante in person was worth any amount of effort to get there. I'd been in LA on business at the time, and I caught a flight back just in time to head to the club.

After arriving and finding Griff, I'd caught sight of Dante dancing with Griff's friend Nico. I knew he was a player, and once he caught me staring, he pulled Dante in tighter and began kissing his fucking neck while grinding his hips into him. Asshole. I didn't put it past Nico to do that shit on purpose, but I was surprised that Dante seemed into it. His hands came up to thread into Nico's hair, and he wasn't doing anything to discourage the grinding.

If either of them thought I was going to stand there and let it happen, they were both mistaken. I yanked Nico away and took his place against Dante. His arms went around me and he sank into me. *Ohhh fuckkkk*, he felt good. Right where he belonged.

And when he asked me to leave? There was no amount of self-control on earth that would allow me to refuse such an offer.

"Let's go," I said, grabbing his hand and dragging him toward

Griff and Sam. "I'm taking him home." They both looked at me with knowing smiles and gave me a thumbs up.

Dante muttered something under his breath, so I leaned in to ask him to repeat it.

"I said, I'm not a goddamned kid who needs his parents' permission to leave with a guy."

"Dude, I told them you were with me so they didn't wait around wondering where you were. It's just common courtesy when you came here with them," I said.

"Oh, well. Fine. I guess," he mumbled. Fuck, he was even cute when drunk. I thought back to whether I'd even seen him drunk before and didn't think so.

Once we got back to his apartment, the alcohol had knocked him for an additional loop and he slurred. There was no way I would make out with him while he was drunk since there was a good 75 percent chance he would hate me again in the morning as it was. But I was damned sure going to stick around and take any excuse to be in his presence for a few more hours until he kicked me out.

When I closed his bedroom door behind us, Dante turned and launched himself at me, catching me off guard and pushing me back against the door. His mouth was on mine, and I was assaulted with tequila tongue and a hundred and fifty pounds of hot, horny man clinging to my front.

My hand went under his ass to steady him, and my other hand clasped the back of his head. Our tongues tangled together; I let myself enjoy the blissful moment of the kiss. How the hell would I control myself if I couldn't even stop from kissing him?

I felt his cock against my stomach and groaned. Jesus, he was as hard as I was. My fingers gripped his ass through his jeans, and I began to move us forward to the bed to set him down.

I pulled myself away from him with a gasp. "Stop," I breathed.

"Shit, why?"

"Because you're drunk and you'll change your mind about this tomorrow."

"No, I won't," he insisted. "I want you. Want you to fuck me, AJ."

"You don't know what you're saying right now."

"Don't tell me what I know," he said with fiery eyes. "I'm horny, you're hot, and I want you to fuck me, goddammit."

"Really, Dante? You want to lose your virginity right here and now while you're still pissed at me and drunk on tequila?" I snapped.

"Uh, *yeah.*"

Fuck.

"Well, it's not gonna happen," I said, reaching down to adjust my angry dick.

Dante's annoyed face morphed into something bordering on evil and he grinned up at me from where he lay on the bed.

"Hmm, then I guess I'll have to just fuck myself."

All the rest of the blood in my body rushed south as if to settle in for the show of a lifetime. That motherfucking tease.

I swallowed and frowned. "Ah, what do you mean, exactly?" I asked.

He shrugged and sat up, unbuttoning his shirt slowly and making sure to run the tip of his finger down the bare skin of his chest before reaching each new button down the line.

His voice took on a sultry tone. "If I can't have someone's big, thick cock in my ass, I think I'll have to improvise."

He stood up to let the shirt drop to the floor and I saw the expanse of Dante's chest complete with the dark happy trail begging for my tongue.

"Dante," I croaked.

"Feel free to stay or go, AJ. Doesn't matter to me either way. Wouldn't want to make you *uncomfortable.*" His eyes lowered to where I palmed my own cock through my jeans.

Why wasn't I jumping his fucking bones right now? Was I trying to be some kind of saint? Couldn't we at least swap blow jobs or something?

I swallowed hard again at the thought of Dante's red lips stretched around my cock. Oh god.

No, I couldn't. I wasn't going to allow us to get intimate without having a conversation about what had happened between us.

I shuffled back to put some distance between us and tripped on the carpet, falling back against his desk and landing my ass on it with a hard jolt.

So maybe I'd just sit and watch. For... reasons.

Dante turned his back to me, showing me the muscles moving in long columns on either side of his spine, his shoulder blades shifting under his skin like wings. I wanted to run my hands over that warm skin and press kisses into the back of his neck.

He leaned over to get something out of his drawer and his jeans tightened across his ass.

Holy hell. His beautiful butt. Dante's gorgeous, perfect, fuckable—

I sighed. Maybe I should leave and put myself out of my misery. That was it. I'd just go. Get on home and rub one out in a late-night shower. Alone.

I compared the two options in my mind. Masturbating solo versus watching Dante shove something into his perfect fucking ass.

Hmm, decisions, decisions.

He came up from the bedside table drawer with a familiar-looking box.

"What's that?" I couldn't help but ask.

"Turgid Love Hammer."

I remembered Tilly's penis party and the gift the woman had given Dante as we left. His other hand held a bottle of lube he placed on the bedside table.

"Have you, ah, used it before?" I asked, crossing my arms where I sat propped against his desk.

"Nope. Nothing has been in my ass besides fingers. But, god, AJ. I want something big and thick in there, you know? Just want to feel full and thoroughly fucked. I've waited *so long*." His voice teased, and every word plucked my strings.

He took the giant cock out of its box and sat it on the table next to the lube before moving his hands to his belt. My fingers twitched as I watched him pull the strap out of the buckle and then slide the belt out of each loop in his jeans. How long was that goddamned belt? It seemed to take forever before it finally clunked to the floor.

I squeezed my eyes closed as his fingers went to his fly. The snicking sound of a zipper brought my eyes open again. I caught sight of a flash of red as the fly of his jeans fell open. He was wearing red underwear? Like, what? A matador teasing a bull?

He turned around and shimmied out of his jeans, adding extra wiggle to his adorable butt to fuck with me. What was left after the jeans were off was the tiniest pair of designer briefs I'd ever seen him wear.

"Jesus fuck," I mumbled.

"You don't like these?" he asked, batting his eyelashes and frowning as he ran a finger back and forth under the waistband of the briefs.

I swallowed. "I don't like that you wore them when shaking your ass for strangers, no."

"Then I'll get rid of them," he said, shucking them down and kicking them into the corner of the room.

And there he was. My Dante, standing in all his naked splendor only five feet away from my aching balls.

"Baby," I breathed. His eyes darkened.

"*Please*, AJ. Please touch me," he begged.

30

DANTE

I awoke to the feeling of strong familiar arms around me and smiled. AJ was there, so I must have still been in a delicious dream. But someone in the dream was playing music with a rhythmic pounding bass line that was mildly annoying.

"Turn it down," I griped halfheartedly. The sound of my own voice exacerbated the pounding, and I felt my eyebrows draw together in frustration.

"Turn what down?" AJ asked, startling me. I shifted around to look at him and realized it wasn't a dream. He was actually there in my bed and the thumping bass got worse.

"The music, the fucking music," I said, scooting back and stumbling out of my bed. I wasn't sure where I was headed first—to find the early morning music asshole or to find the bathroom.

My subconscious must have realized the music was a hangover because I found myself in the bathroom without making a conscious decision. After taking a leak, I washed my face and brushed my teeth. My bottle of pain reliever was not where it lived in my medicine cabinet, and I grunted in frustration before making my way back out to the bedroom.

AJ was still there. It really wasn't a dream. Had it been a dream, he'd have been significantly less dressed. As it was, he wore a T-shirt and presumably at least underwear, although I couldn't see his lower half under the blankets.

I, however, was naked.

"What are you doing here?" I asked. My brain tried to recreate the series of events from the night before. Had I drunk-dialed him? Shit.

"What do you remember?" he asked, rubbing his face and leaning over to the bedside table to check the time on his phone. *Holy fuck*, there was a giant dildo on the bedside table.

"Ahhh…" I couldn't take my eyes off the dildo. "What's that?"

AJ's face looked entirely too smug. "Turgid Love Hammer."

My eyes flashed to his. "Why is it out of the box?"

"Let me recall your exact words," he said, raising the tip of his index finger to his lips in thought. "You said you wanted to be *thoroughly fucked*."

I felt my eyes narrow as my face flushed with embarrassment. "Why are you here, AJ?" I was only half listening for his answer while the other half of my brain scrambled to recollect any situation in which I might have actually shoved a giant dong up my ass in front of AJ Flores. Oh dear god, this wasn't happening. My face kept getting hotter as he studied me.

"You were very drunk. I wanted to make sure you got home safely," he said.

"And then? Why did you stay?"

He looked at me with a raised brow.

"Wait," I said. "We didn't… I mean. You didn't…" My eyes glanced back over to the dildo, and I squinted to see if I could determine its status as having been recently used or not. I couldn't tell. But I did see a bottle of water and my pain reliever there on the bedside table.

AJ sat up and leaned against the headboard with a sigh. "No, Dante. We didn't, and you didn't. You passed out before things got that far. After you shucked off your underwear, you lay on the bed and grabbed the bottle of lube. Before you even opened the cap, you'd fallen asleep. Honestly, I should have snapped a picture. You were adorable—hugging the lube bottle to your chest like a teddy bear."

Oh my god.

I rolled my eyes. "Fuck you."

His eyes darkened. "Can we talk. Please?"

I wanted to tell him no. Hell no. But before the words came out, I paused. What exactly did I want?

I wanted AJ. But I didn't want the reminder of my past. And I wasn't sure I could have one without the other. Still, AJ had made sure I made it home safely and didn't take advantage of me, so maybe he deserved a chance to explain.

"What did my mother say when she hired you?" I asked, surprising myself. I felt tears spring to my eyes, and I turned around quickly to hide them from AJ. I fumbled through my dresser for a pair of pajama pants and slid them on before getting a hold of myself and sitting down on the bed next to him.

My biological mother, Janet Lawton, had been the quintessential pastor's wife. Sweet, demure, obedient. She filled her dutiful role to a T. She hosted ladies guild meetings and arranged for the altar flowers. She comforted mourning widows and helped watch over neighbors' kids when their parents were sick. She was a friendly but quiet woman, who didn't seem to express any opinions that weren't my father's.

For the first thirteen years, I'd thought I loved her. And maybe I had. But when my father punished me with belts, his hand, the withholding of a meal, she never helped me or went against him. She never even gave me concerned glances sending me an unspoken message of support. And when I began to learn more about the world around me, I realized that wasn't okay. Not helping someone in need was akin to being complicit. Standing by to watch a child being beaten or starved was almost the same thing as doing the beating and starving yourself.

So when AJ told me my mom had hired them to rescue me and remove me from my father's church basement that night? It didn't compute, which caused me to do what I always did—force it out of my mind. Ignore the new information and pretend it didn't exist.

Sitting there on my bed with AJ, I was surprised the question about my mother was the first thing out of my mouth. But I shouldn't have been. The information had gutted me. It was like drowning and then finding out in heaven someone had tossed a lifeline to you thirty seconds too late.

"Do you really want to hear this, Dante?" he asked quietly.

"I don't know."

I wanted to crawl into AJ's personal space and curl up against his body. Feel his arms wrap around me and hold me tightly while he told me about my mother. But I didn't move. I didn't want to send him mixed messages, and I was still so mad at him for... something. I wasn't sure if it was because he hadn't told me who he was or because now I knew he'd seen me at my worst—broken and humiliated on the floor of that basement bathroom at the hands of my own father. How could AJ ever look at me without seeing that image?

How could I ever be with him knowing he'd seen me like that?

"Tell me," I said.

"She called my dad a year before that, actually. You'd been sent to conversion camp and she was worried about you. She'd heard rumors about what they did there and just wanted him to perform a well check to make sure you were okay."

I thought about my time at a place called Youth Can Change. That one hadn't been as bad as the shit that went down under my father's watch, but it was still no picnic.

"Did he come to the camp?" I asked in surprise.

"No. She said she'd call back with the details of where you were, but she never did. My dad had no idea where to look."

I felt my jaw clench at the idea of enduring an entire extra year of my father's wrath because of my mom's fear. Apparently, it took actual broken bones and blood before she finally pulled the trigger on the extraction.

I blew out a breath.

"Then what?" I asked.

"Then she called a year later in tears. Said she'd been wrong. That it was bad. You needed help and she didn't know where else to turn. Apparently everyone in town was friends of your father's and there was no one else to call."

"It *was* bad," I agreed in a quiet voice. "Really bad."

31

AJ

I couldn't sit there any longer without touching him. I leaned toward him slowly and reached out a hand to take his. Dante's eyes were far away in memory and he let me take his hand and pull him closer to me. Once he relaxed against my side, his face went automatically into my neck and I wrapped my arms around him.

"I'm so sorry, Dante," I breathed against his ear. "I'm so sorry for everything."

I felt the warm tears hit my neck and slide down.

"Why didn't she help me, AJ?" His voice broke as he cried into my neck. "For fifteen years she just stood there and let me take it. The yelling, the hitting, and the fucking brutal isolation of being home-schooled in that house. I had *no one*. No one on my side."

He sobbed, and my heart felt like it was being ripped from my chest.

"You have me now. You have the Marians. All the kids at the shelter who look up to you and adore you. There are so many people who love you, Dante."

He pulled back and looked up at me with wet eyes. Even covered in snot and tears he was beautiful. His eyes were bright and his lashes held sparkling drops. His cheeks were flushed and his hair stuck up on one side.

"How do I just put the past behind me again? When you took me out of there, you made me swear I'd put it all behind me and start fresh. Well, I fucking did that, AJ. I dealt with it and then packed it away. But now? Now when I look at you all I see is that night."

The statement wrecked me and I knew my heart couldn't take much more of this. The combination of seeing him hurt and knowing my presence only contributed to it was too much.

"That's exactly why I didn't want to tell you." My voice cracked and I drew a trembling breath. "Because I knew you wouldn't want anything to do with me after that."

Dante studied me before whispering words I'd expected.

"I think you should go."

THAT TIME WHEN I LEFT, I didn't try to speak to him or look for him again. If staying away from Dante meant keeping him from another reminder of his painful past, then I'd do it. Even if it tore me apart.

I threw myself into my work and tried hard not to see Dante's face on every child I rescued. We had four jobs in as many weeks, and I flew all over the country to make it happen. I already knew how common it was that teen girls ran away with older boyfriends, but it was still disheartening after I'd had to rescue a particularly young one. The girl had been fourteen and the boyfriend twenty-eight. Somehow they'd managed to evade the authorities, but once we found them, we were able to call in the local cops and have the man arrested for kidnapping.

The whole situation made me wonder if I'd ever have kids of my own. I couldn't even imagine what it was like to lose a child to their stupid teenaged decisions.

It was during one of those trips that I caught a news clip about Richard Lawton. I was in the Atlanta airport heading home when I saw one of the television monitors flash a photo of the reverend on the screen. The clip mentioned the Reverend Richard Lawton, a state representative from Gordon, Indiana, was running for a seat in the US House of Representatives on a big conservative platform of family values. The reporter mentioned that with his campaign relying heavily on support from other family values organizations, there was increased pressure on Reverend Lawton to speak publicly about his teenaged son who'd gone missing eight years before.

"Reverend Lawton has always declined speaking publicly about such a personal family matter," explained the reporter. "Although a missing child report was filed, there was heavy speculation at the time that the boy, named Daniel Lawton, had chosen to run away from home. With Reverend Lawton's potential rise to national politics, chatter has renewed about whatever happened to Daniel Lawton. The man would be twenty-three today."

Oh shit. I pulled out my phone to call my dad.

"Angel?" Dad said when the call connected.

"Dad, I'm looking at CNN right now and—"

"I know, son. Your mother and I are watching it too."

"What do we do?" I asked, feeling fucking helpless.

"I'm not sure what you mean," he said.

"Lawton's a monster," I growled. "We have to stop him."

Dad's voice was kind and gentle, but the message was brutal because it was true. "Our job is extraction, Angel. We don't get to decide what happens after that."

I understood what he was saying, that there wasn't much we could do about it. It was up to the people of Indiana to rally the troops. But that felt wrong.

"Dad, people need to know what kind of monster that guy is."

"And what is that?" he asked. It was obvious he knew the answer and was building to a point.

"A child abuser," I barked. Several heads swiveled in my direction, causing me to wince and lower my voice.

"And how do we prove that exactly without exposing Dante to a national press fiasco?" Dad asked. I could tell by his voice he was as unhappy with the situation as I was.

But he was right, and there was no fucking way I was willing to throw Dante to the wolves.

THE FOLLOWING week I was called out on a difficult extraction mission in Utah. It was a boy from a fundamentalist sect in a tiny, secluded town run by a small group of very powerful church leaders. The situation was hard anyway, but it reminded me so much of Dante's experience, it haunted me.

The boy's name was Ammon and he was terrified. When we'd removed him from the small mobile home where he'd been kept, he broke down in tears and started apologizing.

I wanted to hug him or hold his hand, but I knew touch comfort wasn't what every kid needed. So instead I handed him a balled up fuzzy fleece jacket under the guise of maybe needing warmth on the trip.

He frowned, pushing it back toward me, clearly anxious about taking something that didn't belong to him.

"Don't worry," I reassured him. "This jacket belongs to you now."

He hesitated a moment before clutching it to his chest and trying to relax. It was a trick I'd figured out years ago. Fold the fleece up the right way and it felt like a stuffed animal or a pet. Something the kids could hold on to when they were scared and could take with them after the mission was over.

I'd been carrying them with me on missions ever since.

After a while, I noticed Ammon tracing his fingers over a number embroidered on the chest.

1-800-273-8255

It took him a little while longer to get up the courage to speak. "What's this for?" he asked in a quiet voice.

I smiled softly. "My mom embroidered that. It's the number for the National Suicide Prevention Lifeline in case you're ever stuck and need help."

He nodded, turning the information over in his head. And then he curled on his side, using the balled up jacket as a pillow, and dozed off.

Once I was sure he was asleep I whispered the same words I'd told Dante years before and repeated to every kid since: *You're safe now.*

32

———————

DANTE

I was at my parents' house for Marian Sunday dinner when I saw my biological father's face staring back at me from the television.

"Reverend Richard Lawton, best known for his large devout church following in Gordon, Indiana, is ramping up his campaign for US Congress. Reverend Lawton first caught our attention when the governor of Indiana praised him last year for his controversial work with gay youth in his small comm—"

"Turn it off!" I barked, startling everyone in the kitchen into stunned silence. I turned on my heel and made a beeline for the family room. Once there, I threw myself down on one of the sofas face-first and put my arms over my head to try and block out any residual noise that might remain from the broadcast.

I could no longer hear the television, but I could hear my family's murmured expressions of *what the fuck just happened.*

That had probably been the first time in all these years I'd raised my voice in front of them. I knew what was coming. Or, rather, *who* was coming.

Sure enough, Griff came in and sat down on the sofa by my hip, reaching out to pull my arms away from my head.

"Go away," I grumbled.

"No way," he said with a smile. "You're a Marian, remember? We don't go away. We're like a nasty case of crabs."

"You should have just let me go the day we met," I said halfheartedly. He knew I didn't really mean it.

"Pfft. You were way too fucking cute to let you kill yourself. Besides, I wanted to set you up with Nico," he teased.

I shuddered. "Ew, gross."

"And you know I was never going to stand for being the youngest Marian kid. I needed a baby brother."

"We both know Jude's still the baby brother even though I'm ten years younger than he is," I said, repeating a favorite family joke.

"True. Remind me to ruffle his hair when he gets here," Griff said. His smile faltered. "Tell me about the guy on TV, Dante."

And there it was. After all these years, my past family was clashing into my present one. I knew Griff would never let me get away with holding out on him again, and it was time to stop letting the past control me. I needed to get this out in the open.

"He's my biological father."

Silence for a beat, and then Griff let out a breath and ran his fingers through his hair.

"Shit, Dante. I'm sorry. Jesus. Reverend Lawton, really? That guy's a monster."

I nodded and felt my jaw twitch as if trying to decide between clenching and chattering with nerves.

"I didn't know he'd gone into politics," I admitted. "I tried to forget about him."

"So, what happened?" he asked. "You ran away from home?"

"Not really, no. I was taken away. Rescued."

His forehead wrinkled and I could tell he was trying to piece together everything I'd ever told him about my past. Which, admittedly, wasn't very much.

My chest felt tight at the memory of my rescuer, and I rubbed over my heart with my hand.

"The tattoo," he said quietly. "Your angel. The person who took you away and brought you to us?"

The way he said "to us" warmed my heart. How fucking lucky was I?

"Yes," I said. "And I recently found out who that angel was."

"Who?" he asked, studying my face. I lifted my eyebrow at him. "Oh," he said when the pieces clicked in place. "*Oh.*"

"Yeah."

"Holy shit, Dante. That's like the most romantic fucking story ever," he said with a grin. "What did you say when you realized you'd hooked up with the guy you'd thought about all these years?"

He made it sound like it was a good thing.

"I told him to go fuck himself, Griff. He lied to me."

"What? He didn't tell you who he was? Didn't you recognize him? I don't understand."

"Never mind. I don't want to talk about it. It's over. He reminds me too much of that time anyway, so it doesn't matter," I said, feeling exhausted.

"That's a bunch of bullshit," Griff said matter-of-factly.

"Well, bullshit or not, I don't want to talk about it."

Griff studied me until I began to squirm.

"So then what are you going to do about your bio dad? He's like the modern-day king of conversion therapy, Dante. And he's running for congress."

I shot him a glare and he laughed.

"What? Dante, you didn't want to talk about AJ, so I'm just changing the subject. Now we're talking about Lawton."

I pushed up to sit and crossed my arms with a huff. "What do you expect me to do about it? I'm just one guy. And, honestly, I put that shit in my past for a reason."

Griff looked at me with surprised eyes for several beats before his face seemed to turn to disappointment. Like I'd let him down. I knew he'd never say such a thing, but he was clearly thinking it.

Nerves shimmied through my gut. What the hell did he expect

me to do? Come out publicly against the man? I looked back up at him.

"What, associate myself with a monster and become a national celebrity for having been abused and humiliated as a child? No fucking way. No, thanks." I tried to keep my teeth from grinding together but it was difficult.

That must have gotten his attention because his face softened. "Come on," Griff said, patting my arm. "Burgers are almost ready and the TV is turned off. Let's go out there and see how big Wolfe's gotten since we saw him last."

I ran my hands over my face and took a cleansing breath. "Please keep this shit to yourself, Griff, okay? I don't want to talk about it, and I don't want them all looking at me with pity in their eyes."

"Sure thing," he said. "I'll distract them with my beauty and wit instead, how about that?"

I rolled my eyes and tried suppressing a laugh. "Perfect. In other words, you'll be you."

"Works like a charm," he teased.

I SPENT the next several weeks trying my hardest to force my life back into its nice little predictable box. Job I loved? Check. Fun family gatherings? Check. Friday night pizza and hangout with my room-mates? Check. Love life? Well... that one had always sucked. And not in a good way.

I couldn't stop thinking about AJ—missing him, wanting him. It wasn't just because of the sex. Not that I didn't fantasize about my mouth on his cock or vice versa, but I missed talking to him and being heard by him. I missed being able to ask his input and advice. He was smart, kind, and funny. He always kept his eye on me and seemed to care about how I did. Even though we'd only spent a week together, it was one of the best weeks of my life. Having him with me had just felt good. It had felt... right.

When he realized we'd been accidentally swept away on Aunt

Tilly's joyride, instead of freaking and bailing, AJ had gotten on board and taken charge. He'd refused to leave her alone, and made sure we were all okay.

When he learned not one but twenty Marians were joining us at the Bellagio, he still hadn't bailed. He'd stayed and met my family with charm and grace. When he realized I'd been swarmed that day in the lobby with the paparazzi, he'd come after me and pulled me out of there, reminding me to breathe and let it go, sharing with me his own experiences with panic attacks.

He'd wanted me to see where he grew up, for god's sake. And when I rejected him, he'd tried so hard to get me back. And then I'd gotten drunk and thrown myself at him, and he hadn't taken advantage of the moment.

Fuck. He was a good man. And as Griff pointed out, he was actually the person I'd fantasized about since that horrible night eight years ago. What the hell was my problem?

I decided it was time to go back to therapy. As much as I didn't want to admit I needed it, I definitely did. So in August, I began seeing my counselor again and told her everything. She already knew about my childhood shit, but I told her about AJ and finding out who he really was.

She helped me figure out what really bothered me about it. I'd thought it was trust, but it turned out to be fear. I was afraid AJ saw me as broken or weak or someone to be pitied. I hated people pitying me. And I didn't like the idea of him knowing I was some kind of freak from a backward upbringing.

I also cared enough about him to want him to find someone healthy and whole, and I sure as shit wasn't feeling healthy or whole these days. Since the morning AJ had woken up in my apartment, he'd kept his distance anyway. So it was probably a moot point.

I figured AJ had decided to stay firmly in my past when one night as I was working late at Marian House, I heard the outer door buzz. I walked out to answer it and saw it was AJ with a teenage boy. My heart leapt into my throat at the sight of AJ after all these weeks, and I rushed to open the door.

He looked amazing. He wore a dark suit and had on dark-rimmed eyeglasses. I'd never seen him in his glasses since he hadn't had them with him the night we took off in Tilly's van. I knew he normally wore contacts, but seeing him in a suit and glasses left me breathless.

"Hey," I said as AJ led the boy into the lobby.

"Hey, you're just the person I hoped to see. I have someone who needs your help. Can we go back to your office?" AJ asked.

He was acting completely businesslike to the point of being aloof, and I didn't like it at all. Gone were the soft smiles and twinkling eyes that seemed reserved just for me. In their place was a man on an assignment. Nothing more. It was enough to make me feel empty inside. It was like having the shell of my very favorite person right in front of me but realizing the shell was empty. There was nothing inside for me.

"Sure, follow me," I said.

I led them down the hall into my office where I closed the door behind us and gestured for them to have a seat. After they were seated on the sofa, I took the armchair next to it. This kind of situation was the very reason I'd insisted on having room for some comfortable furniture in my space. Intakes were stressful enough for kids as it was, but sitting on the opposite side of a desk from an adult could be very intimidating.

Once seated, AJ spoke up. He was all business, and it was clear this wasn't his first rodeo. I realized the young man must have been a client of AJ's—someone he rescued and brought here.

AJ spoke. "Dante, this is Ammon. Ammon, this is the executive director of Marian House, Dante Marian."

I realized I hadn't even spared a second thought for the poor kid he'd brought with him. That wasn't like me at all. I shook off my mental fog and reached out to smile and shake hands with Ammon in welcome. The young man was scared to death and I noticed him clutching a fleece jacket in his arms as if it was a lifeline. The poor guy must be feeling overwhelmed.

After I asked if he wanted a drink or anything, he declined politely and went back to looking at his kneecaps. He reminded me so much of myself, it was spooky. My heart went out to him. Being in a strange place with nothing but strangers around was terrifying.

"Ammon," I said softly, "I'm so glad you're here. I know it's a lot right now for you to take in, but this is a safe place and you are completely in control of what happens here. We'd love to find you a comfortable bed to sleep in tonight if that's okay with you. And in the morning I can introduce you to AJ's aunt, Londa, who is just about the most loving woman you'll ever meet. She and I will help you in any way you need. Okay?"

The boy nodded and blushed, looking pretty much miserable the way I remembered feeling. It was almost enough to make me want to bail. Simply walk out the door and find somewhere to hide away from the memories of when I was in Ammon's situation.

I locked eyes with AJ and knew he was remembering the same thing. Remembering me as that broken boy who had hit rock bottom and had almost given up hope.

But I wasn't that kid anymore. I was the adult. And it was my job to stick it out and make this right. For Ammon. To prove to him that he'd get through this and things would get better.

AJ cleared his throat, laying a gentle hand on the kid's forearm to get him to look up. "Ammon, I brought you here because it's a great place for kids like you. It's safe and has the resources to help you start over. But most of all, it has Dante." He paused and glanced over at me before continuing. My heart raced like a kid's at Christmas, but AJ remained all business.

"One of the best things about this place is that it's run by someone who knows exactly what it's like to be in your shoes. Dante went through hell, same as you, at the hands of his father and a church that had lost its way. If you stay here, you'll learn it's possible to move past all that. After coming here at the age of fifteen, Dante worked his tail off in school and got not only a bachelor's degree but a master's degree in order to help other people like himself. The entire time he was in school, he also volunteered here, helping others."

My throat felt so thick I thought I wasn't going to be able to swallow anymore. AJ went on.

"He came from the same dark place, Ammon. But look at him now. He's become an amazing, loving man and a leader in our community. Everyone who knows him adores him and looks to him for guidance."

My jaw tightened out of fear I would blurt out something stupid. AJ didn't even look at me when he stood up.

"I have to go now." His voice cracked and he turned away for a moment. He seemed to pull himself together because when he turned back, he looked determined. "After I leave, Dante's going to tell you I exaggerated everything I said about him. I didn't. Listen to what he says, Ammon, and you'll do amazing things—just like he has."

Before I could open my mouth to speak, he was gone. I sat there frozen in shock before Ammon cleared his throat and squirmed in his seat.

"Oh, ah, sorry, Ammon. Let's get you a bunk," I said.

After showing him around and helping him find a bed and clean pajamas, I lingered in the bunk area until I knew he was asleep. Once I was sure he was settled for the night, I made my way back toward my office. Londa stood in my office doorway, waiting for me.

"Hey," I said. "I thought you'd gone home hours ago."

"Want to join me for a cup of hot tea?" she asked. I nodded and followed her to the big industrial kitchen where we helped ourselves to what we needed. Once we sat down at a cafeteria table, she asked how I was doing.

"I don't know, not great, I guess," I admitted.

She smiled again and looked down into her coffee. "I've tried not to get in your business."

"What do you mean?" I asked.

"I know something's been going on with you, and you're not really the type who likes to be pressed about things."

I couldn't help but laugh at the understatement. "You know me that well, huh? I'm sure you're having thoughts though. Go ahead and tell me. I value your opinion. And you've known me a long time."

Londa studied me a minute before answering. "I'm torn between what my heart wants to say and what my brain wants to say, Dante."

"Why don't you tell me both?"

"My brain wants to tell you to stay the hell away from my nephew so you don't break his heart again," she said.

My own heart began thumping harder in my chest.

"And what does your heart say?" I asked quietly.

"Sweetie, my heart wants to smack you upside the head for denying yourself something that's obviously meant to be. Your whole family told me how happy you two seemed together in Vegas. And now you've both been miserable since then."

"AJ's miserable too?" I couldn't help but ask.

She lifted an eyebrow at me and pursed her lips. "You fishing?"

I barked out a laugh. "You sound just like him. I guess I am fishing. He seemed so put together when he dropped that kid off tonight. It looks like he's moved on. Maybe I should too."

"Looks can be deceiving. You want my advice? Life's too short for this bullshit. You want a good man to spend your life with and warm your bed at night? You can't find one better than my Angel. You want to live alone and go to sleep every night with nothing but old ghosts in your bed? Then keep yourself to yourself. It's your choice, Dante."

33

AJ

When Labor Day weekend rolled around, I looked forward to several days off. Griff had invited me to visit him and Sam at the vineyard and I had to admit, the offer was tempting. I knew it was the beginning of the white wine harvest, and Griff's brother Blue offered to show me around. Since I hadn't lived in California long, I'd never visited a winery.

After Londa mentioned going to the Marian family barbeque at Rebecca and Thomas' house on Labor Day, I assumed Dante would stay in town to be with his family, so I gladly accepted Griff's invitation to head to Napa.

When I pulled up to the Alexander Vineyard, I followed signs to the main lodge hotel building. I texted Griff to let him know I was there. Since it was so late, he told me to grab my room key from the front desk and he'd find me the following morning.

The young woman at the desk seemed to be waiting for my arrival and had my room key ready.

"That's it?" I asked. "You don't need a credit card?"

She laughed. "No, sir. Griff says you're family. Let me know if there's anything you need."

The idea that Griff had overcome his anger at me to even invite me there made me happy, but to be considered somehow part of the Marian family? That made me feel a combination of elation and sadness. I still missed Dante so much I could barely stand it.

I managed to smile back at her. "Thanks."

After making my way down the hall, I found the right room number and swiped the key card to get in. I noticed the room's light was already on and I stepped forward to let the door close behind me.

I wasn't alone. There on the bed was Dante. He'd apparently fallen asleep reading and lay there curled up in jeans and a T-shirt with no shoes on. What the hell was he doing at the vineyard? Just the sight of him made my entire chest seize up and I couldn't move. The woman at the desk must have given me the wrong key card.

I turned to leave when I heard his voice, rough from sleep. "Wait."

My eyes squeezed closed as my heart pounded. He wanted me to stay. I didn't dare hope too hard because what if he was just asking me to wait so he could find out what I was doing in his room?

After turning back to him, I began to apologize. "I'm sorry, I didn't know you were in here. The woman at the front desk must have—"

"No, she got it right," he said. "This is your room. I was waiting for you. Must have fallen asleep." He sat up, knocking the paperback to the floor. I stepped forward to grab it and put it on the bedside table. My heart was thumping out of control at this point because there he was, curled up in bed within striking distance. Had my hands ever itched that much to touch someone before? I didn't think so.

When I looked back at him, I noticed his hair stuck up on one side just like I'd seen many times before. He was the most beautiful human being I'd ever known.

"You were waiting for me?" I asked, trying not to get hopeful.

"Yes. Will you come sit with me for a minute?" he asked, patting the spot next to him on the bed.

I slipped off my shoes and climbed onto the bed, being careful not to touch him.

"Are you okay?" I asked. "I've been thinking about you and hoping you were doing well." What was I doing? Babbling? Jesus.

He smiled. "No, actually. I haven't been doing well. That's why I'm here."

My heart dropped. "Oh. I'm sorry, Dante."

He turned to face me, crisscrossing his legs into a pretzel and tentatively reaching out to take hold of one of my hands. The feel of his skin sent shivers up my arm, and I forced myself to be patient.

"AJ, I owe you a very big apology," he began.

"No, you don't—"

His free hand came up to stop me.

"Yes, I do. Just let me talk for a minute. I didn't handle myself well when all of the shit from my past came back up. It hit me out of the blue and really brought back lots of crap—not only memories, but also bad habits. One of those bad habits was tunneling into myself when things get scary." He took a deep breath before continuing. "When I was little, expressing emotions wasn't something I was encouraged or really allowed to do much of. So when I felt them, I hid away rather than let anyone see what I felt."

It made complete sense, so I squeezed his hand to let him know I understood without interrupting him.

"I also have a nice history of avoiding putting my heart out there, obviously, because I'm not used to trusting people not to hurt me. I mean, I've gotten better over the years. Lots of therapy and the Marians have helped. But when all of this shit came up and you and I hadn't known each other very long..." He paused and looked down at our hands before lifting a shoulder. "It was just so easy to use your confession as an excuse to run."

While Dante talked, my heart rate kicked up until it thumped in anticipation. Was he apologizing to get closure or to give us another chance?

He let out a breath and smiled at me again. "So, I'm sorry for running. And I have two things to ask you that are unrelated."

Please let one of them include naked body parts, please let one of them include naked body parts...

"I need your help confronting my father," he said.

The sound of a vinyl record scratching shot through my brain.

"What?" I asked.

Dante gripped my hand harder before leaning toward me, his expression earnest. "I can't let him keep doing what he's doing. I'm going to confront him, AJ. But I don't think I can do it without your support."

"You know I'll do anything to support you, but what made you decide this?"

"He needs to be stopped. I should have done this a long time ago."

Before I could say anything, Dante held up a finger. "Correction. I couldn't have done this a long time ago. I was a kid myself. I have to keep reminding myself I'm only twenty-three," he said with a laugh. "Sorry. Sometimes my therapist's voice interrupts me when I'm going down a path of blaming myself for all the world's problems."

"I think I want to kiss your therapist," I said with a wink.

Dante's face grew serious and I braced myself for the second thing.

"Kissing. That's actually the second thing."

My stomach jangled with nervous excitement, and I couldn't help but babble again. "Well, I thought you said your therapist was a woman, but I can try," I teased.

He laughed and nudged my shoulder. "I'd prefer you didn't. Plus, I don't think her wife would appreciate it very much."

I smiled. "I guess not."

Dante looked at me and his eyes seemed to reflect the heat I was sure blazed in my own. "I want to be with you. To try this again, I mean. If... that is, if you haven't given up on me yet."

Thank fucking god. I wanted to scream and shout, but instead, I let out a deep breath, realizing there was still more stuff I needed to tell him.

"Dante Marian, I will *never* give up on you. I would really, really like to try this again if you're willing. But first, there are some more things we need to get out in the open."

"Okayyyy," he said with a worried tone.

I squeezed his hands in reassurance. "This is stuff about me and my past, not you."

He nodded, and I took a deep breath. "I didn't tell you why my father and I do what we do for a living. Well, my dad's retired now, but he kind of got into private personnel recovery because of me."

Dante looked up at me. "What do you mean?"

"My dad was in the Marines and did personnel extraction stuff with them, so when he got out, he was recruited to work for one of the companies that does the same kind of thing but for corporate kidnap, ransom, and extortion insurance. Like the big oil executives carry when they travel overseas. When dad retired from the military, we moved from Camp Pendleton to Chicago. My dad traveled a lot with his new job in the private sector, and my mom was busy with my sisters. I was that stupid age of like thirteen or fourteen when I got into shit with some bad kids. We stole stuff and did drugs. I hung out with them because they seemed to be the only kids who tolerated the new guy. Before I knew it, I cared more about being with those idiots than my own family.

"One night we snuck out late and ended up getting caught by the cops with some drugs. We were arrested and charged. My parents lost their shit and made drastic changes. Dad relocated us to Aster Valley. Just up and moved us. He had a good friend whose family owned the lodge there and told us what a safe place it was to raise a family. I was shocked. To go from living in San Diego, to Chicago, to *Aster Valley, Colorado*? It was like hell on earth for a teen boy who liked excitement and danger and shit."

I sighed and ran my hands through my hair. "So I bailed. I ran away and tried to get back to my friends in Chicago. I had enough money for a bus ticket, but when I hooked back up with my friends, I realized I'd been shortsighted. I could only stay with each kid for, like, a few days before their parents got suspicious."

Dante grabbed hold of my hands again, and I smiled at him.

"By the time my dad and his buddies found me, it had been three weeks and I was living in this nasty broken-down apartment with a bunch of random strangers. A 'friend of a friend of a friend' kinda thing. I was exhausted, hungry, scared, and lonely, but I was way too stupid and embarrassed to call my family and ask them to come get me. It took me all of five seconds to realize how fucking lucky I was that someone came and got me out of there. That someone cared enough to take me away from that shit and let me start over."

"What happened next?" Dante asked. "Did you have to go to rehab?"

I shook my head. "No. Luckily I hadn't done enough drugs to get addicted to anything. For me, it was more the thrill of being bad. Of doing something against the rules. And maybe that's something I *am* addicted to. But now I get to do it for a living," I said with a wink.

"Anyway, Dante, that's my extraction story. After I returned home and settled into my new school, the guys who'd helped Dad find me in Chicago called him back to ask him to start a private recovery group for cases like ours. Most of them worked for the original company in Chicago and just switched from corporate international work to private, family work. So that's how the company started. When I graduated high school, I moved to Chicago for college and interned with them. I already knew that's what I wanted to do, but they insisted on a degree. That's how I ended up there again the last few years. Now all those guys are retiring, and it's really just me. My hope was to create this group for Joel at On Your Six and then stay to manage it."

"You don't want to keep running your own business?" he asked.

"No. I hate the pressure of working solo. Plus, it's hard to handle the extractions as well as the paperwork, insurance, banking, and shit. Right now, my dad still handles all of that. But he'd like to retire for real. Which means I'd have to do it or find someone to do it for me."

Dante thought about this a minute and I realized I was holding my breath, waiting to see if my story changed anything between us. Then he tilted his head, considering me. "You've always seemed so strong. So together. And yet you needed rescuing just like me."

I shrugged. "We all need help at some point, Dante."

He lifted my hand and pressed his lips to my knuckles. "Thanks for telling me, AJ. And thank you for saying all those nice things about me the other night when you brought Ammon to us."

Dante crawled toward me and settled into my lap, wrapping his arms around my neck.

"I missed you so fucking much," I admitted in a low voice.

"Me too. I'm so sorry, AJ. I'm really good at cutting off my nose to spite my face."

The sheepish grin Dante gave me was the cutest fucking thing ever, and I wanted to capture it in my memory bank for all time.

"Can we agree to stop the apologies?" I asked. "And maybe replace them with some of the kissing you mentioned?"

"I guess so." Dante smirked, leaning in.

When our lips met, it was like coming home.

34

DANTE

Thankfully, things turned light and flirty between us as we teased each other's mouths and took our time kissing.

Eventually, I pulled AJ's shirt off so I could have more skin to run my hands over. He wound up doing the same to me and we lay side by side on the bed, alternately talking and kissing as the night wore on.

At one point, AJ mentioned wanting to hop in the shower before going to sleep.

"I just got back from a business trip this afternoon and I feel all sweaty from the plane ride."

"Can I join you? Might need some help reaching your hidden spots," I suggested.

His face lit up. "Absolutely."

When we stepped into the shower, I dropped to my knees. I wanted AJ's cock in my mouth, like, yesterday.

"Oh fuck," he gasped as I licked up his length. His hands landed on my shoulders, and my fingers gripped the backs of his thighs.

I went to town on his cock and devoured it—sucking, licking, and teasing, using my fingers to toy with his sac and jack him along with my mouth. Within moments, he came down my throat as I hit my own peak and blew all over the goddamned shower floor.

My cheeks flushed as I peered up at him and shrugged. "I guess watching someone else come is kind of a turn-on. Who knew?" I joked.

His eyes darkened, and his hands came up to run through my hair. "Me."

We cleaned ourselves up and stepped out of the shower, drying off and brushing our teeth before returning to the room. I sat on the edge of the bed naked, and AJ stepped forward to stand between my legs.

My fingers grasped his firm cheeks and squeezed as I leaned forward to drop kisses along his abdomen and over his hip. In the dim light I could still see a small scar on his chest; I reached a hand up to caress that spot.

He grabbed me under the arms and thrust me farther up the bed before crawling on top of me like a predator. AJ's smile was wide and his eyes teased.

"When I saw you dancing with Nico that night, it really bothered me," he said. "I know I told you that already, but I thought maybe you two were going to get together."

"Really? What made you think that?" I asked in surprise. His proximity made my heart race, and I reached out to run my hands up his chest to his shoulders.

"I don't know. Just jealousy, I guess."

I couldn't help but laugh. "Nico's like a brother to me. Plus, he's a hot mess."

AJ shifted to lie next to me on his side, one leg draped over mine and his fingers tracing delicious patterns over my chest.

"I heard he's a tattoo artist. Is he the one who did this?" he asked, moving his fingers to my angel tattoo. Goosebumps prickled under his touch, and I felt my stomach muscles go tight.

"Mm-hm," I murmured.

"Tell me about it," he prompted in a low voice. "Who designed it? I love it."

"Blue and Griff helped design it after I told them what I wanted."

"You wanted an angel to watch over you?"

"I wanted you," I admitted in a rough voice. "You're my angel. Always have been."

He rolled farther over on top of me again and we locked eyes. I felt impaled by his intense gaze, so I looked away. AJ's hand came out and moved my face back around to look at him.

"I want you too," he said before dropping his mouth onto mine to follow through on his words.

I brought a leg up between his so I could arch my cock against his hip. "Want you to fuck me," I breathed. Enough with the emotional conversation bullshit. It was too much. I wanted mindless sex. Physical pleasure to take me out of my head.

AJ's grin returned and I sensed his unspoken agreement to my mood shift. "Bossy bottom," he teased before kissing me again. I leaned over to grab condoms and lube I'd brought and handed them to him. His eyes darkened again and I saw lust shimmer through them.

I hoped to god this was it. Finally a chance to feel him inside me. The only person I'd ever imagined allowing inside of my body. Just the thought of it actually happening made me hard as a rock again. I clamped a hand at the base of my cock to calm down while AJ climbed back onto the bed.

"Turn over onto your stomach," he said.

I did as he commanded and felt him shift beside me. A warm hand landed on my back and began to massage my muscles.

"What are you doing?" I asked.

"Going to give you a massage first. Just relax."

"No way. I can't relax. I want to jump your fucking bones."

AJ laughed and I felt him lean over to nip one of my ass cheeks. "You'll get your chance to jump my bones, but first I want to relax you and make you feel good."

My frustration simmered below the surface, but I decided not to be a dick about it and go with the flow. "Okay. Maybe I shouldn't complain about getting a massage," I mumbled.

"Yeah, maybe not," he said with a laugh.

AJ climbed up and straddled my ass, causing me to hitch in a breath when I remembered he was naked too. His warm cock brushed against the cool skin of my ass and I groaned. How the hell would I survive a massage with his junk nestled in my ass crack?

He began kneading my shoulders and every time he leaned forward, I felt his hot length press against me. Holy fuck, I was going to come like an idiot again. I needed a strategy to cut this massage session short.

Hmm, I thought. *What if I...?*

"*Jesusfuckingchrist*, Dante," AJ gasped as I clenched my ass around his shaft.

"Hm?" I asked innocently, turning my head around to look at him. "What?"

His eyes narrowed, so I clenched again and then pressed my ass up into him in a cat stretch. "God, you feel good," I murmured. "Your cock in my ass. Makes me have all kinds of thoughts, AJ."

"Dante," he warned. "I was giving you a massage, remember?"

"Mm-hm, and it feels *sooo good* too," I agreed. "Please continue."

I settled back down into the mattress as his hands began moving on my back again. It really did feel good, so I began to moan my appreciation. I may or may not have made the moans dirtier than I normally would have, and I may or may not have wiggled and squeezed my ass some more until I felt AJ's cock instinctively rock into the cleft in response.

"Fine," he finally growled. "You win." AJ crawled off me and grabbed my ass cheeks with his hands before leaning down and laying into me with his mouth.

"Oh fuck, fuck!" I yelped, almost leaping off the bed from the sensation. AJ's strong arm came around my hips to hold me still as he continued rimming me with the most glorious, wet tongue imaginable.

By the time he was through, I was a shaking, mumbling blob of hot need. All I felt was a billion zinging nerves that seemed to originate in my ass and travel to the very edges of my sanity.

The next thing I knew, AJ had lubed up his fingers and began pressing them inside me one by one.

"*Mpfh*. Mm-hmm," I muttered. When his finger grazed over my prostate, I almost lost my shit. "Oh *GOD*."

"That's it, baby, that's the good stuff," I heard him say through a smile.

"Again," I managed to blubber. "*Please*."

He stroked the right spot again and I felt my eyes roll back. It reminded me of the time Simone had described women who weren't sure if they'd ever had an orgasm. "Honey, if you're not sure, then the answer is no. You haven't," she'd said.

That's how I felt about whether my prostate had ever been stroked. No, it hadn't.

The ecstasy of that feeling helped me take more of his fingers until I felt the stretch turn into a burn. I tried not to worry about being able to take his cock, but I couldn't help it.

"Turn around, Dante," he whispered into my ear. "I want to see you."

I turned onto my back and looked up at him. His face was bright and his eyes sparkled. He was the most beautiful man I'd ever seen, and in that moment I knew I wasn't looking at the stranger who'd saved me all those years ago but at the man he was now.

I smiled up at him and whispered, "Kiss me some more."

His smile widened and he dropped his face to brush his lips against mine. We kissed until I felt drunk and dizzy and then he leaned back to put on the condom.

"You sure about this, Dante?" he asked, brows furrowed in concentration and concern.

I was torn between wanting to snarl at him for treating me like a child and wanting to tackle him back onto the bed and fuck him instead of the other way around. Rather than doing either of those things, I narrowed my eyes at him and stared him into submission.

He acquiesced with a quick wink before leaning down to kiss me again. His fingers snuck back to my hole and worked it again before I felt the head of his cock take their place.

Fucking finally.

AJ pushed my knees up and leaned back to focus on what he was doing. I enjoyed watching his facial expressions as he crinkled his forehead in concentration. His hands rested gently on my knees and I reached out to put mine on top of his, causing him to look back up at me and smile. He grabbed one of my hands and brought it up for a quick peck of his lips before setting it back down and grasping my cock instead.

His hand stroked me, trying to help keep me hard as I felt the stretch of his cock pushing in. I watched his face as I focused on the sensations. I could tell his only concern was for me, for how I felt and what I was experiencing.

I brought a hand up to his stomach and ran it along the ridges of his muscles.

As he rocked his hips back and forth to press his cock even farther inside me, I breathed in and out carefully, locking eyes with him and trying to stay relaxed. It was a strange feeling, really. Being stretched past the point of comfort but also wanting more of it. Of him.

I closed my eyes and arched my head back, inhaling a deep breath and pushing out against the pressure of him pushing in. I felt the warm puff of his breath against my cheek as he leaned in and brushed his lips past my face to murmur his encouragement in my ear.

"You feel so good, baby," he whispered. "So fucking gorgeous, Dante. Watching my cock slide into your body is the hottest thing ever. Want more of you. You're so tight. *So tight*. God, you feel incredible. I want to make you feel as good as you make me feel. Shhh, relax. That's it. Just like that. Mmm-hmm."

His hand made slick strokes on my cock as he spoke and I felt my dick harden and my balls tighten. I'd never before felt so close to a person. To trust someone enough to let him inside of me, knowing he'd never do anything to hurt me. It was strangely intoxicating. Was this what true intimacy was?

"AJ," I breathed.

"Hmm?"

"Want to stay like this forever," I said.

I felt his warm tongue on my earlobe and his teeth clamped lightly onto it, making a tiny click sound as his teeth brushed against my earring. "Me too."

As his hips rocked him deeper and deeper, his hands stroked me faster and faster. I was overloaded with the feel of him—cock in my ass, hand on my dick, mouth on my ear.

I brought my legs around his waist and used them to pull him in tighter. My hands came up to cup his face and kiss him deeply. As he shifted, he pegged my prostate and I threw my head back with a cry. "Oh god, fuck!"

AJ pulled out of me and bent down to put his lips on my cock. I almost came apart at the sudden replacement of his hand with his hot mouth, but it was only seconds later I came apart for real. I writhed on the bed through one of the most intense orgasms I'd ever had, and I felt the spectacular pulses deep in my ass in a way I never had before.

After I came, I lay gasping on the mattress while AJ loomed above me looking satisfied. I noticed his hand around the base of his cock obviously trying to stave off his own release. Fuck that. I tackled him onto his back, ripped off the condom, and returned the favor, engulfing his shaft with my mouth and sucking him off quickly.

His hands were light on my head as I swallowed his release and continued small sucks and licks until his breathing steadied. Once he seemed somewhat recovered, I climbed up to lay my head on his shoulder. We both still tried to catch our breath and the air around us was hot and humid from our exertions.

I felt AJ's hand brush through my hair before I heard him speak. "Sorry," he said in a quiet voice.

I turned to look at him, unsure I'd heard right. "Good god, for what?" I asked.

"Sorry I pulled out and finished you off with a blow job."

I barked out a laugh. "Are you crazy?"

His face was already red from the orgasm or he might have

blushed. "No, I just feel bad because I kind of promised you sex and then—"

My laughing stopped, replaced by disappointment at his discomfort. "AJ, we *did* have sex. Great sex. And I had an orgasm. A pretty damned good one. Stop whatever it is you're doing right now with the second-guessing. Did you enjoy it?"

"Of course I did. Couldn't you tell?"

"Looked that way to me. Do you think *I* enjoyed it?" I asked with a lascivious grin.

He smirked. "No. You looked bored to tears."

"I was. It was all I could do to fake my way through it."

"Shut up," he said, tackling me back onto the bed and kissing me some more. When he took a break and pulled back, his face in shadows in the dimly lit space. "Dante, thank you for bringing me here. And for trusting me again."

I reached up to wrap my arms around him in a tight hug, forcing him to tuck his face into my neck. "Honestly, AJ, I don't think I could stop trusting you if I tried."

35

AJ

Had this been a romance novel, I would have said that night was the best I'd slept in weeks with Dante nestled against me. But it wasn't, and I didn't. At some point in the middle of the night I heard a cry and wound up with a sharp elbow in the face.

"What the hell?" I gasped out of a dead sleep, hand coming up to cradle my injured cheekbone.

Dante was flailing around and drenched in sweat. "Shit, Dante. Wake up," I said, reaching a hand out to grab one of his arms.

"Dante," I barked. My face throbbed; I realized he'd probably given me a black eye. "Babe, wake up."

He finally woke up and looked around. "AJ?"

"Yeah, it's me. You had a nightmare."

"Shit."

"Yeah," I muttered, leaning over to turn on the lamp. "What's going on?"

He groaned and rubbed his face. I continued to hold a hand over my injured eye, and he looked at me funny.

"What was the bad dream about?" I asked.

"The same one I've had forever. About being stuck in a crowd. I thought after all the fucking counseling I've had, the nightmare would stop. But I think it's just part of my life now."

"I'm sorry. Come here," I said, reaching out to pull him against me.

"What happened to your face? You're squinting."

"I accidentally ran my eye into your elbow," I said after kissing his cheek. I would have winked at him but my winker was offline.

"Dammit, AJ. I'm sorry." He reached out to cup my cheek and peered at the injured spot. "Shit. It might be a shiner."

"That's okay. Wouldn't be my first. And think of the stories I can make up now about you roughing me up in bed," I teased. "Catch your breath so we can go back to sleep. It's not quite morning yet."

"No, I'm going to go get you some ice for that eye. Stay here." Dante got up and found some pajamas in his bag before making his way out of the room.

DESPITE THE ICE pack Dante brought back to the room and held on my face, I still ended up with a nasty black eye.

"You know, this reminds me of Simone. She got a black eye in bed once," Griff said over a late breakfast on the patio off the lodge lobby the next morning.

"You're kidding?" I asked. "Who the hell gave her a black eye?"

"My brother," Tristan said, taking a sip of coffee and frowning. "Supposedly it was an accident."

"I thought your brother was married," I said.

"He is now. This was before that. Dante hasn't told you about Simone and John?" Blue asked.

"I try not to remember Simone with John," Dante interjected. "No offense, Tristan."

"None taken. Although since he and Sheila married, he's almost like a different person. I think they're good for each other. But I have to admit I'm damned glad neither of them plans on having kids."

I looked over at Blue and Tristan's daughter, Ella, who was busy trying to shove half a banana in Griff's face. She had Blue's strawberry-blond hair, and it curled in loops around her head, catching the sunlight as she laughed. Griff made exaggerated faces at her, trying his best not to wind up covered in food.

"Speaking of Simone," Sam said. "We tried to fix her up with one of my sous chefs, but she said she's giving up dating."

Dante laughed. "That's just what she told you to get you to stop fixing her up."

"No," Griff said. "I think she's done for a while. She seemed really depressed about it, and I know she's had a string of bad dates this summer."

Blue took Ella from Griff and removed the banana from her hand before standing up. "I still think Thad's right and his friend Bell would be perfect for her. I don't know why she's so resistant to letting any of us set her up."

Tristan shot Blue a look, and Blue blushed. "But it's her life I guess," he muttered. "None of my business."

This time it was Sam's turn to laugh. "Yeah, because Marians are *so* good at staying out of each other's love lives."

Tristan stood up. "I don't know. I'd say we Marians have a pretty high success rate in the love life department," he said, leaning over to kiss his husband. "Isn't that right Ella?" The baby giggled and it was the best sound in the world.

"We're going to take her back for a nap. See you this afternoon for the vineyard tour," Blue said.

Once they were gone, Griff leaned over and put his hand on my arm.

"Are you mad at me for getting you up here under false pretenses?" he asked with a grin.

I barked out a laugh. "Hell fucking no. Are you crazy?" I looked over at Dante, who blushed crimson. "Best surprise roommate ever."

"Oh my god," Dante muttered into his hands. Sam laughed too and shot a wink at me.

I reached over and grabbed Dante's hand, pulling it up to kiss it. "Sorry, Dante, I didn't mean to make you blush."

He blushed deeper, and I loved every minute of it.

"Yes, you did," he groaned.

Griff and Sam continued laughing. I squeezed Dante's hand. "Okay, maybe I did. But only because you're so damned cute when you blush."

"I have to go," he said, pretending to push his chair back.

I stopped him with a growl. "Stay. I'll try to behave," I promised.

"No, you won't," Dante said with a laugh.

We continued to joke around with Griff and Sam until it was time for the vineyard tour. After learning more than I ever thought I wanted to know about grapes and wine, I finally got Dante back to the privacy of our hotel room and blessedly naked.

I'd like to say we saw more of Dante's brothers that weekend, but we didn't. I'd like to say we spent some lovely time outside enjoying the beautiful September weather, but we didn't.

We spent the rest of the time wrapped around each other's naked bodies, diving into each other as often as our stamina would allow and relishing the tender renewal of our relationship.

WHEN MONDAY AFTERNOON ROLLED AROUND, we decided it was time to head back to the city. Dante had originally caught a ride to the vineyard with one of his brothers, so he was able to ride back with me. We hadn't gone far when Dante turned in his seat to face me, his expression serious.

"I want to talk about my biological father," he said.

I moved my hand from the wheel and took his, holding it gently. I knew how difficult it was for him to talk about his past. "Okay."

He blew out a long breath. "I want to confront him. And I need your help to do it."

I squeezed his fingers to show my support. "What made you decide to do something?"

"I recently read an article about working with troubled youths who've been in conversion camps. And, I mean, it's not like I didn't know they still existed, but reading that article in relation to my job as the head of an LGBTQ youth program was like a slap in the face about my own hypocrisy. It made me realize how many kids are going through this shit right now while I sit back and do nothing," Dante turned to look out the window. "Here I claim to want to help gay youths, yet I'm unwilling to step out of my own comfort zone to stop one of the country's antigay mouthpieces."

His earnestness made me fall for him even more, but I also knew the heartache and disappointment that came with rescuing a kid only to realize how many more you hadn't been able to reach.

"You can't save every child from conversion therapy, Dante," I told him softly.

"I know that, but what if I just save one? Wouldn't it still be worth it?"

He looked down at our joined hands, drawing an index finger along the top of one of my fingers before looking back up at me. "Wasn't I worth it?"

God, the man had the ability to stop my breath on a dime. I pulled his hand to my lips and kissed it. "Of course you were worth it, Dante Marian. Jesus. You know better than to even ask."

He smiled a sweet smile. "I was one of the lucky ones who got saved, and look what a difference it made to just me. One person can make a difference. And now it's my turn to be that one person for others."

Cars went by in the glow of the late afternoon sun. I felt a combination of pride and excitement at the words Dante was finally saying.

"If my biological father gets elected, he can influence policy. He'll push for more conversion programs." He shook his head, cheeks flushed with conviction. "I've been running from my past, thinking I could put it behind me. But I can't. And I don't want to any longer."

He turned back toward me, his jaw set and eyes bright with intention. "Richard Lawton is dangerous and I plan to do anything I can to keep him from getting elected and doing to other kids what he did to me."

Dante ducked his head as though suddenly shy again. "You in?"

Looking at this beautiful, passionate man made my heart beat a silly rhythm. How the hell did I get so lucky? I squeezed his hand tightly. "Of course I'm in. What's our plan?"

36

DANTE

Deciding to give things with AJ another try was the best damned thing I'd done in a long time. I wanted to kick myself for being such an idiot before and thinking I could stand to live without him. Maybe I was selfish, but I wanted it all. And having Angel Julian Flores was step number one.

Step number two was making sure Reverend Richard Asshole Lawton never set foot in the US House of Representatives. But I was still focused on step number one when AJ and I arrived back at my apartment.

We jumped each other's bones the minute my bedroom door closed behind us and had finally emerged a couple of hours later to a round of applause by my fucking roommates, Robbie and Jason, who sat on the sofa watching a football game.

I wasn't sure it was possible for my face to get that hot, so I quickly shuffled my tender ass to the kitchen to shove my face into the freezer and cool off. AJ followed me with a lazy chuckle. Or, what was more likely, a proud chuckle.

Braggart.

"What are you laughing about?" I muttered to the frozen peas.

"You and your splotchy neck," he said, walking up behind me and kissing the neck in question. "Cute as shit."

I grumbled some more before finding some edamame to steam for dinner. "You okay with something small? I'm not really that hungry."

"Yeah, sure."

After rustling up some odds and ends for us, we sat down at the table. I'd grabbed my laptop so I could book the flight to Indiana for the big confrontation with the Lawtons.

"I'm going to go on Saturday so he's more likely to be home," I said, trying not to think about it too hard. "I tried to find his campaign schedule, but it didn't show much for this weekend."

"You mean *we're* going to fly up on Saturday."

"No." I shook my head. "No way. I don't want you anywhere near there."

AJ took my hand. "Babe, I'm not asking to come with you," he said. "I'm telling you I'm coming with you."

He peered at me with those beautiful hazel eyes until I rolled my own boring brown ones. "If you weren't so hot, I'd fight you harder on this. But it's going to be an overnight trip and, well, I've seen firsthand how well you perform in a hotel bed."

AJ coughed out a laugh. "Jeez, no pressure or anything. Now I'm feeling a little stage fright."

I shrugged. "Don't worry. You'll think of something."

I spent the rest of the week so focused on the looming trip that the only thing that could take my mind off it was AJ and dear god was he good at that. Once we landed in Indiana, however, my nerves kicked into overdrive.

When we checked into a hotel in Bloomington, I couldn't stop pacing as I worked up the nerve to drive to Gordon.

AJ stepped in front of me and placed his hands on my shoulders. "You can do this. I'll be with you every step of the way."

I shook my head. "You're staying here."

He quirked an eyebrow as if to say, *You're adorable but so fucking wrong about that.*

I stared him down. "AJ, I need to do this on my own. I can't talk to them while I'm sitting there with my fucking gay boyfriend, okay?" I blurted.

He glared back at me for a split second, clearly ready to go head to head with me until my words hit him and he cracked a smile.

"What did you just call me?"

I thought back. "My... my boyfriend," I repeated. Dammit, had I overstepped? Hell no I hadn't. "You're here with me. I think that qualifies you as my boyfriend."

He stepped forward and wrapped his arms around my waist, pulling me in and rubbing his crotch against mine. Neither of us was hard, but it was sexy nonetheless.

"No, you called me your *fucking* boyfriend," he said with a teasing grin. "Maybe we should see if that title's accurate before we get back in the car."

"Seriously? Right now?" I asked. "Do you have any idea how freaked out I am?"

His face got serious and he leaned in to rest his forehead against mine. "I do, Dante. That's why I'm trying to make you laugh. And I'd really like to suck you off before we go because I think it'll help take the edge off. That, and I really like having your cock in my mouth."

I blew out a breath. Jesus, after that comment things might have gotten hard after all.

"This isn't really the time," I said. But my heart wasn't in the rejection, and he knew it. Plus, getting a little action would delay the upcoming confrontation in my hometown, and that was A-okay with me. "And even if it was, I'd want to suck you off, not the other way around."

He lifted the side of his lips in a quirky grin of victory.

My hands came up to grasp the sides of his neck and his own came around to cup my ass and pull me tighter against him. I felt the growing outline of his cock and groaned. Suddenly, I had this crazy desire to hear him beg.

I fumbled with his fly until his pants were open and my hand reached in to find his cock. It was thick and full, warm and silky smooth. I pulled at it gently and felt it harden even more.

"Please, Dante," he breathed against my skin. "Want you so much. *Please.*"

Well, that didn't take long.

His words went straight to my own cock until it strained against my fly.

I moved him over to the foot of the nearest bed and snuck my hands under his boxers to slide his underwear and pants to the floor. Once I pushed him to sit, I knelt down in front of him and opened my mouth on his cock. I ran a giant lick along the length, making it jump up in response.

I took him into my mouth and sucked up and down his length, reaching to fondle his balls with one hand and stroke the base of his cock with the other.

"Fuck, baby," he breathed. "That feels so good. Please don't stop."

The words came out in a rush of pleading, and I smiled against his girth. I took a few more swipes with my tongue before moving my mouth over to drop some kisses on his hip and the inside of his thigh. I returned to his cock and began sucking again in earnest. AJ cried out, cursing and begging. His fingers raked into my hair but remained gentle on my head.

He kept calling me baby, and the word zapped me in the fucking heart every time he said it. I deep throated him and swallowed, finally pushing him over the edge until he shuddered and came down my throat.

"Oh my god," he murmured. "Oh my *god.*"

He leaned forward and found my face in the dark with his hands to draw me up for a kiss on the mouth. "Dante, that was amazing."

AJ kissed me and I ended up straddling him where he still sat on the end of the bed. He felt so good.

"C'mere," he said, lifting me off his lap and moving me up the bed until my head was on the pillows. He moved back down and stripped my clothes off, running hands up my legs as he came back up to slip my shirt over my head.

"You feel amazing, Dante," he said with a rough voice. "I want to run my hands all over your body."

"Yes, please," I breathed, causing him to chuckle.

His hand moved down to cup my cock and I almost squeaked in excited relief. Instead, I pushed up into his hand with my hips. He groaned and wrapped his fingers around me, tugging. I spread my legs apart to give him easier access. After getting revved up sucking his dick, I wanted him to return the favor so badly I was willing to cry like a baby to make it happen.

AJ's mouth nibbled on my neck and I began to tremble with antic-ipation and excitement. My cock was so hard it dripped, and my balls already felt tight. His long fingers stretched out to stroke them, and I was wracked with a full-body shudder.

"AJ, *fuck*, please just—" I whimpered.

His mouth crushed mine again. I was breathless with need. "Just what, baby? What do you want, beautiful Dante?" he whispered. "Anything. It's all yours."

I felt my eyes sting as his tender words brushed over me. "You," I breathed.

He moved to kiss his way back down my chest as I groaned with relief. Once his mouth landed on my stiff cock, I was practically done for. He took several sucks and pulls before sticking a finger in his mouth and then sliding it down to press against my ass. I vaguely wondered if I could still enjoy a slim finger now that I'd had a deli-cious fat cock up there. What if it wasn't the same and I no longer enjoyed the finger? What if—?

Holyfuckingshit. My entire body arched with delicious pleasure.

"Again, more, please," I begged, grabbing for his hand to press it tighter to me.

AJ smiled up at me and raised an eyebrow at me. "You like that, huh?"

He slid his long finger in farther this time and my eyes rolled back in my head as hot cum shot out of me, landing all over my chest and even on my shoulder.

I vaguely noticed his wide-eyed reaction before a satisfied smirk overtook his face.

My breathing was strained and irregular as I struggled to regain my composure.

"Jesus, you're so beautiful when you come, Dante," he murmured against my ear as he ran fingers through the trail of fluid on my front.

I turned my head to kiss him on the lips. "Thank you," I said with a smile.

He brought a hand up to brush my hair away from my face. "Stay here," he said before getting up and retrieving a towel from the bathroom. He wiped me down before climbing into bed beside me.

"This okay?" he asked. "Can I hold you for a bit before we go?"

"Of course," I said, shocked he even had to ask. Couldn't he tell I was nuts for him?

He wrapped his body around mine and pulled me in tight. "Mmm, I love holding you like this," he rumbled.

"Mmm-hmm," I murmured, realizing I'd gone from feeling freaked to feeling relaxed and happy.

THE RELAXED FEELING wore off about the same time we crossed the city limits into Gordon and I was thrown back into my childhood. Everything looked the same as it had growing up. Hardly anything at all had changed in eight years. Maybe it would have been easier if it had. Seeing it the same as it had always been made me feel like I was that kid again.

I navigated to my old street by memory. The house had been freshly painted and looked more vibrant than I remembered. There was an unfamiliar pair of vehicles in the driveway, and I realized belatedly they'd have different cars by now.

Once we parked, AJ reached a hand out to take mine, and I automatically jerked mine away from him before realizing what I'd done.

His eyes widened in shock, and we just sat there, staring at each other.

"F-freak. I'm so sorry," I croaked. "I'm so sorry, AJ."

He stared at me for another beat before his face relaxed and he pulled his hand back to his lap. "No, Dante, I'm the one who's sorry. I don't want to make you feel uncomfortable, okay? No touching. I got it. And I'm staying in the car like you asked."

"AJ—"

"I know, babe," he said quietly. "It's okay, I promise."

My chin trembled because I was downright terrified. "I can't do this," I whispered, glancing up at him with what surely looked like desperation in my eyes. "Can we please go home?"

I could see he was upset too, but he tried to hide it. "Dante Marian, you are one of the bravest men I know. You can do anything you set your mind to. I'll be right here waiting for you."

My teeth came out to rake over my lip as I nodded. "Okay."

I got out of the car on shaky legs before making my way to the porch. It was very strange to knock on the front door of a house you'd lived in for fifteen years without having to knock first. But it was no longer my home, so I knocked and waited.

The faded red brick beneath my shoes was so familiar, I felt like I could trace the cement grout with my fingertips by memory. The door opened and I stood face to face with my biological mother.

My hand shot out to grab the wrought-iron railing beside me, and I gripped it as tightly as I could. My mother stood there, looking at me in confusion for a few moments until her eyes widened with dawning recognition, like she was looking at a ghost which, of course, she was.

I cleared my throat. "Um, hi. It's, ah, Daniel."

"*Richard,*" she shouted without taking her eyes off me. It might have been the only time I'd ever heard her shout, and I jumped in surprise. My heart felt like it would burst through my chest and take off on flapping wings through the golden silver maple tree in the yard.

"What?" I heard him yell back, and all my blood went cold. I felt dizzy with fear, and its intensity hit me all at once. I glanced over to the car and got a nod of encouragement from AJ. I thought about waving frantically at him to come the heck over there and help me, but I refrained.

"Ah, could I maybe, come in for a few minutes?" I started to add, "mom," to the end of the question but the word froze in my mouth. Apparently I couldn't bring myself to call her anything. What did I call her when she hadn't been my mom for all those years? Janet? Ugh.

She turned out of polite habit and led me to the formal living room where she took a seat on the floral chintz sofa. There were a pair of matching sky blue wingback chairs on either side of the sofa and I chose one to keep myself separated from her.

Just after I sat down, *he* came rushing around the corner asking, "What is it?"

He came to a complete stop when he saw me and his mouth fell open.

We stared at each other for a few moments until he muttered, "Well, I'll be."

My mother—I mentally shook my head, *Janet* I reminded myself —wrung her hands and kept popping up from where she sat perched on the very edge of her spot on the sofa. "Should I get some...? I mean, would you like something to drink?" She seemed nervous and unsure, which shouldn't have come as a surprise to anyone, but she also seemed to be teetering between Janet, the woman who did what the reverend said, and Janet, the woman who'd lost her only child eight long years ago.

Finally she cracked and lurched at me, wrapping her arms around my neck and going in for a hug.

"Oh!" I squeaked. It took all my self-control not to throw her away from me. Instead, I ducked away from the hug as quickly as I could and shrunk away from her, farther into my chair. "Ah, yes, please. Some water would be good," I said.

I could see the hurt in her eyes, but she nodded and left the room.

Then it was just the two of us. Me and the man himself. I felt like I might be sick all over the carpet.

"So, Daniel. You're back," he began with a suspicious look in his eyes. "What do you want?"

I cleared my throat. I could do this. AJ told me I was brave, right? I could do this.

"Yes. I'm back. I want to talk to you about your campaign," I said.

His eyes narrowed. "Whatever you're thinking about, don't you dare," he warned, taking me by surprise.

Eight years ago I would have cowered at his tone. But now I held my ground. "You need to withdraw your bid for Congress and stay out of politics," I told him. "If you do that and stop your abusive conversion therapy practices, I'll never bother you again."

He bit out a laugh. "Ha! Or what? You think one visit from my long-lost wayward son is going to convince me to give up the chance to make a real difference in this country? Do you have any idea how many people agree with me and are just waiting for me to help turn things around?"

I felt my hands curl into fists and I forced them flat. "Before I came here, I thought of how I would respond to any argument you'd come up with and then I realized nothing I say is going to change your beliefs. So it's a waste of breath. If you do not end your campaign within a week, I'll book an interview on national television."

I stood up to leave, having said what I came there to say.

"Sit," his voice boomed. Before the word was even fully pronounced, my ass was in the chair out of habit, and I hated myself for it.

I felt my nostrils flare as I looked up at him.

His expression was smug and it brought back many memories of times I'd seen that arrogance before. "You think I don't know what happened to you that night, Daniel?" he asked.

"It's Dante now," I said defiantly.

He laughed again. "Right. Dante *Marian*."

Hearing that word out of his mouth was like hearing a baby cry in an abandoned building—unexpected and downright chilling.

I felt my jaw tighten and my nostrils flare as I realized just how easily he could still throw me off-guard with a few simple words. "How do you know my name?" I asked.

He leaned back and crossed his arms, drawing out his next words for maximum effect. "Son, I've known where you were since a month after you left. The homosexual capital of the world, San Francisco."

The revelation was a punch in the gut. "And you didn't come look for me?"

"Why should I have? You were an embarrassment. You brought all of this on yourself and then you had the selfish audacity to involve your family. Time after time we gave you chances to change. We tried everything. Spent thousands of dollars to send you to the best programs, and for what? So you could humiliate us by throwing yourself at one of the football players?" He said the last part with disgust, as if he had actual dirt on his tongue.

He leaned toward me, a cold smile spreading across his lips. "When your mother confessed to what she'd done, calling that man to come get you, I had half a mind to thank her. Suddenly we didn't have to deal with you always trying to be the center of attention and we could concentrate on what we were sent here on earth to do."

I sat there in shock, not even knowing where to begin. My brain was still cycling well enough to realize Janet had not come back with the water. Shouldn't have surprised me, really. She knew her place while the reverend conducted business.

"So, that's it then," I said. "I guess there's no need to wait. I'll just go ahead with the interview." I stood and started toward the door.

"Oh, I don't think you will, actually." It was the tone of his voice that caused me to hesitate. Lawton stood, strolling closer. "You wouldn't want me to out AJ Flores as a drug-addicted homosexual kidnapper, now would you?"

I whipped around to stare at him.

"What?" I sputtered. "That's just ridiculous. You're grasping at straws."

"You don't think I did my own opposition research before announcing my candidacy? I know all about your life, *Dante*."

He moved to the window, glancing toward the rental car and AJ sitting inside. "Your, ah, *friend* there has a juvenile record. I'm a state congressman and half my friends are in law enforcement. I can get my hands on any information I want. He was convicted of drug possession. And that was before he stole my son from the house of the Lord and indoctrinated him into the homosexual lifestyle. And, for all we know, that pervert is still doing things like that today."

He clasped his hands behind his back and shrugged, feigning innocence. "Why, just last week someone took a photo of him bringing a nice young boy to a known den of homosexuals. The boy was reported as missing from his church retreat compound."

He pointed out the window toward AJ. "*That man steals young boys from churches and turns them gay.* How do you think that's going to play out in your little television interview?"

I stood frozen, completely shell shocked.

"You can't prove any of that," I blurted. "That's the most ridiculous, grasping—"

"Who in the world do you think my family values constituents here in Indiana are going to believe, Daniel? A raging homosexual who works to encourage young people to embrace the lifestyle there in San Francisco or a trusted, dedicated servant of the church and well-respected congressman of the great state of Indiana?"

My mouth hung open and not a single word came out. I was having a hard time breathing.

Then his entire demeanor changed and he smiled again. "Now listen, I don't want to argue with you after all this time. I'd be happier if we could make amends and somehow work together to try and clean up this country's woes. But first, I need you to think about what you want. If your goal is to help kids, maybe you're better off letting AJ keep his job and rescue children in need. If you interfere with my campaign, he'll no longer be able to do that, and I'll be replaced on the ticket with someone just like me."

He clapped a hand on my shoulder and squeezed painfully tight.

Tears sprang to my eyes and, as I'd done a million times before in front of that man, I silently begged them not to overflow and show my weakness.

"Think about it before you do something stupid, son."

Just then, my moth— Janet, came back in the room with fake cheer just like she always had. I couldn't help but feel betrayed by her for being so weak and staying with him while he continued his awful bigotry. How could she have stayed with him all this time?

"Dante here was just saying he wanted to join us for Sunday services tomorrow, isn't that right, son?"

I clenched my fists and walked out the door.

AJ

Waiting for Dante to walk out of that house was excruciating. It took forever, and there was absolutely no end in sight. Then, suddenly, he was there.

The guy was white as a ghost and his legs worked double time. I'd already shifted to the driver's seat in anticipation of an emotional exit so I started the ignition and pulled out the moment his door was closed.

He breathed heavily and shook, but I didn't dare reach over to touch him, even though I was desperate to. He'd freaked out when I'd tried to hold his hand earlier, so I gave him some space to catch his breath as I focused on getting us out of there as quickly as I could.

A few minutes outside of town, Dante pointed to a small unpaved road and told me to pull over. He got out of the car and stumbled into the grass as if he was going to be sick. I bolted after him as fast as I could, standing beside him and resting my hand on his back. Thankfully, nothing came up and he stayed there, bent over with his hands on his knees.

"Oh shit," I muttered, returning to the car to grab a bottle of water from the cupholder. He was bawling by the time I got back and he turned to face away from me, holding a hand back to stop me from coming closer.

"I'm not staying away from you right now," I told him. "*Please* don't make me stay away from you right now."

He turned the saddest eyes on me I'd ever seen. I grabbed him and held him against me.

We didn't speak. I simply let him cry it out until the sobs wound down and his breathing was steady again. When he spoke, his voice was hoarse.

"He knew where I was the whole time," he said in a whisper. "And he never came for me."

That cruel bastard.

"Oh, baby," I said, cupping the back of his head. "I'm so sorry."

I kissed the side of his head before continuing in a softer voice. "I think it was probably a good thing he didn't come for you. Don't you agree?"

I felt him nod his head against my chest. "That's not the point," he said. "Of course I'm glad I ended up with the Marians. But how the hell is that supposed to make me feel?"

I stroked his hair with my fingers the way I knew he liked. "Do you want to tell me what happened?"

"He's a monster."

I certainly wasn't going to argue with that. After waiting a little while to see if he wanted to say more, I realized he was worn out and most likely still processing what happened. "Come on. Let's get back to the hotel and order room service. We can talk if you want or not talk if you don't want. It's up to you."

He didn't let go for a few more minutes until finally he pulled away. "Okay. Let's go."

ONCE WE WERE BACK at the hotel and room service arrived, we sat at the small table in the room and ate in our pajamas. Dante had on a hoodie sweatshirt and seemed to be treating it like a turtleshell.

He wound up telling me more of what Lawton had said to him, and I was as shocked as he was. I couldn't believe that bastard tried to use me and our relationship against him.

"Are you fucking kidding me?" I barked. Dante jumped in his seat and glared at me. "Sorry. But what a presumptuous bastard. I mean, Jesus Christ."

Dante snorted. "If only he could hear you say the lord's name in vain. That would just add to the rosy picture he painted of you."

Now it was my turn to glare. "He can kiss my *homosexual* ass."

Dante laughed again. "I should have told him I've kissed your homosexual ass many times. And liked it."

"You should have. We should go back tomorrow and tell him," I suggested. "Because there are a few other things I'd like to tell him as well."

I didn't realize the hard edge that had crept into my voice until Dante reached over and grabbed my hand. "Calm down. Just... I'm fine, okay? It's over."

I got up to put the dishes outside the room while Dante crawled onto the bed. Even though I grumbled about it, I reluctantly agreed. "We're not going to church tomorrow, are we?" I asked.

A pillow came out of nowhere and caught me in the back of the head. "Ow!"

"Hell no we're not going to church tomorrow, asshole."

"Thank fuck," I muttered before climbing in beside him. "I'm a little rusty on my New Testament."

"That wouldn't be a problem. Reverend Lawton thinks that part is more of an optional epilogue. He concentrates more on the first bit. The 'older and wiser' section."

I shuddered. "That's too bad. The New Testament has some cool stuff in it—love, forgiveness, doing unto others. Radical notions, you know?"

Dante nodded. "Enough about that. I need escapist fantasy. What movie do you want to watch?"

I grabbed the remote out of his hand and flipped through the options.

"Anything with Wentworth Miller," I suggested. Dante turned to me with a scowl.

"Nice, jackass."

"What? You don't think he's hot as shit?"

"Of course I think he's hot as shit."

I turned and pointed my index finger in his face. "Hold up. You agree the guy is fuckable, yet I'm not allowed to say it out loud?"

"How about something with Orlando Bloom?" he suggested.

"If he has long blond hair and pointy ears, yes. Otherwise, no."

"Mark Wahlberg?" Dante asked.

"Marky Mark, yes. Mark Wahlberg, no. What about Matt Damon?"

"Gah, he's kinda old, don't you think?"

"Fuck, Dante—"

He turned to me with a huge grin and bright eyes. "Okay. Let's do that," he said before landing his mouth on mine.

38

———————

DANTE

s much as I wanted to put it off, I knew I was going to have to make a decision about how to deal with my father. But since the ultimatum he'd given me involved AJ, it wasn't something I could decide on my own. Not that I would have anyway.

AJ was all for me going to the press as planned, regardless of what that might mean for his reputation and career.

As much as I loved that he was willing to make that sacrifice for me, there was one other ultimatum from my father that I hadn't told him about. Before I left the house, my father had told me that if I didn't show up for Sunday service the next morning as the reunited prodigal son then he would go to the press with his own story.

He'd tell the world about the 'lost sheep of his flock' and how I'd run away to San Francisco to be with all the queers.

I'd recognized the emotional manipulation right away and knew there was no way I would ever step foot in his church again. I'd have to let the chips fall where they may.

But that meant I spent the next two weeks anxiously waiting to see if my father planned to follow through with his threat. It didn't help that AJ kept getting called out of town on work trips. He still checked in every spare moment, wanting to make sure I was ok, and I assured him I was fine.

Then on Friday, two weeks after I'd confronted my father, the other shoe dropped. A reporter from one of the big cable news shows called and asked if I wanted to join my father for his prime time interview the next night.

They made it sound like they were genuinely interested in hearing my story, but it was obvious they were really hoping to juice the ratings by pitting me and Richard Lawton against each other across the interview couch. No way, no thanks.

I turned them down, but the thought of my father telling those lies on TV made me feel ill. I spent the rest of the day waiting for AJ to return from his trip and alternating between vowing to forget all about the interview and wondering if I should warn my family.

So it was no surprise that when AJ arrived from the airport that evening I lost my shit.

"Come on. We have to go to my parents' house," I said, grabbing his hand and turning him around in the doorway to my apartment. "Just leave your stuff."

"Huh? What?" he said, dropping his bag and following me. "What's happening?"

"Why didn't you answer your phone at the airport?" I asked as we made our way downstairs and out to my car.

"Battery died. Remember I fell asleep with the line open last night? I didn't get to charge it before my meeting this morning."

"Lawton is going on television tomorrow night," I blurted. "We have to warn my family."

"What? Jesus Christ, Dante, I knew this would happen. Why didn't you beat him to the punch?" He slammed the seatbelt into its clasp and ran his hand through his hair before slapping his hand down on the dash. "Goddammit."

Instead of yelling back at him, I stayed quiet and drove.

After a few minutes, he reached over and put his hand on the back of my neck. "I'm sorry, Dante. I shouldn't have yelled at you. How are you feeling about all this?"

I blew out a breath. "Shitty, honestly. Pretty damned shitty."

"What do you think he's going to say?"

"If he so much as mentions your name, he's done. There's nothing to hold me back once he does that. I'll go fucking apeshit," I confessed. And, truly, that was my biggest fear.

"Weren't you planning on doing that anyway?" he asked.

I clenched my teeth. "I don't know."

AJ said nothing, and I could tell he was trying very carefully to keep his cool.

"Maybe he is stepping down. Maybe this interview is his announcement."

"Dante, what did the network person say when they called you?" AJ asked. "Because it would seem to me if they called you at all, it's a clear indication he's not stepping down quietly. He's talking to them about Daniel."

"Maybe he's stepping down, not quite so quietly," I suggested, knowing I was full of crap. "Maybe he's going to spin some BS about stepping down because he's just been reunited with his son and he needs family privacy at this time."

AJ looked at me with such disappointment in his eyes I almost couldn't take it. Luckily, he turned to look out the window so I didn't have to see it anymore.

We drove the rest of the way in silence, and when we got to my parents' house in the suburbs, Mom and Dad were finishing up a late dinner with Simone, Jude, and Derek.

"Look who's here," Mom said with a big smile when I let myself in the front door. She got up to come around the table for a hug and kiss and I held on to her for a few extra beats. When she pulled back, her brows were furrowed. "You okay, sweetie?"

I nodded. "Yeah, kind of. Well, not really. Actually, no. Listen, I need to talk to you guys about something important. Am I interrupting anything? Sorry for showing up unannounced like this."

"Nonsense," Dad said. "This is your home, Dante, have a seat. Hi, AJ. How was your trip to LA?"

I looked at AJ. How the hell did my parents know he'd been to LA for work?

"It was good. Thanks for setting that up." AJ turned to me. "Your dad connected me with a youth organization in LA that tries to keep tabs on runaways. Sometimes we get their parents as clients. Anyway, tell them your news. Want me to grab you a drink?"

I nodded. "Just water, thanks."

He helped himself to a beer and bottle of water from the kitchen before returning to sit around the dining room table. I secretly felt a little giddy he was comfortable enough at my parents' house to help himself to the drinks. It felt like a serious relationship thing. Not that I would ever say something so silly out loud, of course, but I enjoyed it nonetheless.

After taking a deep breath, I began. "I've never told you guys where I came from, but it's getting ready to be made national news tomorrow night, so... I can't keep it a secret anymore."

My parents' faces showed concern, and Mom reached out to put her hand on my arm.

"You know whatever you have to tell us will not change how much we love you, right?" she said.

"Unless you're really a Kardashian, in which case I can't decide if I'd love you more or less," Simone said.

"A Kardashian, Simone?" Jude interjected. "Really? With that ass? Please."

Simone shrugged but then nodded in agreement.

AJ finished taking a sip of his beer and couldn't let that slide. "Watch your mouth. The man has a stellar ass."

Simone and Jude shuddered in disgust while Derek nodded in agreement.

"Thanks for that, I guess," I said. "Anyway, my biological father... wait. I don't even know where to start this." I looked at AJ. "Where do I start?"

He looked at my family. "Well, you know the part from his speech at the gala. He was raised by a harsh man. He grew up in a little town in Indiana. He was the only child of a very powerful preacher who led an extreme congregation."

"Kind of a fundamentalist," I added, feeling nervous and scattered. "And his beliefs were very old school." I looked back to AJ for help. "I can't—"

He reached over to hold my hand. "It's okay, baby. Take your time. Everyone in here loves you."

I swallowed, wondering if he was including himself in that statement. "He was, ah, physically and emotionally abusive--"

"Extremely abusive," AJ added.

I nodded. "And when I started being attracted to boys, it got much worse. He sent me to conversion camps, but when that didn't work, he and his friends tried making their own conversion happen in the church basement."

I avoided eye contact with my family members because I knew I couldn't take whatever looks they had on their faces. Whether they looked at me with love or pity, I knew it would wreck me and I wouldn't be able to continue.

"I was very isolated," I added. "I only had friends through the church group and church events. But that included most of the town. My biological father was also the town mayor, and his best friends were the cops, the doctor, the judge. You get the idea."

"Honey, what about your mother?" Mom asked. "Didn't she look out for you?"

I shook my head. "No. Not until the last day. I'd been at a church car wash with the other teens on a Saturday. There was this boy there who'd flirted with me on and off for weeks. I kept trying to ignore him, not because I wasn't interested, but because I was afraid if we were caught, he'd become a target of the same conversion efforts. His dad was definitely not the kind of guy who'd be open minded about his son liking boys. Anyway, after the car wash he asked if I'd walk home with him. I was going that way anyway. We walked past the high school just chatting, you know? I asked him what it was like at public school and everything. Suddenly, he stopped to ask if he could kiss me. So I said yes."

I took a sip from my water bottle. "It seemed like as soon as our lips touched, I was jumped. The entire football team ambushed me."

It was still so embarrassing to remember.

"I was an idiot. To this day I don't know if it was a setup or not. But either way, I knew—*I knew*—nothing good could come of it. Kissing that kid."

AJ scooted his chair closer and put his arm around me, pulling me in and taking over. "He ended up with broken ribs and three broken fingers. Black eyes, a cut on his face, you name it. A cop found him shortly after, but instead of taking him for medical attention, he took him to dear ole dad over at the church."

I squeezed his leg. "I guess that's when my mother finally thought enough was enough. She hired AJ's dad's extraction company to get me out."

AJ explained what that meant and told them about delivering me to his sister Kelly, who was a doctor. Kelly had patched me up and then flown me to Londa.

Simone was flabbergasted, which was a rare occasion. "So AJ was the one who brought you here all those years ago? I thought you just met at the gala."

I let out a laugh. "Same here. I had no idea AJ was the same guy who rescued me. Not until after Vegas," I said.

"And that's why you broke up," Dad said, giving me a sympathetic smile. "You were angry."

I nodded.

"So what's tomorrow night?" Simone asked, bringing us back around to the purpose of my visit.

My lips twisted. "Tomorrow night my biological father is going on national television to tell the world *his* side of the story. Or what he claims is his side. In reality he plans to lie about it all. Anything to get elected, of course."

I wasn't sure what kind of reaction I expected from my family. I knew they loved me and I hoped my story wouldn't change that. Even so, a small part of me was still worried. I'd spent my first fifteen years with parents who cared so little for me that they didn't even bother to come after me when I disappeared.

Sometimes, it was still difficult to believe I could be worthy of love.

Of course my mother knew exactly what to say to dispel all my fears. She straightened, her expression fierce as she leaned across the table and placed a strong hand on my arm. "Dante Marian, you tell us what you need us to do."

Jude and Simone nodded while Derek clutched his hands into fists so hard his knuckles cracked.

My chin wobbled at the reminder that I was no longer Daniel Lawton, but Dante Marian. And being a Marian meant unconditional love and acceptance.

I let out a wobbly laugh, my heart so full it almost burst. "Just be my family," I told them.

My father reached across the table, laying one hand on my arm and the other on AJ's shoulder. "Always. We love you, son."

Tears pricked my eyes and AJ pressed a kiss to my temple, squeezing me tight against his side.

"Besides," Simone snorted. "You couldn't get rid of us if you tried."

39

AJ

I was proud of Dante. Despite how difficult it was, he told his parents everything and let them love him afterward. When we got back to the apartment, he seemed lighter. We were in his room getting into bed when I realized he was way chattier than usual.

"Part of me feels like I should have done that sooner, you know? It kind of feels like I held this big piece of myself back from them all this time. I never saw it that way. I just wanted to keep my past in my past."

"They definitely seemed relieved to finally know where you came from. And knowing them, they're off group-texting some kind of massive Marian support rally for their baby boy," I teased. "You know being at their place tomorrow during the broadcast is going to be insane."

"Ugh, don't remind me," he muttered, peeling off his shirt and dropping it into a laundry basket on the floor. At the sight of his angel tattoo, my dick woke up and took an interest in what was happening.

"I was surprised you agreed to go over there. I thought you were going to skip watching it altogether."

His hands moved to the button on his jeans, and I stopped what I was doing to watch.

"I was. I don't want to see that bastard spouting a bunch of bull-shit about me. It's just going to upset me," Dante said as he lowered his zipper and shimmied the jeans down his lean legs.

"We don't have to go," I reminded him. "You can still say it's too much."

"Nah, it's important to Mom and Dad. If I'm there, they'll know I'm not standing on a bridge somewhere." It was a joke, but it still squeezed my heart.

"Do you want to call Dr. Elkins?" I asked softly. "Maybe get an appointment for Monday just in case you want to talk to her?"

He looked up in surprise before his face softened into a smile. "Already done. But thank you, AJ. That's very thoughtful. I hope you're not really worried about me like that. I'm okay."

"I know. I just want to make sure you stay okay. This is going to be hard."

Dante walked over to me and took my hands. "You don't have to stick around for all this shit, you know. It's a lot. I would totally understand if you wanted to take a step back for a little bit."

I couldn't decide if his words made me sad or angry. "Dante, what the hell? Do you think I'm the kind of person who bails when things get rough?"

He put a hand on my chest. "Calm down. I just wanted you to know I'd understand. This is a pretty shitty thing to be going through when you're just starting out in a new relationship. We've only been together for, like, ten seconds. Like I said, it's a lot to deal with this early on."

I slid my arms around his waist. "Dante, you've been in my heart for eight years; you just didn't realize it. And unlike the Marians, for those entire eight years, I *have* known about your past. This is not new for me. The only part that's new is finally having you on board too. And I hate to break it to you, but I'm not going anywhere." I smiled at him. "So now, if you don't mind, I'd like to see your butt. Preferably naked and elevated with a neon sign blinking the word 'enter' with a big-ass arrow pointing to your—"

Dante laughed and slapped my chest. "I got it. Horny much?"

"What? You don't want that? Okay. How about just show me your dick? I'd be cool with that too. Or I could show you mine."

"Ooooo, I'd like that. I've never seen a grown man's cock before. Will it scare me?" he teased, running fingertips up and down my chest.

"It's big for sure, so it might. Mine is pretty intimidating actually. Maybe if you touched it before looking right at it…"

My hands moved to my own fly and I began undoing buttons.

"I don't know, AJ. What if it comes at me? I've heard those things can stab people over and over."

"Have you ever heard the expression 'hurts so good'? It's kind of like that. It's a good stab. Here, let me show you." I shucked off my pants and underwear, shedding clothes until I was naked and stroking my own cock in front of him.

He bugged out his eyes when he looked down at my moving hands and clapped a hand over his mouth dramatically before dissolving into a fit of laughter.

"I'm sorry, AJ. I'm way too turned on to keep this up. Can we just get to the fucking?"

I looked at him like he was crazy. "The answer to that question will always be yes."

Dante removed the rest of his clothes and walked over to his bedside table to get out condoms and lube.

I stroked my cock some more as I watched his bare back and ass move. He had the kind of ass I couldn't keep my eyes off. I wanted to lick it and bite it, fuck it over and over until I couldn't move.

"I can feel you staring at my butt," he said over his shoulder.

"That's only because you know me so well. As if you'd ever present your naked ass to me and I wouldn't stare."

"How do you want me?" he asked.

There were so many ways I could answer that question.

From behind, on your back, riding me, sitting on my face, happy, healthy—

By my side forever.

I groaned. "Whichever way makes you feel good, babe. Any way is fucking fantastic for me."

Dante lay back on the bed, pulling me on top of him before bringing his hands up to my face and cupping my cheeks so he could pull me down for a kiss. We kissed like that for a long time, deep, meaningful kisses meant to seal unspoken promises made of love, steady companionship, commitment.

When he pulled away, his eyes were dark and sparking with desire. Our cocks lay full and ready between us, and I wanted to roll my belly along his hard shaft to make him moan.

I felt his hands slide down my back to grasp my ass cheeks and I hummed in appreciation. I loved it when he grabbed my ass. And I'd noticed over time the action was more decisive, like he owned it.

"I want you, Dante," I whispered.

He rolled me over and began to trail wet kisses down the side of my neck, my chest, my abdomen, and to my cock.

"Yes," I hissed, arching up into his hot mouth. "Suck my cock. Fuck, that feels amazing." I groaned. I ran my fingers through the smooth strands of his hair.

His hand clasped my balls as his nose began a path between my cock and my thigh until his tongue took the place of the hand on my sack. Dante pushed my legs up to my ears.

Within moments, his tongue was inside me and I was crying out ridiculousness about his magic mouth. I reached back over my head to grab the pillow so I could bite it. That was the only microsecond's thought I gave to the fact Dante had roommates who didn't need to hear AJ's rim job in surround sound.

When he slowed down, I flipped him back over and returned the favor, chuckling between sucks and nips on his ass out of sheer happiness we were alone together and naked. Dante looked dazed after a few minutes, and by the time I was ready to slide into him, he was halfway blissed out and begging for it.

I suited and lubed up before stretching up to check in with him higher on the bed. "You okay, baby?" I asked with a grin.

"Nuh-uh. Get your dick in my ass," he said gruffly. "Don't be a cocky bastard."

I nudged my cock against his ass and his eyes rolled up.

"Fuck me, *please*," he begged, trying to shove his ass onto me at the same time my hands tried to hold him steady.

"I can't wait to get into your hot little body," I said, teasing him with a slap of my dick against his desperate hole.

"Prove it," he growled.

I leaned in and put my mouth next to his ear while I pressed my cock firmly against his entrance. "You're the most beautiful man I've ever met, Dante Marian." And then I thrust forward.

"*Gahhhhhh*," he cried. "Yes. Oh god, *yes*."

I began to move and he began to whimper. My hips rolled in a languid teasing dance that drove him to the edge of sanity. All the while I thrust into him, he locked his eyes on mine and kept them there. It was the most intense lovemaking I could ever imagine. By the time I worked up my pace to a fevered pitch, tears smarted in Dante's eyes and my heart felt like it was going to explode.

"Angel," he whispered.

My hand stroked his cock as his tight channel made my entire body feel like it was going to turn inside out when I came. I remember him crying out my name and hitting himself in the chin with cum as I pushed even deeper one last time for my own release.

After it was over and I'd cleaned us up, we lay in a stupor together just enjoying the relaxed feeling of satisfaction in each other's arms.

I wound up tracing his angel tattoo with my finger.

"Mmm, feels good, Angel," he mumbled, turning to kiss the top of my head before drifting off to sleep.

My heart squeezed at the sound of my name on his tongue, and I knew I'd never tire of falling asleep in Dante Marian's arms.

THE FOLLOWING night we gathered at the Marians' for the broadcast. I sat on one of the big sofas in the family room and held Dante tucked against my side the entire time. He stayed very quiet, and his family gave him a wide berth. I got the sense they were used to his moments of withdrawal and knew how to handle him with kid gloves.

Tilly, Granny, and Irene were there, which ended up being a good thing because they took the spotlight off Dante. Granny wound up telling everyone about Tilly's recent booty call with Senator Cannon.

Griff laughed. "Really, Aunt Tilly? You're opening up that can of worms again?"

"He's a good lay. What do you want from me?" she muttered before taking a sip of her wine.

Jude choked on his tea and glanced at his husband, who just laughed. Thankfully, the little kids were all in the back of the house with Pete's girls.

"So he takes her to some winery in Napa and she spends the entire time bitching about their substandard varietals," Granny said, rolling her eyes. "The woman clearly doesn't know when to keep her mouth shut."

Irene shot a look at Granny.

"What?" Granny asked.

"Pot, this is kettle, you're black."

The entire room erupted with laughter, which was a welcome stress reliever. Finally Blue piped up. "That man seriously took you to someone else's vineyard? Which one?"

"How the hell should I know? Besides, we spent the whole time in the room anyway. Less grapes, more nuts if you know what I—"

Thomas interrupted her. "Yes, Tilly. I believe we all know what you mean."

40

DANTE

I looked at the people gathered, grateful my family had the ability to both rally around a member in need and also do it with humor. By the time the interview began, I was relaxed into AJ's side on the sofa, sipping my second beer.

When the Lawtons appeared on screen, I felt the eyes of my family flicker between the TV and me. I kept my eyes forward, handing off my beer to AJ to set down for me.

"Tonight we're here with Reverend Richard Lawton and his wife, Janet Lawton. Reverend Lawton is currently a member of the Indiana state House of Representatives and is running for the US House of Representatives this fall. Reverend and Mrs. Lawton, welcome."

"Thank you, Marla, we're happy to be here," Richard Lawton said.

It was obvious he would be doing all the talking while his dutiful wife sat supportive and silent by his side.

"According to your campaign manager, you're running on a platform of family values and religious freedom. Is that right?"

"Yes," Lawton said. *He was clearly comfortable in front of the camera and launched seamlessly into his campaign pitch.*

"We come from a small town in Indiana that tries to keep the American family at the center of things. I believe if we can bring that same focus back

to America on a national level, it will help solve some of the cultural destruction happening in our country today."

"Define what you mean when you say 'cultural destruction,'" the interviewer asked.

"Well, Marla, right now in our country we're dealing with so many negative influences tearing families apart—drugs, sex, pornography, the Internet, social media. Kids today are being ripped away from their families at a young age by strong external influences outside their control. It's up to the American government to step in and help families fight back."

"And how do you propose doing that? What type of changes would you like to see happen if elected to Congress?"

The interviewer lobbed a few softball questions, letting Lawton spout his talking points before getting to the meat of the interview.

She leaned toward him, a gleam in her eye and I held my breath, knowing what question was coming next.

"Reverend Lawton, you've also fought publicly against gay marriage and gay adoption rights. Would you like to tell our viewers more about that?"

"Yes, thank you. This is a subject close to my heart, actually. My wife, Janet, and I have experienced firsthand how homosexuality can destroy a family. You see, our only child, Daniel, was lured down the path of homosexual tendencies at a young age. Despite homeschooling and keeping a close eye on him, he somehow got access to information tempting him to explore same-sex attraction.

"When he was only fifteen years old, he disappeared from our lives. At the time—this was eight years ago—I was the mayor of Gordon and was able to use the entire might of our law enforcement resources to look for him."

Marla frowned. "But he was never recovered, isn't that right?"

"That's right. You know, Marla, we were devastated. To lose your only child at such a tender age is truly heartbreaking. And I'll be honest, my faith in the Lord was tested. I knew He was testing me, and yet I struggled to determine why. What was I supposed to learn from this? It took me a while, but I finally figured it out."

"And what was that?" Marla asked.

"He took my only son away to light a fire under me. A fire to work hard to make sure no other family loses their child to these horrible influences."

The camera panned out and showed Janet Lawton dabbing at tears and nodding along. The interviewer continued after a beat.

"Reverend Lawton, you've gained national attention for your support of conversion therapy camps. Can you tell us a little more about that? Do you think it would have helped in the case of your own son?"

"It did work for Daniel. We saw a drastic change in him after camp, and he worked hard to live his life on the straight and narrow. But one night after a church event, another boy in town made a pass at him. It's my understanding that when Daniel rebuffed the boy's advances, the kid beat him up. It was awful. If only you'd seen my poor boy. We think it was just too much for him. He'd fought so hard for so long. Four days later, our Daniel was gone."

At that point, Reverend Lawton looked up from his clasped hands straight into the camera.

"So you see? Saving our country's children is crucial to keeping the family together and protecting our future. Once I'm elected to the US House of Representatives, I will make it my mission to save this country's youth from the scourge of homosexuality and other alternative lifestyle choices. They are our future, and we have to protect them."

BY THE TIME the interview was over, I found myself planted face-first in AJ's armpit. I'd stopped watching at some point and turned my face into him to escape the sight of such hypocrisy.

I could feel AJ's entire body trembling with rage, and I reached one hand up to rest against the side of his neck. His pulse thundered under my thumb and I knew exactly how he felt.

"What a fucking megalomaniac asswipe!" Simone shouted, jerking everyone out of their stunned silence.

I didn't come out of my hiding spot to see, but I heard everyone start moving around and talking. AJ tightened his grip and curled his body around me.

After a good stern internal lecture, wherein I reminded myself I was a good person and being gay was okay, I began to calm down. It pissed me the hell off that my biological parents still had the power to make me feel small and wrong, but I at least had some coping skills now to fight against those feelings.

I took a breath, peeling myself out of AJ's pit and climbing onto his lap, right there in front of everyone. I'd never done anything so open and forward in front of my family in my life. I smiled at him and kissed him on the lips for all I was worth before leaning back and thanking him.

"What the hell?" he stammered in surprise. "That was unexpected."

"Just needed to see if it was all worth it," I said with a shrug.

"What do you mean?" he asked. I could see everyone watching us out of the corner of my eye.

"All of this, every single bit, is because I'm gay. Because I want to be with a man. Now that I have the man I want to be with, I just realized it was all worth it, Angel Flores." I leaned in and kissed him again—tongue and everything. His hands tightened around me as I felt his lips turn up in a smile.

I wanted to tell him I loved him, but that was something for him alone. Not something to share in front of my family on a night tinged with sadness.

After the kiss, my family started whooping and hollering, and my brothers kissed their husbands until finally Tilly lost her shit.

"Cut that crap out before I have to go find my Womanizer," she barked.

"It's probably in your purse," Irene said helpfully.

"No, it's not," Granny said around a mouthful of potato chips. "It's in mine."

41

———

AJ

A week later, Dante still hadn't publicly responded to the interview and I started to wonder if he was ever going to. I knew it wasn't my decision to make, but I hated seeing him still so afraid of his biological father. I wasn't even sure if he realized he was still letting Richard Lawton control him after all this time.

It didn't make sense to me. Dante was so strong, so passionate about protecting kids, so determined to stop this guy. So why was he staying silent?

Normally I wouldn't have pushed him on the issue. I'd have given him time to retreat and reconsider. But then I realized that wasn't fair to either of us. He wouldn't want me to tiptoe around him as though he wasn't capable of confronting these issues.

I finally decided I would ask him about it. I had a work trip that evening, but stopped by his office at Marian House on my way to the airport. I walked in to find him staring at his phone, an odd expression on his face.

"Everything ok?" I asked.

"Yeah," he said, looking up at me. "Tilly just called to tell me Senator Cannon invited her to fly to DC this weekend for a charity gala Saturday night. He's giving the keynote," Dante said. "Apparently Lawton is giving the introduction."

"You're kidding?" I asked.

"Nope."

"What's the charity?"

"America's Youth Service Coalition. It's a big catchall charity with programs for getting kids into volunteer work both to teach them how to contribute to society but also to help keep them out of trouble."

"I know it," I said with a smile. "It's a good organization."

"Yeah, I thought so too until I found out they picked such a homophobe to take the microphone," he said.

"Well, you know how those things work. Sometimes it's all about politics. Like if last year's keynote was given by a lefty, this year's might have to be given by a righty to keep both sides happy. They probably have one do the intro and the other give the speech then switch off the following year."

"I just can't believe that asshole has been given a microphone in the youth community. It grates on me, you know?"

I stood up to close his office door before turning to put my hands on his desk and lean down to make eye contact with him.

"Then why don't you do something about it, Dante?" I asked. "What are you waiting for?"

"Nothing," he said with a shrug. "I decided to stop fighting him."

I stood there and let the words replay in my mind before losing my cool. "Are you joking? Since when? Why?"

"Since the interview. Because I realized I can't win. No matter what I say, he'll come back and pervert it."

"You're kidding, right? You're giving up because, what? You think it won't work so why even bother? That's bullshit, and you know it."

He looked up at me, defiance clear in his brown eyes. "You don't understand, AJ."

"Really? Try me. Help me understand. Because right now it looks a lot like you're afraid."

"Good, now you finally believe what I've been trying to tell you.

Despite how many times you've tried saying otherwise, I'm not strong, AJ. I'm not the man you think I am."

I threw up my hands in frustration. "Bullshit. *Jesusfuckingchrist*, Dante. That man is still controlling you. This fear you have of him is so strong, it's still keeping you in chains. Don't you see that? You're afraid if you raise your head up too high, he's going to slap you back down again. You can't let him continue to ruin your life like this. Fight for what you believe in, goddammit. You've spent years fighting to support LGBT kids, and now you have the opportunity to keep an antigay politician out of Congress. Yet you're sitting here letting him intimidate you from afar."

Dante stood up from his chair and rested his hands on his desk. His eyes glittered with anger and part of me was happy to see it. Anger was powerful. Anger took action while fear ran away to hide.

"Fuck you, AJ. I'm doing this because I care about those kids. If I go public, then all that shit comes out about your past, and you no longer get to keep your job helping kids. Then what happens to those children who need your help, huh? What about those kids? And what about the kids here at Marian House who will be under the spotlight the minute my identity goes public? I *am* thinking about fighting for these kids, AJ. It's *all* I think about."

I put my hands on Dante's desk and leaned toward him until our noses were practically touching. "Don't you dare use me and the kids here at Marian House as an excuse for your inaction. If you're too chickenshit to speak out or if you've decided it's what's best for your own mental health, then own it, Dante. But don't make up a bunch of bullshit about doing what's best for the kids. Don't turn and run because that's the easier path. You're stronger than that and we both know it."

Dante's jaw clenched as he glared at me. "I don't need a lecture from you right now."

My phone buzzed in my pocket and I looked at the screen. It was a text from Joel asking if I was on my way to the airport.

"I have to go," I said. "Maybe you could use some time to think anyway."

"Maybe so."

"Dante—"

"Just go, AJ. I don't need this right now, I really don't. You're right. Maybe it's a good thing for us to get a little space."

I studied him, trying to determine if he was saying that out of anger or if he really meant it.

"Okay, goodbye, I guess." I turned to leave without touching him.

He sighed. "AJ, wait. Talk to me."

I felt a headache coming on and I realized it was from stress. I wasn't sure I could continue to watch Dante live in fear. He was riding a roller coaster that was fun and free one minute and twisted and scary the next. He deserved so much better than that, but no one could force him off the coaster but himself.

Was I willing to wait around to see when and if he ever made the change?

I threw my hands up. "I don't know how to make you see how strong you are. And I don't know if I can stay and watch you think less of yourself."

"What exactly are trying to say?" he asked. "That this is it between us?"

I blew out a big breath and threw my hands up. "I don't know, Dante."

"When will I see you again?"

"I don't know."

AJ was a controlling bastard. If he thought for one minute I would let him control me the way I'd let my biological father control me, he was an idiot. I didn't need another man with strong opinions in my life.

I left my office fuming mad. I was so angry at him for lecturing me and for acting like he would give up on me after so many times of saying he never would. Fucking asshole.

When I rounded the corner to the lobby, I almost took out Griff. "What the hell?" I barked.

After Griff stumbled back and caught his balance, he raised an eyebrow at me. "In a hurry?" he asked with a smirk.

"What do you want?" I snapped.

"Well, I was going to take you to Mom and Dad's for dinner, but now I want all the juicy details of your fight with the boyfriend."

"Who said we had a fight?" I asked, glaring at him.

"Well, considering I just saw AJ leave with smoke coming from his nostrils and now you just rammed into me and then blamed me for it…"

"Never mind," I muttered. "Nothing good is going to come out of my mouth right now."

"Come on," Griff said, grabbing me by the elbow. "You're coming with me to Mom and Dad's."

I let out a sigh, realizing I didn't have the energy to fight with yet another person I loved in the span of ten minutes. "Fine."

It wasn't until we arrived at our parents' house I realized it wasn't exactly a regular family dinner. It was another home party with Sally the Sex Toy Slinger.

I turned to Griff with a scowl as he burst out laughing. "What the hell, Griff? A sex toy party? Again?"

"Calm down. This one is all about the boys' toys—flavored lube, prostate massagers, cock rings. Come on, I'll grab us some beer so you can relax." He left me standing there while he headed to the kitchen.

"Make it a shot of tequila and you have a deal," I called after him.

THREE SHOTS, two beers, and one pair of edible underwear later, and I was feeling no pain. "Remind me again what sizes this comes in?" I asked, holding up what I thought was a bottle of the strawberry slick we'd sampled.

"That's the ketchup, Dante," Sam said.

"Oh, damn. You're right. I meant this," I said, holding up another bottle.

"That's your beer," Griff added helpfully.

"Shit."

"He means the strawberry lube," Tilly said from her spot in an overstuffed chair nearby. "That stuff goes great on toast in a pinch."

"Remind me again why you're here, old lady?" Blue asked her. He and Tristan had come to town for the event with Griff and Sam. Jude and Derek were there too, along with my roommates Robbie and Jason, and Griff's BFF Nico. Mom and Dad were at Pete's house with all the kids.

"Because Griff booked his party through me, I get free stuff. Isn't that right, Sally?" Tilly asked.

"Absolutely, depending on how much people purchase tonight, you'll earn Pecker Points to spend however you like," she said sweetly.

"I've got my eye on a few things," she said.

"I thought you were out of town?" I asked. "With the Tilly fucker."

Jude's jaw dropped and his eyes flashed to Tilly. "What the hell?" he asked.

"The president's whatever. You know. His cannon," I clarified.

"Where's AJ?" Derek asked.

"Hopefully in hell," I said. "Frotting."

"I think you mean, rotting," Griff said.

"Right. That's what I said. Fr...rotting." I looked at all the accouterments on the table. "What's this one do again?" I asked, pointing to one with lots of buttons.

"I think that works the television, dear," Sally said.

"You sell TVs?" I asked.

Griff put his arm around me. "Maybe it's time I took you home."

"Nah, I can wait for Jobbie and Rason. 'S fine."

I noticed Tilly studying me, and I wondered if she could tell my tongue was numb. Probably not.

"You should come with me," she said.

"Back to my place?" I asked. "Why?"

"No. To the gala."

"I don't understand," I said, wondering if maybe I was drunk.

"Harry suggested it, actually. Thought it might make me feel more comfortable if I brought a friend since he'll have to spend so much time schmoozing. I'd like to bring you. What do you say?"

"Ah, isn't it in DC?" I asked, remembering Richard Lawton was going to be there.

"Yes, but it's not a problem. I'll book you a ticket next to me in first class. We're leaving in the morning. Carl will pick you up at 10 a.m."

"Wait, what?" I asked.

"It's settled. I'll even buy you that strawberry lube you like. I'll order two bottles so you can keep one in the kitchen."

"I don't... what?" I looked over at Griff, who shrugged.

"Sounds like you're going to DC on a date with Tilly and the Senator, baby brother."

"But that asshole's going to be there," I said.

Tilly glared at me. "Don't call him that. He's been very good to me. And he looks mighty fine without his senator suit on."

"I think he means Richard Lawton," Jude said.

"Oh, that fucker. I know he's going to be there. Even more reason for you to go. If someone like him can get included in a fundraiser for America's youth, then someone like you ought to be there to balance the scales."

I had trouble following her logic in my state, but I knew no amount of arguing was going to dissuade her from dragging me along to DC. After a while, and most likely more drinks, I realized the DC gala would be the perfect event to prove to myself and everyone else that I was strong enough to be in the same room with Richard Lawton. I could do this.

Oh, fuck. I could *not* do this.

By the time I sobered up, I found myself in first class, and remembered vaguely spouting off about how I was brave and strong. I tried convincing Tilly it had all been a drunken mistake. She was in rare form and adamantly refused my reasons for not going.

"Stop trying, Dante. For god's sake. Think of this as a networking opportunity. The executive director of one of the preeminent youth charities in one of the country's biggest cities is attending a national gala for one of the country's biggest youth organizations. Yet you're sitting here sighing and fretting like I'm dragging you to the guillotine. Cut the crap and quit your bitching. This is important for your job so you need to suck it up. Plus, I demand a fun travel companion, and you're it."

I sighed. She was right. I needed to look at the gala like an opportunity to meet people who could help affect positive change for LGBT youth. Surely the gala would be big enough to avoid my biological father, and Tilly was right. The networking would be invaluable. I couldn't let Richard Lawton interfere with me doing my job. And, honestly, part of me wanted to prove to AJ that I was the man he thought I was.

I missed him so fucking much. Every part of me demanded that I fix things with him and make him understand that we were meant to be together. When I got home, I was going to force him to give us another chance.

"You're right. I'm sorry. I'll get my head on straight. Maybe I'm just hungry."

"You want a snack? I have an edible jockstrap in my purse," she offered. "It isn't very filling, to be honest. More like eating a Twizzler."

"This is first class, Aunt Tilly, surely they have something better than a jock for breakfast."

"It's black licorice flavor," she singsonged. As if that was going to sell me on it.

I shuddered. "Gross. No, thanks. Might as well be real jockstrap flavored."

"You know, Dante, there are going to be lots of politicians there at the gala. You could have conversations that could end up influencing policy."

The idea of having to meet so many big players that night had me on edge, and I wanted to change the subject. Thankfully, the flight attendant chose that moment to take our order for lunch and offer a snack. Because we were flying American Airlines, the snack was hot nuts. Before she had a chance to make a joke about it, I shot Tilly a glare. "Don't."

"Fine. But, speaking of hot nuts, Harry wants us to meet his kid." She opened the magazine on her lap and started flipping through it.

"Ah... uh... but isn't his kid the, um..." I stammered.

"Yes, Dante. We're having a drink at the White House before the gala. Hope you brought something besides those jeans."

I DON'T REMEMBER MUCH about meeting the president. I was mostly star-struck and tongue-tied. He was a good man, a moderate who appealed to the masses politically but also had a charismatic personality. He was very welcoming and introduced us to his wife and their two teen daughters. I was left in awe of where my life had brought me and the opportunities that had been afforded to me because of my meeting the Marians.

By the time we got to the gala, I was riding high on the knowledge that if I could stand in the White House and speak to the president, I could damned well stand in the same ballroom with Lawton. Sure, it was going to be tough, but I'd prove AJ wrong and do good things for the children of Marian House by meeting some influential donors.

It wasn't until I saw his smug face standing on the stage welcoming everyone to the event that I realized I'd been fooling myself.

As Lawton began to speak about youth in service, he crossed the line that had me seeing red.

"I lost my own son several years ago to the negative influences that society..." The monster rambled on about the evil of idle children and the importance of structure and service. His tone of voice indicated how very devastated he was that his beloved child had been ripped from the safety of his arms. *Bullshit.*

I didn't realize I'd reached out for Aunt Tilly's arm until she turned her head to look at me. We stood near the front with Senator Cannon before it was his turn to speak.

"I need to say something," I blurted. "Please let me up there."

Senator Cannon looked at me with wide eyes, but Tilly's held more of a twinkle.

She placed a hand on the senator's arm and gave him a look. "Let him speak, Harry. Please."

He looked at me and nodded, causing me to wonder just how far gone the man was for my great-aunt. I didn't have much time to think about it because the reality of what I'd decided to do began bearing down on me. I needed to stay strong.

If I told my story and the people of Indiana still elected him, fine.

Then it would be out of my hands. But if I stayed quiet and he won the chance to affect national policy, I'd always wonder if I could have made a difference.

If I was really going to do this, it would require me to face one of my biggest fears.

43

———

AJ

I was on a layover in the Atlanta airport on my way home when I got the text from Griff. As I walked between gates in the terminal, I texted back and forth with him.

Griff: *FYI — Dante went to DC with Tilly to attend the youth gala with Senator Cannon. Lawton's going to be there.*

AJ: *How did that come about?*

Griff: *Honestly, I think Tilly's up to something. Trying to force the issue.*

AJ: *Like how?*

Griff: *No idea. But I don't think she just wanted a travel companion. And I'm worried about Dante being there with Lawton.*

AJ: *Thanks for the heads-up.*

I stopped and looked up from my phone to see how far away I was from my departure gate. The gate in front of me was for a flight to

Reagan International Airport in DC. I laughed at myself and shook my head before responding.

AJ: *Guess I'm on my way to DC.*

~

THANK GOD FOR GRIFF. While I was on the plane, he contacted Tilly to get my name on the guest list, and he found me a tux on short notice. By the time I got to the hotel, I was running late. I took the time for a quick shower and shave before slipping into the tux and rushing to the gala venue.

Once I passed through the security line to get in, I was taken aback by the crowd. There had to be close to two thousand people there. I'd never seen so many people in one ballroom.

When I entered the room, the lights were already dimming and Reverend Lawton was walking on stage. My eyes searched frantically for Dante, but I couldn't find him anywhere. There was no way to pick one little guy out of this enormous crowd. I could only hope Tilly was with him for this part.

Reverend Lawton read off the teleprompter. "...While as individuals we may not agree on every detail of how to best help our country's greatest asset, we all have the best in our minds and hearts for the children of America. Please welcome Senator Harold Cannon."

As the senator took the stage and shook Reverend Lawton's hand, I saw a familiar head of white hair on the edge of the stage from the direction the senator had climbed onto the stage. Tilly. There was a brown-haired man next to her; my sixth sense kicked in. Dante. Good, he was with Tilly. I could relax.

Senator Cannon began to speak.

And I stopped relaxing.

"The organization asked me to speak to you tonight about how service-oriented children can grow up to be community leaders. Before heading over here tonight, I was lucky enough to watch one such leader in action. Instead of standing here telling you his story,

I've asked him to tell you himself. Dante Marian is the executive director of Marian House, the largest LGBTQ youth shelter in my home state of California. Dante, come on up here, son."

I watched Dante, *my* Dante, turn and kiss his aunt on the cheek before taking the stage.

After trying in vain to get closer, I gave up and watched as he thanked the senator and stood at the podium before looking out into the ballroom.

And then he froze, and I knew right then he wanted to bolt.

44

———————

DANTE

I'd been so fucking brave just moments before. But when I stood at the podium and looked out at the sea of strange faces, I knew I couldn't do it. I wanted to run.

My eyes flicked frantically around the room looking for exits. Everything inside of me begged for escape. Finally, I realized where the closest door was, but someone was blocking it.

The man who was both my past and my future. My Angel.

His eyes focused intently on me, and I noticed concerned creases in his forehead. I never wanted to be the cause of his beautiful face creasing with worry. As my brain frantically searched a million directions for what to say, my gaze settled on that one face. I would tell that one person, the love of my fucking life, why everything was going to be okay and he could stop worrying. I wouldn't need a prepared speech. I'd simply talk to *this one guy*.

"My name is Dante Marian," I told the man. "And I'm here to tell you my story."

His eyes widened in surprise and the light picked up golden flecks in their hazel depths. They were exquisite and familiar, and I felt myself relax into their depths with a smile.

45

AJ

He was fucking adorable, and I wanted to tell him how amazing he was. How proud I was of him. How much I head-over-heels loved him.

"First of all, I'd like to thank Senator Cannon for inviting me tonight and allowing me to speak. Second, I'd like to thank all of you for supporting youth in service. Obviously this issue is important to me."

I saw movement off the side of the stage where Reverend Lawton had exited after his introduction. No doubt he was freaking out and wondering if he could stop a potential disaster. I wondered what Dante would say.

"It's important to me because I believe children who benefit from the service of others are this country's biggest resources for future nonprofit leaders. I am where I am today because someone helped me. When I was fifteen, I left a physically and emotionally abusive father and wound up at the shelter in San Francisco, now known as Marian House. I was so messed up, I found myself standing at the edge of the Bay Bridge in preparation of ending it all.

"It was another child from the shelter—not an adult, not a parent or guardian—who stopped me and talked me down. He convinced me to just give it one more day. So I did. I gave it another day, and another, and another until I realized I never wanted to find myself on that bridge again. I was so grateful to that kid who'd shown up for me."

He took a breath and smiled. "That kid's name is Griff, and he now writes and illustrates graphic novels for kids. His purpose in publishing those books is to help kids like us understand that we don't have to be defined by any one thing. He went from living on the streets to teaching children around the world how much they matter.

"He found purpose, education, direction, and love in a homeless shelter. Just think about that for a minute. He climbed up the ladder and then *reached back down*."

Dante looked around the room, making eye contact with several people before continuing.

"I watched him do it, and I wanted to be just like him. So what did I do? I worked hard at the shelter while pursuing a master's in nonprofit management so I could help grow the program. I feel particularly qualified to help these kids, not because of my education, but because I've been there. I know what it's like to feel unloved and unwelcome in your own home. To feel pain at the hands of the people who are supposed to love you. To need help when you have nowhere else to turn."

He took another deep breath and smiled again. "So that's my big idea. It's not original. Harness the children who are out there in need, and serve *them*. In the process of serving them, give them the chance to pay it forward. I promise you, most of them are chomping at the bit to do so.

"So many times we focus on getting kids involved in service without realizing there are also kids *already involved* in service—on the receiving end. But they don't just want to receive help. They want to give help too. And they don't just need to be loved, they need to *give* love as well."

He looked up and smiled sheepishly at that. I looked around at the crowd watching Dante and saw eyes focused intently on his story.

"It's up to us to show them how. We need to be the models of loving behavior. We need to show them how to have empathy for others and how to harness that empathy into action. We start by walking the walk. By loving and serving others. By raising our children to believe that's just what you do when you are a good person, you love and serve others. Period.

"Thank you for serving others, especially our children, and thank you for showing up again and again to help remind us why working together as a community is powerful. My hope tonight is for each of you to have the opportunity in the days/weeks/years to come to help a child climb the ladder of success, so they, in turn, can reach back down and help pull someone else up too.

"My name is Dante Marian."

He took a breath and steeled himself in a way that tipped me off to what he was going to do next.

"But it used to be Daniel Lawton."

46

DANTE

U ntil the moment I said the name, I was halfway convinced I would chicken out. I was so proud of myself. I'd held it together and said what I wanted to say.

I stepped off the stage and walked straight through the parting crowd to where AJ stood. Without giving it a second thought, I launched myself into his arms and kissed him right there for all the world to see.

There were raised voices asking questions and cameras crowding around us, but I just stayed there in the most incredible lip lock with the only person on earth who needed to know in that moment that I was okay.

I was better than okay. I was in love with an amazing man, and I was pretty sure he was in love with me too.

"Dante," he breathed against my lips.

"AJ?" I asked, my voice cracking on the word.

"Baby, I'm so proud of you." He moved from the kiss to a hug and his lips brushed my ear as he spoke.

I moved my own lips to his ear and said, "I love you so much, Angel."

His entire body sagged into mine. "I love you too, Dante."

~

WE MADE it back to my hotel room unmolested, and AJ didn't waste any time sliding my tuxedo jacket off.

"So, that thing you said after you kissed me," he said in a sexy-as-shit voice.

"Go on," I said, pulling his jacket off too and then moving my hands to his bow tie.

"What was it again?" he asked, reaching around my waist to remove my cumberbund.

"What was what?"

"I seem to recall something about the L-word," he teased.

"Angel Flores, are you fishing?"

"You are so fucking cute right now I want to eat you."

"You're welcome to," I said. "Just sayin'."

He grinned a crocodile grin. "I'll keep that in mind."

Once both bow ties were gone and the cumberbunds followed, we each began plucking off cufflinks and studs, dropping them in a glass tumbler on the table.

"Were you trying to ask me something? What was it again?," I encouraged, pulling his shirt out of his waistband and pushing it down his arms to the floor.

"You're distracting me. I forgot where I was going with this."

"No, you didn't. You were going to tell me you loved me."

We were both bare chested now, and I took the opportunity to run my hands over the defined edges of AJ's pecs and abs, moving my fingers in circles around his nipples and enjoying the sound of his breath hitching. I could see the vaguest twitch of the fabric in the front of his pants, and I wanted to see more.

My fingers moved lower to open his fly and reach inside. AJ's hand came out to stop me before I touched him. "Wait," he rumbled.

"What is it?" I asked.

"I love you."

I stood there and blinked at him.

"Did you hear me?"

"No."

"Yes, you did."

"No, I really didn't. Didn't hear a thing. Tell me again about the love thing."

"See? I told you you heard me," AJ said, poking my chest.

"Dude, is it too much to ask for you to say it again? This is my fucking moment," I demanded.

AJ's eyes widened in surprise. "But we already said it, earlier. You don't remem—?"

"Hmm, did we? I don't recall."

"Fine. Dante Jackass Marian, I love you."

"Huh?" I asked with a shit-eating grin. "I didn't quite hear—"

"Shut up." He snorted, tackling me onto the bed. We wrestled around until I wound up on top of him. Our chests heaved from the exertion, and I had to swallow before speaking.

"Angel Big Dick Flores, I love you too," I said. And then I kissed that motherfucker to within an inch of his life.

We ordered room service champagne before proceeding to talk and laugh and make love long into the night.

EPILOGUE
AJ - THANKSGIVING

Getting Dante Marian away from his job and his family had proved to be a total bitch. I had a surprise planned for him, but it was going to have to happen in front of the entire damned Marian clan. I decided to embrace the idea and quickly got them all on board with the plan.

After work one day I showed up at Marian House and walked into his office. He was squinting at some numbers on his computer and didn't look anywhere near ready to shut it down for the holiday weekend.

"Let's go," I said, coming around and grabbing the mouse from his hand.

"Hey Angel, what are you doing here?" Dante asked in confusion. "I thought we were meeting at home at six to drive to Napa."

"Baby, it's half past six. Your bag is in the car. If this computer isn't shut down in thirty seconds, I'm yanking the cord from the wall."

"But—"

I yanked the cord from the wall and grabbed him, slinging him over my shoulder and carrying him out of the building. Several kids sat in lounge chairs in the entryway and hooted and hollered as we came through.

"Dante's getting lucky!" One kid yelled.

"Go git you some, Mr. Marian," another teased.

"Think AJ's the spanking type?" I heard one kid ask another. I looked over and saw Ammon blushing a deep shade of red even though his face was alight with laughter. I shot him a wink and saw him laugh even harder. It warmed my heart, and I knew I'd be saying a special thanks for that the following day at the big Marian turkey dinner..

"Happy Thanksgiving everyone," I called out as we passed them. Dante was still sputtering in righteous indignation and his fingers were digging into my sides as he clutched me to keep from falling. "I'll return Mr. Marian on Monday."

When we arrived at the vineyard we joined everyone for food and drinks in the big lodge lobby. Thomas and Rebecca had arranged for a photographer to take a giant family portrait of everyone, and word had gotten around that they were supposed to all wear their family reunion T-shirts.

Dante squirmed on the sofa next to me. "Shit," he muttered.

"What's wrong?" I asked.

"I couldn't find my damned shirt and forgot to ask Mom for a new one. Think they brought extra?"

He tugged at his bottom lip with his teeth and I reached out a finger to stop him. "Relax, I already asked Blue and he brought one for you."

Dante's face softened. "Thanks. That was really sweet of you. I'm sorry I've been so preoccupied this week."

Three weeks before, when Richard Lawton had lost his election in a crushing defeat, the media had hounded Dante night and day for his reaction. He was only just now able to concentrate and make up for lost time at work.

"I understand. It's okay." I reached over and slid my palm against the side of his face. "At least I have a few special ways of making sure your attention is solely focused on me once you do finally leave the office and come home," I said with a grin.

Normally, I would have expected him to roll his eyes at me, but this time he leaned against my palm and then turned to kiss it before kissing me on the mouth. We must have kissed long enough to catch someone's attention because I heard a catcall from behind me.

It was Pete. "Go change your damned shirt baby brother. After our picture, Tilly's friend Sally is coming to demo something. I think it's Tupperware."

I knew he was teasing but it still cracked me up. I stood and pushed Dante away from me to change. Once he was back and the photographer had all of the Marians lined up just how he wanted, he stopped to assess the scene.

I sat back on one of the sofas and watched. They were all lined up in front of the gorgeous stone fireplace and I was overcome with what an amazing family they were. Everyone wore their Made Marian shirts, and I caught Blue and Tristan sharing a special look.

Someone made a sound and I turned to look at Dante. His forehead was crinkled and he looked upset. I quirked a brow to ask him what was wrong.

"AJ needs to be in the picture," he said, loud enough for everyone to hear.

"Who, me?" I asked, pointing to my chest.

His eyes narrowed as he looked around, daring anyone to object. "Yes, you."

Without taking my eyes off him, I stood pulled off my cashmere sweater as I approached him.

He looked at me like I was crazy, but as soon as he saw what I was wearing under my sweater, he froze.

"Wh-what are you doing?" he squeaked. "What are you wearing? Where did you get that?"

I looked down at my shirt. It was his family reunion T-shirt, only I'd added a little something with a permanent marker. The shirt said *Made Marian*, but I'd written *I want to be* above it.

I shrugged. "What do you think?"

"I... I love it. Obviously. But... what... I mean, what do *you* think?" he asked. He was so flushed and flustered, I wanted to laugh. I got down on one knee and reached into my pocket.

"I think the shirt about says it all, really," I said with a grin, pulling the small box out of my pocket and holding it out to him. "But if you still need more proof, I have this."

Dante lunged at me, landing full force against my body, and almost knocking me on my ass, causing his whole family to erupt in laughter. His mouth latched on to mine in a fevered attack of tongue and nipping teeth.

"Oh my fucking god," he said. "I love you so much."

"Is that a yes?"

"Of course it's a yes." He beamed and kissed me some more before pulling back with a giant grin. "Now get in this photo where you belong."

So I did.

~

UP NEXT: *A Very Marian Christmas,* in which Tilly's Love Junk connection goes a little off the rails. The entire Marian clan places bets on who can set sweet Noah up with the perfect man by Christmas. Meanwhile, check out Lucy's website for tons of freebies including a free short story set in the Made Marian world!

LETTER FROM LUCY

Dear Reader,

Thank you so much for reading *Delivering Dante*, the sixth book in the Made Marian series!

The series continues with *A Very Marian Christmas*, a tale of a newcomer to the Marian clan who inadvertently discovers himself the center of a Marian matchmaking scheme during the holidays. Poor Noah gets roped into working for Sally the Love Junk Lady and hilarity ensues. Will he fall for one of the men the Marians set him up with? Or will Pete Marian's co-worker, Luke, who just so happens to be Noah's brother's BFF finally notice little Noah isn't so little anymore?

Please take a moment to write a review of *Delivering Dante* on the site where you found it as well as Goodreads. Reviews can make all of the difference in helping a book show up in book searches.

Feel free to stop by my website and drop me a line or visit me on social media. To see inspiration photographs for all of my novels, visit my Pinterest boards.

Finally, I have a fantastic reader group. Come join us for exclusive content, early cover reveals, hot pics, and a whole lotta fun. Lucy's Lair can be found on Facebook.

Happy reading!
Lucy

ABOUT THE AUTHOR

Lucy Lennox is a mother of three sarcastic kids. Born and raised in the southeast, she now resides outside of Atlanta finally putting good use to that English Lit degree.

Lucy enjoys naps, pizza, and procrastinating. She is married to someone who is better at math than romance but who makes her laugh every single day and is the best dancer in the history of ever.

She stays up way too late each night reading M/M romance because it is delicious.

For more information and to stay updated about future releases, please sign up for Lucy's author newsletter here.

Connect with Lucy on social media:
www.LucyLennox.com
Lucy@LucyLennox.com

KEEP IN TOUCH WITH LUCY!

Join Lucy's Lair
Get Lucy's New Release Alerts
Like Lucy on Facebook
Follow Lucy on BookBub
Follow Lucy on Amazon
Follow Lucy on Instagram
Follow Lucy on Pinterest

Other books by Lucy:
Made Marian Series
Forever Wilde Series
Aster Valley Series
Twist of Fate Series with Sloane Kennedy
After Oscar Series with Molly Maddox
Licking Thicket Series with May Archer
Virgin Flyer
Say You'll Be Nine

Visit Lucy's website at www.LucyLennox.com for a comprehensive list of titles, audio samples, freebies, suggested reading order, and more!